PENGUIN BOOKS

BETWEEN SHADES OF GRAY

Born and raised in Michigan, Ruta Sepetys is the daughter of a Lithuanian refugee. Ruta lives with her family in Tennessee. *Between Shades of Gray* is her first novel.

In memory of Jonas Šepetys

PENGUIN BOOKS

Published by the Penguin Group
Penguin Books Ltd, 80 Strand, London WC2R ORL, England
Penguin Group (USA) Inc., 375 Hudson Street, New York, New York 10014, USA
Penguin Group (Canada), 90 Eglinton Avenue East, Suite 700, Toronto, Ontario, Canada M4P 2Y3
(a division of Pearson Penguin Canada Inc.)
Penguin Ireland, 25 St Stephen's Green, Dublin 2, Ireland (a division of Penguin Books Ltd)
Penguin Group (Australia), 250 Camberwell Road, Camberwell, Victoria 3124, Australia
(a division of Pearson Australia Group Pty Ltd)
Penguin Books India Pvt Ltd, 11 Community Centre, Panchsheel Park, New Delhi – 110 017, India
Penguin Group (NZ), 67 Apollo Drive, Rosedale, Auckland 0632, New Zealand
(a division of Pearson New Zealand Ltd)
Penguin Books (South Africa) (Pty) Ltd, 24 Sturdee Avenue, Rosebank, Johannesburg 2196, South Africa

Penguin Books Ltd, Registered Offices: 80 Strand, London WC2R ORL, England

www.penguin.com

First published in the USA by Philomel Books,
a division of Penguin Young Readers Group 2011
Published simultaneously in Great Britain in Puffin Books 2011
Published in Penguin Books 2011
5

Printed in Great Britain by Clays Ltd, St Ives plc

ISBN: 978–0–670–92085–3

between shades *of* gray

RUTA SEPETYS

PENGUIN BOOKS

ARCTIC OCEAN
IRELAND
ENGLAND
THE NETHERLANDS
NORWAY
SWEDEN
FRANCE
GERMANY
BALTIC SEA
FINLAND
AUSTRIA
POLAND
LITH.
LAT.
EST.
ITALY
BELARUS
UKRAINE
ROMANIA
RUSSIA
GREECE
BLACK SEA
TURKEY
MEDITERRANEAN SEA
KAZAKHSTAN
CASPIAN SEA
SYRIA
IRAQ
IRAN
INDIA

This map is intended to convey the great distance Lina and her family traveled. It is not meant to accurately represent all country borders.

Day 1	Kaunas, Lithuania	Day 6	Smolensk, Russia
Day 3	Vilnius, Lithuania	Day 21	Cross the Ural Mountains
Day 4	Minsk, Belarus	Day 30	Omsk, Siberia
Day 5	Orsha, Belarus	Day 42	Altai Labor Camp

A TIMELINE

Day 306	Altai Labor Camp	Day 350	Ust Kust, Siberia
Day 313	Biysk, Siberia	Day 380	Yakutsk, Siberia
Day 319	Makarov Camp	Day 410	Cross the Arctic Circle
Day 320	Banks of Angara River	Day 440	Trofimovsk, North Pole

This map is intended to convey the great distance Lina and her family traveled. It is not meant to accurately represent all locations.

thieves and prostitutes

THEY TOOK ME IN MY NIGHTGOWN.

Thinking back, the signs were there—family photos burned in the fireplace, Mother sewing her best silver and jewelry into the lining of her coat late at night, and Papa not returning from work. My younger brother, Jonas, was asking questions. I asked questions, too, but perhaps I refused to acknowledge the signs. Only later did I realize that Mother and Father intended we escape. We did not escape.

We were taken.

June 14, 1941. I had changed into my nightgown and settled in at my desk to write my cousin Joana a letter. I opened a new ivory writing tablet and a case of pens and pencils, a gift from my aunt for my fifteenth birthday.

The evening breeze floated through the open window over my desk, waltzing the curtain from side to side. I could smell the lily of the valley that Mother and I had planted two years ago. *Dear Joana.*

It wasn't a knocking. It was an urgent booming that made me jump in my chair. Fists pounded on our front door. No one stirred inside the house. I left my desk and peered out into the hallway. My mother stood flat against the wall facing our framed map of Lithuania, her eyes closed and her face pulled with an anxiety I had never seen. She was praying.

"Mother," said Jonas, only one of his eyes visible through the crack in his door, "are you going to open it? It sounds as if they might break it down."

Mother's head turned to see both Jonas and me peering out of our rooms. She attempted a forced smile. "Yes, darling. I will open the door. I won't let anyone break down our door."

The heels of her shoes echoed down the wooden floor of the hallway and her long, thin skirt swayed about her ankles. Mother was elegant and beautiful, stunning in fact, with an unusually wide smile that lit up everything around her. I was fortunate to have Mother's honey-colored hair and her bright blue eyes. Jonas had her smile.

Loud voices thundered from the foyer.

"NKVD!" whispered Jonas, growing pale. "Tadas said they took his neighbors away in a truck. They're arresting people."

"No. Not here," I replied. The Soviet secret police had no business at our house. I walked down the hallway to listen and peeked around the corner. Jonas was right. Three NKVD officers had Mother encircled. They wore blue hats with a red border and a gold star above the brim. A tall officer had our passports in his hand.

"We need more time. We'll be ready in the morning," Mother said.

"Twenty minutes—or you won't live to see morning," said the officer.

"Please, lower your voice. I have children," whispered Mother.

"Twenty minutes," the officer barked. He threw his burning cigarette onto our clean living room floor and ground it into the wood with his boot.

We were about to become cigarettes.

2

WERE WE BEING ARRESTED? Where was Papa? I ran to my room. A loaf of fresh bread had appeared on my windowsill, a large wad of rubles tucked under the edge. Mother arrived at the door with Jonas clinging close behind her.

"But Mother, where are we going? What have we done?" he asked.

"It's a misunderstanding. Lina, are you listening? We must move quickly and pack all that is useful but not necessarily dear to us. Do you understand? Lina! Clothes and shoes must be our priority. Try to fit all that you can into one suitcase." Mother looked toward the window. She quickly slid the bread and money onto the desk and snapped the curtains shut. "Promise me that if anyone tries to help you, you will ignore them. We will resolve this ourselves. We must not pull family or friends into this confusion, do you understand? Even if someone calls out to you, you must not respond."

"Are we being arrested?" began Jonas.

"Promise me!"

"I promise," said Jonas softly. "But where is Papa?"

Mother paused, her eyes blinking quickly. "He will be meeting us. We have twenty minutes. Gather your things. Now!"

My bedroom began to spin. Mother's voice echoed inside my head. "Now. Now!" What was happening? The sound of my ten-year-old brother running about his room pulled a cord within my consciousness. I yanked my suitcase from the closet and opened it on my bed.

Exactly a year before, the Soviets had begun moving troops over the borders into the country. Then, in August, Lithuania was officially annexed into the Soviet Union. When I complained at the dinner table, Papa yelled at me and told me to never, ever say anything derogatory about the Soviets. He sent me to my room. I didn't say anything out loud after that. But I thought about it a lot.

"Shoes, Jonas, extra socks, a coat!" I heard Mother yell down the hallway. I took our family photo from the shelf and placed the gold frame faceup in the bottom of the empty suitcase. The faces stared back at me, happy, unaware. It was Easter two years before. Grandma was still alive. If we really were going to jail, I wanted to take her with me. But we couldn't be going to jail. We had done nothing wrong.

Slams and bangs popped throughout the house.

"Lina," Mother said, rushing into the room, her arms loaded. "Hurry!" She threw open my closet and drawers, frantically throwing things, shoving things into my suitcase.

"Mother, I can't find my sketchbook. Where is it?" I said, panicked.

"I don't know. We'll buy a new one. Pack your clothes. Hurry!"

Jonas ran into my room. He was dressed for school in his uniform and little tie, holding his book bag. His blond hair was combed neatly over to the side.

"I'm ready, Mother," he said, his voice trembling.

"N-no!" Mother stammered, choking on the word when she saw Jonas dressed for academy. She pulled in an uneven breath and lowered her voice. "No, sweetheart, your suitcase. Come with me." She grabbed him by the arm and ran down to his room. "Lina, put on shoes and socks. Hurry!" She threw my summer raincoat at me. I pulled it on.

I put on my sandals and grabbed two books, hair ribbons and my hairbrush. Where was my sketchbook? I took the writing tablet, the case of pens and pencils and the bundle of rubles off my desk and placed them amongst the heap of items we had thrown into my case. I snapped the latches closed and rushed out of the room, the curtains blowing, flapping over the loaf of fresh bread still sitting on my desk.

~

I saw my reflection in the glass door of the bakery and paused a moment. I had a dab of green paint on my chin. I scraped it off and pushed on the door. A bell tinkled overhead. The shop was warm and smelled of yeast.

"Lina, so good to see you." The woman rushed to the counter to assist me. "What may I help you with?"

Did I know her? "I'm sorry, I don't—"

"My husband is a professor at the university. He works for your father," she said. "I've seen you in town with your parents."

I nodded. "My mother asked me to pick up a loaf of bread," I said.

"Of course," said the woman, scurrying behind the counter. She wrapped a plump loaf in brown paper and handed it over to me. When I held out the money, she shook her head.

"Please," whispered the woman. "We could never repay you as it is."

"I don't understand." I reached toward her with the coins. She ignored me.

The bell jingled. Someone entered the shop. "Give your parents our very best regards," said the woman, moving to assist the other customer.

Later that night I asked Papa about the bread.

"That was very kind of her, but unnecessary," he said.

"But what did you do?" I asked him.

"Nothing, Lina. Have you finished your homework?"

"But you must have done something to deserve free bread," I pressed.

"I don't deserve anything. You stand for what is right, Lina, without the expectation of gratitude or reward. Now, off to your homework."

3

MOTHER PACKED AN EQUALLY large suitcase for Jonas. It dwarfed his small, thin frame and he had to carry it with both hands, bending backward to lift it off the floor. He didn't complain of the weight or ask for help.

The sound of breaking glass and china wailed through the house in quick intervals. We found our mother in the dining room, smashing all of her best crystal and china on the floor. Her face glistened with sweat, and her golden ringlets fell loose over her eyes.

"Mama, no!" cried Jonas, running toward the broken shards that littered the floor.

I pulled him back before he could touch the glass. "Mother, why are you breaking your beautiful things?" I asked.

She stopped and stared at the china cup in her hand. "Because I love them so much." She threw the cup to the floor, not even pausing to see it break before reaching for another.

Jonas began to cry.

"Don't cry, darling. We'll get much nicer things."

The door burst open and three NKVD officers entered our house carrying rifles with bayonets. "What happened here?" demanded a tall officer, surveying the damage.

"It was an accident," Mother replied calmly.

"You have destroyed Soviet property," he bellowed.

Jonas pulled his suitcase close, fearful that any minute it, too, might become Soviet property.

Mother looked in the foyer mirror to affix her loose curls and put on her hat. The NKVD officer slammed her in the shoulder with the butt of his rifle, throwing her face-first into the mirror. "Bourgeois pigs, always wasting time. You won't need that hat," he scoffed.

Mother righted and steadied herself, smoothing her skirt and adjusting her hat. "Pardon me," she said flatly to the officer before fixing her curls again and sliding her pearl hatpin into place.

Pardon me? Is that really what she said? These men burst into our home at night, slam her into the mirror—and she asks them to pardon *her*? Then she reached for it, the long gray coat, and suddenly I understood. She was playing the Soviet officers like a careful hand of cards, not quite sure what might be dealt next. I saw her in my mind, sewing jewelry, papers, silver, and other valuables into the coat under the lining.

"I have to use the bathroom," I announced, trying to divert the attention from my mother and the coat.

"You have thirty seconds."

I shut the bathroom door and caught sight of my face in the mirror. I had no idea how quickly it was to change, to fade. If I had, I would have stared at my reflection, memorizing it. It was the last time I would look into a real mirror for more than a decade.

4

THE STREETLAMPS HAD been turned off. It was nearly black in the road. The officers marched behind us, forcing us to keep pace with them. I saw Mrs. Raskunas peer out of her curtains. The moment she saw me looking, she disappeared. Mother nudged at my arm, which meant that I should keep my head down. Jonas was having a hard time carrying his suitcase. It was banging against his shins.

"Davai!" commanded an officer. Hurry, always hurry.

We marched into the intersection of the street, toward a large dark object. It was a truck, surrounded by more NKVD. As we approached the rear of the vehicle, I saw people sitting inside on their luggage.

"Boost me up before they do," Mother whispered quickly, not wanting an officer to touch her coat. I did as she asked. The officers pushed Jonas up. He fell on his face, his luggage thrown on top of him. I made it without falling, but when I stood up, a woman looked at me and clasped her hand to her mouth.

"Lina, dear. Button your coat," instructed Mother. I looked down and saw my flowered nightgown. In the rush and search for my sketchbook, I had forgotten to change. I also saw a tall, wiry woman with a pointy nose looking at Jonas. Miss Grybas. She was a spinster teacher from school, one of the strict ones. I recognized a few others: the librarian, the owner of a nearby hotel, and several men I had seen Papa speaking with on the street.

We were all on the list. I didn't know what the list was, only that we were on it. Apparently so were the other fifteen people sitting with us. The back gate of the truck slammed shut. A low moan came from a bald man in front of me.

"We're all going to die," he said slowly. "We will surely die."

"Nonsense!" said Mother quickly.

"But we will," he insisted. "This is the end."

The truck began to move, jerking forward quickly, throwing people off their seats. The bald man suddenly scrambled up, climbed the inside wall of the truck, and jumped out. He smashed onto the pavement, letting out a roar of pain like an animal caught in a trap. People in the truck screamed. The tires screeched to a halt and the officers leapt out. They opened the back gate, and I saw the man writhing in pain on the ground. They lifted him up and hurled his crumpled body back into the truck. One of his legs looked mangled. Jonas buried his face in

Mother's sleeve. I slipped my hand into his. He was shaking. My vision blurred. I squeezed my eyes shut, then opened them. The truck jerked forward, moving once again.

"NO!" the man wailed, holding his leg.

The truck stopped in front of the hospital. Everyone seemed relieved that they would tend to the bald man's injuries. But they did not. They were waiting. A woman who was also on the list was giving birth to a baby. As soon as the umbilical cord was cut, they would both be thrown into the truck.

5

NEARLY FOUR HOURS PASSED. We sat in the dark in front of the hospital, unable to leave the vehicle. Other trucks passed, some with people covered in large restraining nets.

The streets began to buzz with activity. “We were early,” one of the men commented to Mother. He looked at his watch. “It’s nearing three A.M. now.”

The bald man, lying on his back, turned his face toward Jonas. “Boy, put your hands over my mouth and pinch my nose. Don’t let go.”

“He will do nothing of the sort,” said Mother, pulling Jonas close.

“Foolish woman. Don’t you realize this is just the beginning? We have a chance now to die with dignity.”

“Elena!” A voice hissed from the street. I saw Mother’s cousin Regina hiding in the shadows.

"Have you any relief now that you're on your back?" Mother asked the bald man.

"Elena!" The voice appeared again, a little louder.

"Mother, I think she's calling you," I whispered, eyeing the NKVD smoking on the other side of the truck.

"She's not calling me—she's a crazy woman," Mother said loudly. "Be on your way and leave us alone," she yelled.

"But Elena, I—"

Mother turned her head and pretended she was deep in conversation with me, completely ignoring her cousin. A small bundle bounced into the bed of the truck near the bald man. His hand grabbed for it greedily.

"And you speak of dignity, sir?" said Mother. She snapped the bundle out of his hands and put it under her legs. I wondered what was in the package. How could Mother call her own cousin "a crazy woman"? Regina had taken a great risk to find her.

"You are the wife of Kostas Vilkas, provost at the university?" asked a man in a suit sitting down from us. Mother nodded, wringing her hands.

~

I watched as Mother twisted her palms.

Murmurs rose and fell in the dining room. The men had been sitting for hours. "Sweetheart, take them the fresh pot of coffee," said Mother.

I walked to the edge of the dining room. A cloud of cigarette smoke hovered over the table, held captive by the closed windows and drapes.

"Repatriate, if they can get away with it," said my father, stopping abruptly when he saw me in the doorway.

"Would anyone like more coffee?" I asked, holding up the sterling pot.

Some men looked down. Someone coughed.

"Lina, you're turning into quite a young lady," said a friend of my father's from the university. "And I hear that you're a very talented artist."

"Indeed, she is!" said Papa. "She has a very unique style. And she's exceptionally smart," he added with a wink.

"So she takes after her mother then," joked one of the men. Everyone laughed.

"Tell me, Lina," said the man who wrote for the newspaper, "what do you think of this new Lithuania?"

"Well," interrupted my father quickly. "That's not really conversation for a young girl, now, is it?"

"It will be conversation for everyone, Kostas, young and old," said the journalist. "Besides," he said, smiling, "it's not as if I'd print it in the paper."

Papa shifted in his chair.

"What do I think of the Soviets' annexation?" I paused, avoiding eye contact with my father. "I think Josef Stalin is a bully. I think we should push his troops out of Lithuania. They shouldn't be allowed to come and take what they please and—"

"That's enough, Lina. Leave the pot of coffee and join your mother in the kitchen."

"But it's true!" I pressed. "It's not right."

"Enough!" said my father.

I returned to the kitchen, stopping short to eavesdrop.

"Don't encourage her, Vladas. The girl is so headstrong, it scares me to death," said Papa.

"Well," replied the journalist, "now we see how she takes after her father, don't we? You've raised a real partisan, Kostas."

Papa was silent. The gathering ended and the men left the house at alternating intervals, some through the front door and some through the back.

~

"The university?" said the bald man, still wincing with pain. "Oh, well, he's long gone then."

My stomach contracted like someone had punched me. Jonas turned a desperate face to Mother.

"Actually, I work at the bank and I saw your father just this afternoon," said a man, smiling at Jonas. I knew he was lying. Mother gave the man a grateful nod.

"Saw him on his way to the grave then," said the surly bald man.

I glared at him, wondering how much glue it would take to keep his mouth shut.

"I am a stamp collector. A simple stamp collector and they're delivering me to my death because I correspond internationally with other collectors. A university man would certainly be near the top of the list for—"

"Shut up!" I blurted.

"Lina!" said Mother. "You must apologize immediately. This poor gentleman is in terrible pain; he doesn't know what he is saying."

"I know exactly what I am saying," the man replied, staring at me.

The hospital doors opened and a great cry erupted from within. An NKVD officer dragged a barefoot woman in a bloodied hospital gown down the steps. "My baby! Please don't hurt my baby!" she screamed. Another officer walked out, carrying a swaddled bundle. A doctor came running, grabbing at the officer.

"Please, you cannot take the newborn. It won't survive!" yelled the doctor. "Sir, I beg you. Please!"

The officer turned to the doctor and kicked the heel of his boot into the doctor's kneecap.

They lifted the woman into the truck. Mother and Miss Grybas scrambled to make room for her lying next to the bald man. The baby was handed up.

"Lina, please," Mother said, passing the pink child to me. I held the bundle and instantly felt the warmth of its little body penetrating through my coat.

"Oh God, please, my baby!" cried the woman, looking up at me.

The child let out a soft cry and its tiny fists pummeled the air. Its fight for life had begun.

6

THE MAN WHO WORKED at the bank gave Mother his jacket. She wrapped the suit coat around the woman's shoulders and smoothed her hair away from her face.

"It's all right, dear," said Mother to the young woman.

"Vitas. They took my husband, Vitas," breathed the woman.

I looked down at the little pink face in the bundle. A newborn. The child had been alive only minutes but was already considered a criminal by the Soviets. I clutched the baby close and put my lips on its forehead. Jonas leaned against me. If they would do this to a baby, what would they do to us?

"What is your name, dear?" said Mother.

"Ona." She craned her neck. "Where is my child?"

Mother took the child from me and laid the bundle on the woman's chest.

"Oh, my baby. My sweet baby," cried the woman, kissing the infant. The truck lurched forward. She looked at Mother with pleading eyes.

"My leg!" wailed the bald man.

"Do any of you have medical training?" asked Mother, scanning the faces in the truck. The people shook their heads. Some wouldn't even look up.

"I'll try to make a splint," said the man from the bank. "Does anyone have anything straight I can use? Please, let's help one another." People shifted uncomfortably in the truck, thinking about what they might have in their bags.

"Sir," said Jonas, leaning around me. He held out his little ruler from school. The old woman who had gasped at my nightgown began to cry.

"Well, yes, that's very good. Thank you," said the man, accepting the ruler.

"Thank you, darling," said Mother, smiling at Jonas.

"A ruler? You're going to set my leg with a little ruler? Have you all gone mad?" screeched the bald man.

"It's the best we can do at the moment," said the man from the bank. "Does anyone have something to tie it with?"

"Someone just shoot me, please!" yelled the bald man.

Mother pulled the silk scarf from her neck and handed it to the man from the bank. The librarian slid the knot from her scarf as well, and Miss Grybas dug in her bag. Blood began to soak through the front of Ona's hospital gown.

I felt nauseous. I closed my eyes and tried to think of something, anything, to calm myself. I pictured my sketchbook. I felt my hand stir. Images, like celluloid frames, rolled through my mind. Our house, Mother adjusting Papa's tie in the kitchen, the lily of the valley, Grandma . . . Her face soothed me somehow. I thought of the photo tucked in my suitcase. Grandma, I thought. Help us.

We arrived at a small train depot in the countryside. Soviet trucks filled the rail yard, packed with people just like ours. We drove alongside a truck with a man and woman leaning out. The woman's face was streaked with tears.

"Paulina!" the man yelled. "Do you have our daughter Paulina?" I shook my head as we passed.

"Why are we at a countryside depot and not Kaunas station?" asked an old woman.

"It's probably easier to organize us with our families. The main station is so busy, you know," said Mother.

Mother's voice lacked certainty. She was trying to convince herself. I looked around. The station was tucked in a deserted area, surrounded by dark woods. I pictured a rug being lifted and a huge Soviet broom sweeping us under it.

"DAVAI!" YELLED AN NKVD officer as he opened the back gate of the truck. The train yard swarmed with vehicles, officers, and people with luggage. The noise level grew with each passing moment.

Mother leaned down and put her hands on our shoulders. "Stay close to me. Hold on to my coat if you need to. We must not be separated." Jonas grabbed on to Mother's coat.

"Davai!" yelled the officer, yanking one of the men off the truck and pushing him to the ground. Mother and the man from the bank began to help the rest. I held the infant while they brought Ona down.

The bald man twisted in pain as he was carried off the truck.

The man from the bank approached an NKVD officer. "We have people who need medical attention. Please, get a doctor." The officer ignored the man. "Doctor! Nurse! We need medical assistance!" shouted the man into the crowd.

The officer grabbed the man from the bank, stuck a rifle in his back and began to march him away. "My luggage!" he yelled. The librarian grabbed the man's suitcase, but before she could run to him, he had disappeared into the crowd.

A Lithuanian woman stopped and said she was a nurse. She began tending to Ona and the bald man while we all stood in a circle around them. The train yard was dusty. Ona's bare feet were already caked in dirt. Hordes of people passed by, threading through one another with desperate faces. I saw a girl from school pass by with her mother. She raised her arm to wave, but her mother covered her eyes as she approached our group.

"Davai!" barked an officer.

"We can't leave these people," said Mother. "You must get a stretcher."

The officer laughed. "You can carry them."

We did. Two men from the truck carried the wailing bald man. I carried the baby and a suitcase while Mother helped Ona walk. Jonas struggled with the rest of the luggage, and Miss Grybas and the librarian helped.

We reached the train platform. The chaos was palpable. Families were being separated. Children screamed and mothers pleaded. Two officers pulled a man away. His wife would not let go and was dragged for several feet before being kicked away.

The librarian took the baby from me.

"Mother, is Papa here?" asked Jonas, still clutching her coat.

I wondered the same thing. When and where had the Soviets dragged my father away? Was it on his way to work? Or maybe at the newspaper stand during his lunch hour? I looked at the masses of people on the train platform. There were elderly people. Lithuania cherished its elders, and here they were, being herded like animals.

"Davai!" An NKVD officer grabbed Jonas by the shoulders and began to drag him away.

"NO!" screamed Mother.

They were taking Jonas. My beautiful, sweet brother who shooed bugs out of the house instead of stepping on them, who gave his little ruler to splint a crotchety old man's leg.

"Mama! Lina!" he cried, flailing his arms.

"Stop!" I screamed, tearing after them. Mother grabbed the officer and began speaking in Russian—pure, fluent Russian. He stopped and listened. She lowered her voice and spoke calmly. I couldn't understand a word. The officer jerked Jonas toward him. I grabbed on to his other arm. His body began to vibrate as sobs wracked his shoulders. A big wet spot appeared on the front of his trousers. He hung his head and cried.

Mother pulled a bundle of rubles from her pocket and exposed it slightly to the officer. He reached for it and then said something to Mother, motioning with his head. Her hand flew up and ripped the amber pendant right from her neck and pressed it into the NKVD's hand. He didn't seem to be satisfied. Mother continued to speak in Russian and pulled a pocket watch from her coat. I knew that watch. It was her father's and had his name engraved in the soft gold on the back. The officer snatched the watch, let go of Jonas, and started yelling at the people next to us.

Have you ever wondered what a human life is worth? That morning, my brother's was worth a pocket watch.

8

"IT'S OKAY, DARLING. We're all okay," said Mother, hugging Jonas, kissing his face and tears. "Right, Lina? We're all okay."

"Right," I said quietly.

Jonas, still crying, put his hands in front of his trousers, humiliated by the wetness.

"Don't worry about that, my love. We'll get you a change of clothes," said Mother, moving in front of him to shield his embarrassment. "Lina, give your brother your coat."

I peeled off my coat and handed it to Mother.

"See, you'll just wear this for a short while."

"Mother, why did he want to take me away?" asked Jonas.

"I don't know, dear. But we're together now."

Together. There we stood on the train platform amidst the chaos, me in my flowered nightgown and my brother in a baby blue summer coat that nearly touched the ground. As ridiculous as we must have looked, no one even glanced at us.

"Mrs. Vilkas, hurry!" It was the nasal voice of Miss Grybas, the spinster teacher from school. She urged us toward her. "We're over here. Hurry now, they're splitting people up."

Mother grabbed Jonas's hand. "Come, children." We made our way through the crowd, like a small boat cutting through a storm, unsure if we'd be sucked in or stay afloat. Red wooden train cars lined the platform, stretching in links as far as the eye could see. They were crudely built and dirty, the kind that would haul livestock. Masses of Lithuanians thronged toward them with their belongings.

Mother maneuvered us through the crowd, pushing and pulling our shoulders. I saw white knuckles clutching suitcases. People were on their knees crying, tying erupting bags with twine while officers stepped on the contents. Wealthy farmers and their families carried buckets of slopping milk and rounds of cheese. A small boy walked by holding a sausage nearly as big as his body. He dropped it and it immediately disappeared underfoot in the crowd. A woman bumped my arm with a sterling candlestick while a man ran by holding an accordion. I thought of our beautiful things, smashed on the floor at our house.

"Hurry!" shouted Miss Grybas, gesturing to us. "This is the Vilkas family," she said to an officer holding a clipboard. "They're in this car."

Mother stopped in front of the car and scanned the crowd intently. *Please*, said her eyes as she searched for our father.

"Mother," whispered Jonas, "these cars are for pigs and cows."

"Yes, I know. We'll have a little adventure, won't we?" She boosted Jonas up into the car and then I heard the sounds—a baby crying and a man moaning.

"Mother, no," I said. "I don't want to be with those people."

"Stop it, Lina. They need our help."

"Can't someone else help them? We need help, too."

"Mother," said Jonas, worried the train would begin to move. "You're coming in, aren't you?"

"Yes, darling, we're coming. Can you take this bag?" Mother turned to me. "Lina, we haven't a choice. Please do the best you can not to frighten your brother."

Miss Grybas reached down for Mother. What about me? I was frightened, too. Didn't that matter? *Papa, where are you?* I looked around the train platform, which was now in complete pandemonium. I thought about running, running until I couldn't run anymore. I'd run to the university to look for Papa. I'd run to our house. I'd just run.

"Lina." Mother stood in front of me now and lifted my chin. "I know. This is horrible," she whispered. "We must stay together. It's very important." She kissed my forehead and turned me toward the train car.

"Where are we going?" I asked.

"I don't know yet."

"Do we have to be in these cattle cars?"

"Yes, but I'm sure it won't be for long," said Mother.

9

THE INSIDE OF THE car was stuffy and full of personal smells, even with the door open. People were wedged in everywhere, sitting on their belongings. At the end of the car, large planks of wood approximately six feet deep had been installed as shelves. Ona lay on one of the planks, peaked, the baby crying on her chest.

"OW!" The bald man smacked my leg. "Watch it, girl! You almost stepped on me."

"Where are the men?" Mother asked Miss Grybas.

"They took them away," she replied.

"We'll need men in this car to help with the injured," said Mother.

"There aren't any. We're sorted into groups of some kind. They keep bringing people and shoving them in. There are some elderly men, but they haven't any strength," said Miss Grybas.

Mother looked around the car. "Let's put the little ones on the top plank. Lina, move Ona on that bottom plank so we can fit some more of the children."

"Don't be a fool, woman," barked the bald man. "If you make room, they'll just cram more people in here."

The librarian was shorter than me and stocky. She was strong and helped move Ona. "I'm Mrs. Rimas," she said to Ona.

Mrs. . . . She was married, too. Where was her husband? Perhaps with Papa. The baby gave a blistering yell.

"Is your little one a boy or a girl?" asked Mrs. Rimas.

"A girl," said Ona weakly. She shifted her bare feet on the wooden plank. They were cut and full of dirt.

"She'll need to eat soon," said Mrs. Rimas.

I looked around the car. My head felt detached from my body. More people pushed into the small space, including a woman with a boy my age. I felt a tug.

"Are you going to sleep now?" asked a small girl with hair the color of pearls.

"What?"

"You're in your nightgown. Are you going to sleep?" She thrust a tattered doll toward me. "This is my dolly."

My nightgown. I was still in my nightgown. Jonas was still in my baby blue coat. I had completely forgotten. I pushed toward Jonas and Mother. "We need to change our clothes," I said.

"There's no room to open our suitcases," said Mother. "And there's nowhere to change."

"Please," said Jonas, pulling my coat tightly around him.

Mother tried to move toward the corner of the car but it was useless. She bent down and opened my suitcase a slight crack. Her hand dipped in and out, searching for something. I saw my pink sweater and a slip. Finally, she pulled out my dark blue cotton dress. She then searched for pants for Jonas.

"Excuse me, madam," she said to a woman sitting in the corner of the car. "Could we trade places with you so my children can change their clothes?"

"This is our spot," announced the woman. "We're not moving." Her two daughters looked up at us.

"I realize it's your spot. It would just be for a moment, so my children have a bit of privacy."

The woman said nothing and folded her arms across her chest.

Mother thrust us near the corner, almost on top of the woman.

"Hey!" said the woman, throwing up her hands.

"Oh yes, so sorry. Just for a bit of privacy." Mother took my coat from Jonas and held it up to shield us. I changed quickly and then used my nightgown to make an additional changing curtain for Jonas.

"He peed," said one of the girls, pointing at my brother. Jonas froze.

"You peed, little girl?" I said loudly. "Oh, poor thing."

The temperature in the car had risen steadily since we had climbed in. The wet scent of an armpit hung in front of my face. We forged our way near the door, hoping for some air. We stacked our suitcases and Jonas sat on top, holding the bundle from our cousin Regina. Mother stood on her toes, trying to look out onto the train platform for Papa.

"Here," said a gray-haired man, putting a small case on the floor. "Stand on this."

"That's very kind," said Mother, accepting.

"How long has it been?" he asked.

"Since yesterday," she said.

"What does he do?" said the man.

"He's provost at the university. Kostas Vilkas."

"Ah, yes, Vilkas." The man nodded. He looked at us. His eyes were kind. "Beautiful children."

"Yes. They look just like their father," she said.

~

We all sat together on the velvet settee, Jonas on Papa's lap. Mother wore her green silk dress with the full skirt. Her yellow hair fell in shiny waves against the side of her face, and her emerald earrings sparkled under the lights. Papa wore one of his new dark suits. I had chosen my cream-colored dress with the brown satin sash and a matching ribbon for my hair.

"What a handsome family," said the photographer, positioning his large camera. "Kostas, Lina looks just like you."

"Poor girl," teased Papa. "Let's hope she grows out of it and ends up like her mother."

"One can only hope," I teased back. Everyone erupted in laughter. The flash went off.

I COUNTED THE PEOPLE—forty-six packed in a cage on wheels, maybe a rolling coffin. I used my fingers to sketch the image in a layer of dirt on the floor near the front of the train car, wiping the drawings away and starting over, again and again.

People chattered about our possible destination. Some said NKVD headquarters, others thought Moscow. I scanned the group. Faces spoke to their future. I saw courage, anger, fear, and confusion. Others were hopeless. They had already given up. Which was I?

Jonas swatted flies away from his face and hair. Mother spoke quietly to the woman with the son my age.

"Where are you from?" the boy asked Jonas. He had wavy brown hair and blue eyes. He looked like one of the popular boys from school.

"Kaunas," said Jonas. "Where are you from?"

"Šančiai."

We looked at each other, silent and awkward.

"Where is your dad?" blurted Jonas.

"In the Lithuanian army." The boy paused. "He's been gone for a while."

His mother looked like an officer's wife, fancy and unaccustomed to dirt. Jonas continued to chatter, before I could tell him to stop.

"Our father works at the university. I'm Jonas. This is my sister, Lina."

The boy nodded at me. "I'm Andrius Arvydas." I nodded in return and looked away.

"Do you think they'd let us get out, even for a few minutes?" asked Jonas. "That way, if Papa is here at the station, he'll see us. He can't find us now."

"The NKVD won't let us do much of anything," said Andrius. "I saw them beat someone who tried to run."

"They called us pigs," said my brother.

"Don't listen to them, Jonas. They're the pigs. They're stupid pigs," I said.

"Shh. I wouldn't say that," said Andrius.

"What are you, the police?" I asked.

Andrius raised his eyebrows. "No, I just don't want you to get in trouble."

"Don't get us in trouble, Lina," said Jonas.

I looked over toward Mother.

"I gave them everything I had. I lied and told them he was

feeble-minded. I had no choice," whispered Andrius's mother. "They would have split us up. Now I have nothing, not even a crumb."

"I know," said Mother, reaching out to the woman. "They did the same with us, and my boy is only ten years old."

Ona's baby wailed. Mrs. Rimas made her way over to Mother.

"She's trying to feed the child, but something's wrong," said Mrs. Rimas. "The baby's mouth won't latch properly."

Hours passed like long days. People cried of heat and hunger. The bald man griped about his pain while others tried to organize the space and luggage. I had to surrender my dirt canvas on the floor and instead used my fingernail to carve drawings on the wall.

Andrius jumped down from the car to go to the bathroom but was punched and thrown back in by the NKVD. We all cringed with each gunshot or scream. No one dared leave the car again.

Someone discovered a hole, the size of a plate, in the corner where the stubborn woman sat with her daughters. They had been hiding the hole and the fresh air that came from it. People descended upon her, insisting she move. After she had been dragged off the spot, we all took turns using the hole to go to the bathroom. Some just couldn't bring themselves to do it. The sounds and smells made my head spin. A young boy hung his head from the car and vomited.

Mrs. Rimas organized the children and began to tell stories. The young kids scrambled toward the librarian. Even the two daughters left their grouchy mother and sat mesmerized by the fantastic tales. The girl with the dolly leaned against Mrs. Rimas and sucked her thumb.

~

We sat in a circle on the library floor. One of the younger boys lay on his back, sucking his thumb. The librarian turned through the picture book, reading with an animated voice. I listened and drew the characters in my little notebook. I drew the dragon and my heart began to beat faster. He was alive. I felt a wave of heat from his fiery breath coming at me, blowing my hair back. Then I drew the princess running, her beautiful golden hair tumbling down the mountainside . . .

"Lina, are you ready to go?"

I looked up. The librarian hovered over me. All of the children were gone.

"Lina, are you okay? You're flushed. You're not feeling ill, are you?"

I shook my head and held up my notebook.

"Oh my word. Lina, did you draw that?" The librarian quickly reached for the pad.

I nodded, smiling.

THE SUN BEGAN TO SET. Mother braided my wavy, sweaty hair. I tried to count how many hours we had spent in the prison box, and wondered how many more we had to go. People ate the food they had brought. Most shared. Some didn't.

"Lina, that loaf of bread," Mother began.

I shook my head. Was that loaf of bread still there, sitting on my desk? "I don't have the bread," I replied.

"All right," said Mother, taking some food to Ona. Her lips pursed, she was disappointed.

Andrius sat with his knees drawn up, smoking a cigarette. He was staring at me.

"How old are you?" I asked.

"Seventeen." He continued to stare.

"How long have you been smoking?"

"What are you, the police?" he said, and looked away.

Night came. It was dark in our wooden box. Mother said we should be thankful they left the door open. I wasn't about to thank the NKVD for anything. Every few minutes I heard their boots marching by. I couldn't sleep. I wondered if there was a moon out, and if so, what it looked like. Papa said scientists speculated that from the moon, the earth looked blue. That night I believed it. I would draw it blue and heavy with tears. Where was Papa? I closed my eyes.

Something bumped my shoulder. I opened my eyes. It was lighter in the train car. Andrius stood above, nudging me with his shoe. He put his finger to his lips and motioned with his head. I looked over at Mother. She slept, clutching her coat tightly around her. Jonas was gone. My head snapped around, looking for my brother. Andrius kicked me again and waved me forward.

I got up and stepped between the human bundles toward the door of the train car. Jonas stood at the opening, clutching the side. "Andrius said that an hour ago, a long train came in. Someone told him it was full of men," whispered Jonas. "Maybe Papa is on it."

"Who told you that?" I asked Andrius.

"Don't worry who told me," he said. "Let's look for our fathers."

I looked down off the train. The sun had just appeared on the horizon. If Papa *was* at the train station, I wanted to find him.

"I'll go and let you know what I find out," I said. "Where is the train that pulled in?"

"In back of us. But you're not going," said Andrius. "I'll go."

"How are you going to find my father? You don't know what he looks like," I snapped.

"Are you always so pleasant?" said Andrius.

"Maybe you can both go," suggested Jonas.

"I can go by myself," I said. "I'll find Papa and bring him to our car."

"This is ridiculous. We're wasting time. I shouldn't have woken you up," said Andrius.

I looked out of the train car. The guard was a hundred feet away, his back to me. I hung down off the edge and dropped quietly to the ground, scrambling under the train. Andrius beat me there. Suddenly, we heard a yelp and saw Jonas jumping down. Andrius grabbed him and we tried to hide behind one of the wheels, peeking under the train. The NKVD officer stopped and turned around.

I put my hand over Jonas's mouth. We crouched near the wheel, afraid to breathe. The officer resumed walking.

Andrius peeked out the other side and waved us on. I crawled out. The back of our train car had Russian writing on it.

"'Thieves and prostitutes,'" Andrius whispered. "That's what it says."

Thieves and prostitutes. Our mothers were in that car, along with a teacher, a librarian, elderly people, and a newborn baby—thieves and prostitutes. Jonas looked at the writing. I grabbed his hand, thankful he couldn't read Russian. I wished he had stayed on the train.

Another line of red cattle wagons sat on tracks behind ours. The doors, however, were closed and locked with large bolts. We looked around, then ran under the other train, dodging the splatters of waste. Andrius knocked on the bottom near a bathroom hole. A shadow appeared.

"What's your father's name?" Andrius asked me.

"Kostas Vilkas," I said quickly.

"We're looking for Petras Arvydas and Kostas Vilkas," he whispered.

The head disappeared. We heard scuffling on the floor of the car. The head reappeared. "Not in this car. Be careful, children. Be very quiet."

We scurried from car to car, dodging droppings and knocking. Each time a head disappeared, I felt my stomach tighten. "Please, please, please," Jonas would say. And then we'd move on, with warnings of caution or messages for loved ones. We reached the seventh car. The man's head disappeared. It was quiet inside. "Please, please, please," said Jonas.

"Jonas?"

"Papa!" we said, trying not to raise our voices. A match scraped across a wood plank. Papa's face appeared in the hole. He looked gray, and his eye was badly bruised.

"Papa, we're in a car over there," began Jonas. "Come with us."

"Shh . . . ," said Papa. "I can't. You shouldn't be here. Where is your mother?"

"In the car," I said, happy yet horrified to see my father's bludgeoned face. "Are you all right?"

"I'm okay," he said. "Are you okay? Is your mother okay?"

"We're okay," I said.

"She doesn't know we're here," said Jonas. "We wanted to find you. Papa, they broke into our house and—"

"I know. They're attaching our train to yours."

"Where are they taking us?" I asked.

"To Siberia, I think."

Siberia? That couldn't be right. Siberia was half a world away. There was nothing in Siberia. I heard Papa talking inside the train car. His arm came out of the hole holding some scrunched-up material.

"Take this jacket and these socks. You'll need them." More noise came from inside. Papa handed out another jacket, two shirts, and more socks. He then handed down a large piece of ham.

"Children, split this. Eat it," Papa said.

I hesitated and stared at the ham my father handed through the same hole people used as a toilet.

"Put it in your mouths right now!" he said.

I tore the thick piece of ham in quarters and handed some to Jonas and Andrius. I put the last piece in my dress pocket for Mother.

"Lina, take this and give it to your mother. Tell her it's okay to sell it, if she has to." Papa's hand came down to me, holding his gold wedding band. I stared at it.

"Lina, do you understand? Tell her it's in case she needs money."

I wanted to tell him we had already traded a pocket watch

for Jonas. I nodded and put the ring on my thumb, not able to swallow the ham past the lump in my throat.

"Sir," said Andrius, "is Petras Arvydas in your car?"

"I'm sorry, son, he's not," said Papa. "This is very dangerous. You must all get back to your train."

I nodded.

"Jonas."

"Yes, Papa?" Jonas said, peering up at the hole.

"You're very brave to have come. You must all stay together. I know you'll take good care of your sister and mother while I am away."

"I will, Papa, I promise," said Jonas. "When will we see you?"

Papa paused. "I don't know. Hopefully soon."

I clutched the bundle of clothes. Tears began dropping down my cheeks.

"Don't cry, Lina. Courage," said Papa. "You can help me."

I looked up at him.

"Do you understand?" My father looked at Andrius, hesitant. "You can help me find you," he whispered. "I'll know it's you . . . just like you know Munch. But you must be very careful."

"But," I started, uncertain.

"I love you both. Tell your mother I love her. Tell her to think of the oak tree. Say your prayers, children, and I will hear them. Pray for Lithuania. Now run back. Hurry!"

My chest hurt and my eyes burned. I started to walk but stumbled.

Andrius caught me. "Are you okay?" he asked. His face looked soft, concerned.

"I'm fine," I said, quickly wiping my eyes and pulling free of his grasp. "Let's go find your father."

"No, you heard him. Hurry, run back. Tell your mother what he said."

"But what about your father?" I asked.

"I'm going to try a few more. I'll meet you back at our car," he said. "Just go, Lina. You're wasting time."

I hesitated.

"Are you scared to go alone?"

"No! I'm not scared," I said. "My father said we should stay together, but we'll go by ourselves." I snatched Jonas by the hand. "We don't need him, right, Jonas?"

Jonas stumbled, looking over his shoulder at Andrius.

"HALT!" a voice commanded.

We were so close, nearly under our train car. NKVD boots marched toward us. I tucked my thumb and Papa's wedding band into my palm.

"Davai!" the voice yelled.

Jonas and I crept out from under the car.

"Lina! Jonas!" yelled Mother, leaning out of the train.

The officer pointed his gun at Mother, signaling for her to be quiet. He then circled around us, his boots coming closer with each turn.

I felt Jonas edge up beside me. I tightened my fist, hoping the guard wouldn't see Papa's ring. "We dropped some things down the bathroom hole," I lied, lifting up the bundle. Mother translated my words into Russian for the guard.

The officer looked at the socks on top of the heap I was

holding. He grabbed Jonas and began searching his pockets. I thought of the ham in my dress. How could I explain a slice of ham in my pocket when we were all so hungry? The guard shoved us both to the ground. He waved his rifle around our faces, yelling in Russian. I huddled near Jonas, staring down the barrel of his gun. I closed my eyes. *Please, no.* He kicked gravel at our legs and then spat, "Davai!" pointing toward the train car.

Mother's face was ashen. She did a poor job of hiding her fear this time. Her hands trembled and she was nearly panting. "You could have been killed!"

"We're okay, Mother," announced Jonas. His voice shook. "We went to find Papa."

"Where is Andrius?" Mrs. Arvydas looked over our shoulders.

"He came with us," I said.

"But where *is* he?" she demanded.

"He wanted to look for his father," I said.

"His father?" She sighed deeply. "Why doesn't he believe me? I've told him again and again that his father . . ." She turned around and began to cry.

I realized I had made a great mistake. I should not have left Andrius behind.

"We found him, Mother. We found Papa," said Jonas.

People crowded toward us. They wanted to know how many men were on the train and if we saw their loved ones.

"He said he thinks we're going to Siberia," Jonas reported. "And he gave us some ham. The three of us ate it, but we saved a piece for you. Lina, give Mother the piece of ham."

I reached in my pocket and handed the piece of ham to Mother.

She saw it, the ring on my thumb.

"In case you need money," I said. "He said you could sell it."

"And he said to remember the oak tree," said Jonas.

Mother took the ring off of my thumb and put it to her lips. She began to cry.

"Don't cry, Mother," said Jonas.

"Girl!" shouted the bald man. "What else did you bring to eat?"

"Lina, give this piece of ham to Mr. Stalas," said Mother, sniffing. "He's hungry."

Mr. Stalas. The bald man had a name. I moved toward him. His withered arms were green and purple with bruises. I held out the piece of ham.

"That's your mother's," he said. "What else do you have?"

"That's all he gave me."

"How many cars were on that train?"

"I don't know," I said. "Maybe twenty."

"He said we're going to Siberia?"

"Yes."

"He's probably right, your father," he said.

Mother's crying subsided. I held out the piece of ham again.

"That's your mother's," said the bald man. "Make sure she eats it. I don't like ham anyway. Now leave me alone."

"He wouldn't come with us," my brother explained to Mrs.

Arvydas. "He and Lina started fighting and he said he was going to check more cars."

"We weren't fighting," I interrupted.

"If they find him wandering around and discover he is the son of an officer—" said Mrs. Arvydas. She hid her face in her hands.

The gray-haired man shook his head and wound his watch.

I felt guilty. Why didn't I stay with Andrius or insist he come back with us? I looked out of the train car, hoping to see him.

Two Soviets pulled a priest down the platform. His hands were bound and his cassock was dirty. Why a priest? But then . . . why any of us?

13

THE SUN ROSE and the temperature in the car climbed quickly. The wet smell of feces and urine hovered over us like a filthy blanket. Andrius had not returned, and Mrs. Arvydas wept so hard it scared me. I felt sick with guilt.

A guard approached the car and handed up a bucket of water and a bucket of slop.

Everyone surged toward the buckets. "Wait," said Miss Grybas, as if she were directing her class. "We must all take just a bit, to ensure everyone can eat."

The slop resembled gray animal feed. Some children refused to eat it.

Jonas found the package from Mother's cousin Regina. Inside was a small blanket, a sausage, and a coffee cake. Mother shared the food, giving small pieces to everyone. The baby continued to wail. Ona twisted and screamed right along with the child, who still refused to eat and looked a darker shade of pink.

Hours passed. Andrius didn't return. Mother sat down next to me. "How did your father look?" she asked, smoothing my braids and putting her arm around my shoulder.

"Not too bad," I lied. I put my head on her shoulder. "Why are they taking us? Is it really because Papa works at the university? That doesn't make sense."

The bald man groaned.

"See, like him," I whispered. "He's not a teacher. He's a stamp collector and he's being deported," I said.

"He's not just a stamp collector," said Mother under her breath. "Of that I am certain. He knows too much."

"What does he know?"

Mother sighed, shaking her head. "Stalin has a plan, my love. The Kremlin will do anything to see it through. You know that. He wants Lithuania for the Soviet Union, so he's moving us out temporarily."

"But why us?" I asked. "They already moved into Lithuania last year. Isn't that enough?"

"It's not just us, dear. I imagine he's doing the same to Latvia, Estonia, and Finland. It's complicated," said Mother. "Try to rest."

I was exhausted but couldn't sleep. I wondered if my cousin Joana was also on a train somewhere. Maybe she was near Papa. Papa said I could help him, but how could I help him if we were really going to Siberia? I dozed off, thinking of Andrius, trying to see his face.

~

As I walked by the piece, my feet stopped. The face. It was enchanting, like nothing I had ever seen. It was a charcoal portrait of a young man. The corners of his lips turned up, yet despite his smile, the pain on his face made my eyes well with tears. The subtleties within his hair blended so softly, yet created strong variation. I stepped closer to inspect. Flawless. How did he achieve such sheer shade without so much as a pause or a fingerprint? Who was the artist, and who was the young man? I looked at the signature. Munch.

"Young lady, follow the group, please. That's part of a different exhibit," said our guide.

Some of the students had complained earlier. How could they complain about a field trip to the art museum? I had been looking forward to it for months.

The guide's shoes clacked down the tile floor. My body moved forward, but my head remained fixed on the drawing, fixed on the face. I rubbed my fingers together. A light touch, yes, but with confidence. I couldn't wait to try it.

I sat at the desk in my bedroom. I felt the charcoal vibrate slightly as I pushed it across the page. The sound it made against the paper gave me chills. I bit my bottom lip. I ran my middle finger along the edge, softening the harsh line. Not quite, but almost.

~

I pushed the tip of my finger through the dirt on the floor, drawing his name. Munch. I would recognize his art anywhere. And Papa would recognize mine. That's what he meant. He could find me if I left a trail of drawings.

WHEN I WOKE, the car was dark. I moved to the front and hung my head over the side for air. My hair swung away from my neck. A rush of air swirled around my face, and I breathed deeply. Gravel crunched. I snapped my head up, expecting to see a guard. No one was there. The gravel shifted again. I dropped my head back down, looking under the train. A dark figure huddled near the wheel. I squinted, trying to focus in the low light. A bloody hand lifted toward me, shaking. I pulled back before realizing.

Andrius.

I turned toward Mother. Her eyes were closed, her arms wrapped around Jonas. I looked out on the train platform. The NKVD marched two cars down, their backs to me. The little girl with the dolly sat on her knees near the door. I put my finger to my lips. She nodded. I lowered myself down off the car, trying not to make a sound. My chest thumped, remembering the guard pointing the gun at me.

I stepped closer and stopped. A truck drove by somewhere outside, its lights momentarily sweeping under the car. Andrius stared off with a blue, battered face. He had swollen pillows for eyes. His shirt was covered in blood, his lips sliced. I knelt down beside him.

"Can you walk?"

"A little," he said.

I peeked out to see the guards. They stood in a group smoking, four cars down. I tapped lightly near the bathroom hole. The grouchy woman's face appeared. Her eyes widened.

"I have Andrius. We need to get him back on the train."

She stared at me.

"Did you hear me?" I whispered. "You have to pull him up. Move!"

Her face disappeared from the hole. I heard scuffling inside the car and glanced down to the guards. I slung Andrius's bloody arm over my shoulder and grabbed him by the waist. We rose and inched toward the door. The gray-haired man hung his head over, signaling for us to wait. Andrius sagged on my shoulder, making my knees bend. I didn't know how long I could hold him up.

"NOW!" said the gray-haired man. I thrust Andrius toward the man who, together with the others, pulled him up.

I peeked out at the guards. Just as I moved, they turned and began walking toward me. Desperate, I looked around. I grabbed on to the undercarriage of the train and lifted my legs up, suspended under the car. The sound of the boots came closer and emerged near the wheel. I closed my eyes. They were speaking in Russian. A matchstick hissed, and a glow appeared on the guard's boot. They chatted in low voices. My arms began to shake, trying to hold on. *Hurry.*

I hung there. My hands began to sweat. I was losing my grip. *Leave.* A deep burning washed through the fibers of my muscles. Their conversation continued. *Please.* I bit my lip. *Move.* A dog barked. The guards walked toward the sound.

Mother and the gray-haired man pulled me up. I slumped against the open door, gasping for air. The little girl with the dolly put her finger to her lips and nodded.

I stared at Andrius. Dried blood caked his teeth and the corners of his lips. His jaw was swollen. I hated them, the NKVD and the Soviets. I planted a seed of hatred in my heart. I swore it would grow to be a massive tree whose roots would strangle them all.

"How could they do this?" I asked aloud. I looked around the train car. No one spoke. How could we stand up for ourselves if everyone cowered in fear and refused to speak?

I had to speak. I'd write everything down, draw it all. I would help Papa find us.

Andrius shifted his legs. I looked down at him.

"Thanks," he whispered.

I WOKE WITH A START next to Jonas and Andrius. The door to our car had been closed and locked. People began to panic.

The engines let out a hiss of steam.

"Please don't move unless you absolutely have to," ordered Miss Grybas. "Make sure the bathroom area stays clear."

"Mrs. Book Lady? Will you tell us a story?" asked the girl with the dolly.

"Mama," whimpered a little voice, "I'm scared. Turn on the light."

"Did anyone bring a lantern?" someone asked.

"Sure, and I have a four-course meal in my pocket, too," said the bald man.

"Mr. Stalas," said Mother, "please, we're all doing the best we can."

"Girl," he commanded. "Look out that little slot and tell us what you see."

I moved toward the front of the car and hoisted myself up.

"The sun is beginning to rise," I said.

"Spare us the poetry," snapped the bald man. "What's happening out there?"

The train hissed again, then clanked.

"NKVD officers are walking by the train with rifles," I said. "There are some men in dark suits looking at the train cars."

We felt a jolt and the train began to move.

"There's luggage everywhere," I said. "And lots of food on the platform." People groaned. The station looked eerie, desolate, frozen with only remnants of the chaos that had taken place. There were single shoes strewn about, a cane, a woman's purse lying open, and an orphaned teddy bear.

"We're moving out of the station," I reported. I craned my neck to look ahead. "There are people," I said. "There's a priest. He's praying. A man is holding a large crucifix."

The priest looked up, flung oil, and made the sign of the cross as our train rolled away.

He was issuing last rites.

16

AS WE ROLLED, I reported every detail from the window. The Nemunas River, the big churches, buildings, the streets, even the trees we passed. People sobbed. Lithuania had never looked more beautiful. Flowers burst with color against the June landscape. We moved along, our cars marked "thieves and prostitutes."

After two hours the train began to slow.

"We're coming into a station," I said.

"What does the sign say?" asked the bald man.

I waited for the train to move closer. "Vilnius. We're in . . . Vilnius," I said quietly.

Vilnius, the capital of Lithuania. We had studied the history in school. Six hundred years ago, the Grand Duke Gediminas had a dream. He saw an iron wolf standing high upon a hill. He consulted a priest about the dream who told him that the iron wolf symbolized a large and formidable city, a city of opportunity.

~

"Lina, may I speak to you, please?"

The remainder of my classmates filed out of the room. I approached the teacher's desk.

"Lina," she said, clasping her hands on the desk, "it seems you prefer socializing to studying." She opened a folder in front of her. My stomach leapt into my throat. Inside were notes I had written to girls in class, along with accompanying sketches. On top of the pile sat a drawing of a Greek nude and a portrait of my handsome history teacher. "I found these in the trash. I've spoken to your parents."

My hands became clammy. "I was trying to copy the figure from a library book—"

She raised her hand to stop me. "In addition to being quite social, however, you appear to be a gifted artist. Your portraits are"—she paused, rotating the drawing—"captivating. They show a depth of emotion well beyond your years."

"Thank you," I breathed.

"I believe your talent is above what we could develop here. There is a summer program, however, in Vilnius."

"In Vilnius?" I asked. Vilnius was a few hours away.

"Yes, in Vilnius. Next year, when you're sixteen, you'd be allowed to enter. If accepted, you'd study with some of the most talented artists in northern Europe. Would that interest you?"

I tried to swallow my excitement long enough to speak. "Yes, Mrs. Pranas, it would."

"Then I'd like to recommend you. You'll fill out an application and submit some samples of your drawings," she said, handing the folder with the notes and sketches to me. "We'll send them off to Vilnius as soon as possible."

"Mrs. Pranas, thank you!" I said.

She smiled and leaned back in her chair. "It's my pleasure, Lina. You have talent. You have a successful future ahead of you."

~

Someone discovered a loose board behind some luggage on the back wall. Jonas crawled back and wiggled it aside.

"What do you see?"

"There's a man in the trees," said Jonas.

"Partisans," said the bald man. "They're trying to help us. Get his attention."

Jonas stuck his hand out of the opening in the board, trying to wave.

"He's coming," said Jonas. "Shh!"

"They're unhooking the cars with the men," a man's voice said. "They're splitting the train in two." He ran back into the woods.

Intermittent shots rang out in the distance.

"Where are they taking the men?" I asked.

"Maybe the men are going to Siberia," said Mrs. Rimas. "And we're going somewhere else."

I preferred the thought of Siberia, if that's where Papa would be.

Metal clanged and screeched. They were dividing the train. There was another sound.

"Listen," I said. "The men." It grew louder. Louder. They were singing, singing at the top of their lungs. Andrius joined, and then my brother and the gray-haired man. And finally, the bald man joined in, singing our national anthem. *Lithuania, land of heroes . . .*

I wept.

THE VOICES OF THE MEN in the other cars had sounded full of pride, full of confidence. Fathers, brothers, sons, husbands. Where were they all going? And where were *we* going, a train car full of women, children, elderly, and infirmed?

I wiped my tears with my handkerchief and allowed others to do the same. When it was handed back to me, I paused, staring at it. Unlike paper, the handkerchief could travel hand to hand without deteriorating. I would use it to draw on for Papa.

While I devised a plan, the women in the car showed constant concern for the baby, who could not seem to nurse.

Mrs. Rimas urged Ona to keep trying. "Come, come, dear."

"What is it?" asked my mother through the darkness of the car.

"It's Ona," said Mrs. Rimas. "Her ducts are clogged and she's too dehydrated. The baby won't suckle."

Despite Mrs. Rimas's efforts, nothing seemed to help.

We rolled for days, stopping in the middle of nowhere. The NKVD wanted to ensure we could not be seen and had nowhere to run. We waited for our daily stops. It was the only time the door would be open to light or fresh air.

"One person! Two buckets. Any dead bodies in there?" the guards would ask.

We had agreed to rotate. That way, everyone would get a chance to get out of the car. Today was my turn. I had dreamed of seeing blue sky and feeling the sun on my face. But earlier, it had begun to rain. We had all scrambled to hold cups and containers out of the little slot to catch the rainwater.

~

I snapped my umbrella closed, shaking the excess rainwater onto the sidewalk. A gentleman in a suit emerged from a restaurant, stepping quickly away from the drops I was splashing about.

"Oh, sir, I'm sorry!"

"No trouble at all, miss," he said, nodding and touching the brim of his hat.

The smell of roasted potatoes and spiced meat drifted out of the restaurant. The sun appeared, spreading a golden filter across the concrete and warming the back of my head. Wonderful—the concert in the park wouldn't be canceled tonight. Mother had planned to pack a hamper with our dinner for a moonlight picnic on the grass.

As I rolled the umbrella and wrapped the closure, I jumped when I saw a face staring at me from the puddle at my feet. I laughed at my disorientation, smiling at myself in the pool of water. The edges of the puddle shimmered beneath the sun, creating a beautiful frame around my face. I wished I could photograph it to draw later. Suddenly, a faint shadow appeared behind my head in the puddle. I turned around. A pastel rainbow arched out of the clouds.

~

The train slowed. "Hurry, Lina. Do you have the buckets?" asked Mother.

"Yes." I moved closer to the door. Once the train stopped, I waited for the sound. Boots and clanking. The door jerked open.

"One person! Two buckets. Any dead bodies in there?" the NKVD commanded.

I shook my head, eager to get out. The guard stepped aside and I jumped down. My stiff legs gave way, and I fell to the muddy ground.

"Lina, are you all right?" called Mother.

"Davai!" yelled the guard, along with a series of Russian expletives before he spit on me.

I got up and looked down the length of the train. The sky was gray. Rain fell steadily. I heard a scream and saw the limp body of a child heaved out into the mud. A woman tried to jump out after the corpse. She was smashed in the face by the butt of a rifle. I saw another body thrown out. Death had begun to gather a crop.

"Don't delay, Lina," said the gray-haired man from our car. "Be swift with the buckets."

I felt as if I were dreaming with a high fever. My head seemed airy and my step unsteady. I nodded and looked up at our car. A group of heads stacked upon one another stared back at me.

Dirt and filth clung to their faces. Andrius smoked a cigarette and looked off the other way. His face was still bruised.

Urine streamed through the bottom of the train car. Ona's baby cried from inside. I saw the wet green field. *Come here*, it beckoned. *Run.*

Maybe I should, I thought. *Do it, Lina.*

"What's wrong with her?" Voices began chattering from the train car.

Run, Lina.

The buckets flew out of my hands. I saw Andrius limping away with them. I just stood there, looking at the field.

"Lina. Come back in, dear," pleaded Mother.

I closed my eyes. Rain splashed against my skin and hair. I saw Papa's face, peering down from the match-lit hole in his train car. *I'll know it's you . . . just like you know Munch.*

"Davai!"

An NKVD officer hovered over me. His breath reeked of liquor. He grabbed my arms and threw me toward the train.

Andrius returned with buckets of water and gray animal feed. "Hope you enjoyed your bath," he said.

"What did you see out there, girl?" demanded the bald man.

"I . . . I saw the NKVD throwing dead bodies off the train into the mud. Two children." People gasped.

The door to our car slammed shut.

"How old were the dead kids?" asked Jonas quietly.

"I don't know. I only saw them from afar."

Mother combed through my wet hair in the dark.

"I wanted to run," I whispered to her.

"I can understand that," said Mother.

"You can?"

"Lina, wanting to get away from this is perfectly understandable. But like your father said, we must all stay together. It's very important."

"But how can they just decide that we're animals? They don't even know us," I said.

"We know us," said Mother. "They're wrong. And don't ever allow them to convince you otherwise. Do you understand?"

I nodded. But I knew some people had already been convinced. I saw them cowering in front of the guards, their faces hopeless. I wanted to draw them all.

"When I looked up at our train car, everyone looked sick," I said.

"Well, we're not," said Mother. "We're not sick. We'll soon be back in our homes. When the rest of the world finds out what the Soviets are doing, they will put an end to all of this."

Would they?

18

WE WEREN'T SICK, but others were. Each day when the train stopped, we'd lean out of the car and try to count the number of bodies thrown. It grew every day. I noticed Jonas kept track of the children, making marks with a stone on the floorboard of the car. I looked at his marks and imagined drawing little heads atop each one—hair, eyes, a nose, and a mouth.

People estimated our path traveled south. Whoever was posted at the little window would call out when we passed markers or signs. My feet were numb from the vibration of the floorboards. My head was curdled from the stench, and I itched terribly. Lice were biting down the side of my hairline, behind my ears, and in my armpits.

We had passed through Vilnius, Minsk, Orsha, Smolensk. I wrote the path of cities on my handkerchief in ink. Each day when the door was open to light, I would add more detail and identifying clues that Papa would recognize—our birthdays, a drawing of a *vilkas*—a wolf. I made markings only in the center, surrounded by a circle of hands touching fingers. I scrawled the words *pass along* under the drawing of the hands and I drew a Lithuanian coin. When the handkerchief was folded, the writing was undetectable.

"Drawing?" whispered the gray-haired man, winding his watch.

I jumped.

"I didn't mean to scare you," he said. "I won't tell."

"I have to get word to my father," I said, my voice low. "So he can find us. I figured I could pass this handkerchief and that eventually, it will get to him."

"Very clever," he said.

He had been kind on the journey. Could I trust him? "I need to give it to someone who will understand the importance and pass it along."

"I can help you with that," he said.

We had been rolling for eight days when the train jerked hard and began to slow.

Jonas was at the little window slot. "There's another train. We're coming up on a train going in the opposite direction. It's stopped."

Our train car dragged, bleeding off speed.

"We're pulling up alongside it. There are men. The windows are open on their cars," said Jonas.

"Men?" said Mother. She quickly made her way to the window, swapped places with Jonas, and yelled out in Russian. They replied. The energy in her voice lifted and she began to speak quickly, pulling for breaths in between questions.

"For God's sake, woman," said the bald man. "Stop your socializing and tell us what's going on. Who are they?"

"They're soldiers," reported Mother, elated. "They're going to the front. There is war between Germany and the USSR. Germany has moved into Lithuania," she shouted. "Did you hear me? The Germans are in Lithuania!"

Morale soared. Andrius and Jonas shouted and whooped. Miss Grybas began to sing "Take Me Back to My Homeland." People hugged one another and cheered.

Only Ona was quiet. Her baby was dead.

THE TRAIN WITH the Russian soldiers rolled away. The doors were opened, and Jonas jumped out with the buckets.

I looked over to Ona. She was forcing the dead child toward her breast.

"No," she said through gritted teeth, rocking back and forth. "No. No."

Mother moved toward her. "Oh, my dear. I'm so sorry."

"NO!" Ona screamed, clutching her baby.

Hot tears stung my parched eyes.

"What are you crying for?" complained the bald man. "You knew it was going to happen. What was the baby going to eat, lice? You're all imbeciles. The thing is better off. When I die, if you're smart you'll eat me if you all want to survive so badly."

He prattled on, grating, infuriating. The words distorted. I heard only the timbre of his voice thumping in my ears. Blood pumped through my chest and rose up my neck.

"DAMN YOU!" Andrius screamed and lurched toward the bald man. "If you don't shut your mouth, old man, I'll tear out your tongue. I'll do it. I'll make the Soviets look kind." No one spoke or tried to stop Andrius. Not even Mother. I felt relief, as if the words had come from my own mouth.

"You're concerned only with yourself," Andrius continued. "When the Germans kick the Soviets out of Lithuania, we'll leave you here on the tracks so we don't have to put up with you anymore."

"Boy, you don't understand. The Germans aren't going to solve the problem. Hitler's going to create more," said the bald man. "Those damn lists," he muttered.

"No one wants to hear from you, understand?"

"Ona, dear," said Mother. "Give me the baby."

"Don't give her to them," begged Ona. "Please."

"We will not give her to the guards. I promise," said Mother. She examined the baby one last time, feeling for pulse or breath. "We'll wrap her in something beautiful."

Ona sobbed. I moved to the open door to get some air. Jonas returned with the buckets.

"Why are you crying?" he asked, climbing up.

I shook my head.

"What's wrong?" he pressed.

"The baby's dead," said Andrius.

"Our baby?" he asked softly.

Andrius nodded.

Jonas put down the buckets. He looked over toward Mother holding the bundle and then at me. He knelt down and took the small stone out of his pocket, making a mark on the floorboards next to the others. He paused for a few moments, motionless, and then began slamming the stone against the markings, harder and harder. He beat the floorboards with such force that I thought he might break his hand. I moved toward him. Andrius stopped me.

"Let him do it," he said.

I looked at him, uncertain.

"Better that he gets used to it," he said.

Used to what, the feeling of uncontrolled anger? Or a sadness so deep, like your very core has been hollowed out and fed back to you from a dirty bucket?

I looked at Andrius, his face still warped with bruising. He saw me staring. "Are you used to it?" I asked.

A muscle in his jaw twitched. He pulled a cigarette butt from his pocket and lit it. "Yeah," he said, blowing a stream of smoke into the air, "I'm used to it."

People discussed the war and how the Germans might save us. For once, the bald man said nothing. I wondered if what he said about Hitler was true. Could we be trading Stalin's sickle for something worse? No one seemed to think so. Papa would know. He always knew those sorts of things, but he never discussed them with me. He discussed them with Mother. Sometimes at night I'd hear whispers and murmurs from their room. I knew that meant they were talking about the Soviets.

I thought about Papa. Did he know about the war? Did he know we all had lice? Did he know we were huddled together with a dead baby? Did he know how much I missed him? I clutched the handkerchief in my pocket, thinking of Papa's smiling face.

~

"Hold still!" I complained.

"I had an itch," said my father, grinning.

"You did not, you're just trying to make this difficult," I teased, trying to capture his bright blue eyes.

"I'm testing you. Real artists must be able to capture the moment," he said.

"But if you don't hold still, your eyes will be crooked," I said, shading in the side of his face with my pencil.

"They're crooked anyway," he said, crossing his eyes. I laughed.

"What do you hear from your cousin Joana?" he asked.

"Nothing lately. I sent her a drawing of that cottage in Nida she liked last summer. I didn't even get a note back from her. Mother said she received it but is busy with her studies."

"She is," said Papa. "She hopes to be a doctor someday, you know."

I knew. Joana spoke often of medicine and her hopes of being a pediatrician. She was always interrupting my drawing to tell me about the tendons in my fingers or my joints. If I so much as sneezed, she would rattle off a list of infectious diseases that would have me in the grave by nightfall.

Last summer she had met a boy while we were on vacation in Nida. I'd wait up every night to hear the details of their dates. As a seventeen-year-old, she had wisdom and experience, as well as an anatomy book that fascinated me.

"There," I said, finishing the drawing. "What do you think?"

"What's that?" asked my father, pointing to the paper.

"My signature."

"Your signature? It's a scribble. No one will recognize it's your name."

I shrugged. "You will," I said.

20

WE TRAVELED FARTHER SOUTH and passed through the Ural Mountains. Miss Grybas explained that the Urals were the boundary between Europe and Asia. We had crossed into Asia, another continent. People said we were on course for southern Siberia, or possibly even China or Mongolia.

We tried for three days to sneak Ona's baby out, but the guard stood near whenever the doors were open. The smell of rotting flesh had become unbearable in the hot car. It made me retch.

Ona finally agreed to drop the baby down the bathroom hole. She knelt over the opening, sobbing, holding the bundle.

"For God's sake," moaned the bald man. "Get rid of that thing. I can't breathe."

"Be quiet!" Mother yelled to the bald man.

"I can't," whimpered Ona. "She'll be crushed on the tracks."

Mother moved toward Ona. Before she reached her, Miss Grybas snapped the bundle from Ona and threw it down the hole. I gasped. Mrs. Rimas cried.

"There," said Miss Grybas. "Done. It's always easier for someone unattached." She wiped her hands on her dress and adjusted her hair bun. Ona fell into Mother's arms.

Jonas clung to Andrius, spending nearly every minute by his side. He seemed angry all the time and so distant from his usual sweetness. Andrius had taught him a few Russian slang words I had heard the NKVD use. It made me furious. I knew I'd have to learn a bit of Russian eventually, but I hated the thought.

One night, I saw the glow of a cigarette illuminate Jonas's face. When I complained to Mother, she told me to leave him be.

"Lina, every night I thank God he has Andrius, and you should, too," she said.

My stomach ate itself. Pangs of hunger came at relentless intervals. Although Mother made an effort to keep us on a schedule, I lost track of time and sometimes dozed off during the day. My eyelids were drooping when I heard it.

"How could you? Have you gone mad?" A female voice shrieked through the train car.

I sat up, squinting to make out what was going on. Miss Grybas hovered over Jonas and Andrius. I tried to make my way over.

"And Dickens nonetheless. How dare you! You are becoming the animals they treat us as!"

"What's going on?" I asked.

"Your brother and Andrius are smoking!" she bellowed.

"My mother knows," I said.

"Books!" she said, thrusting a hard cover in my face.

"We ran out of cigarettes," Jonas said softly, "but Andrius had tobacco."

"Miss Grybas," said Mother, "I'll handle it."

"The Soviets have arrested us because we are knowledgeable, learned people. To smoke pages of a book is just . . . What were you thinking?" Miss Grybas asked. "Where did you get this book?"

Dickens. I had *The Pickwick Papers* in my suitcase. Grandma had given it to me the Christmas before she died. "Jonas! You took my book. How could you?"

"Lina," began Mother.

"I took your book," said Andrius. "Blame me."

"I certainly do blame you," said Miss Grybas. "Corrupting this young boy. You should be ashamed."

Mrs. Arvydas slept on the other side of the car, completely unaware of what had transpired.

"You're an idiot!" I screamed at Andrius.

"I'll get you a new book," he said.

"No, you won't. It was a gift," I said. "Jonas, Grandma gave me that book."

"I'm sorry," said Jonas, looking down at his chest.

"You should be!" I yelled.

"Lina, it was my idea," said Andrius. "It's not his fault."

I waved him away. Why did boys have to be such idiots?

21

WEEKS. I LOST TRACK of how long we had been traveling. I stopped watching for bodies to be hurled from the cars. Every time the train pulled away, we left a litter of corpses in our wake. What would people think if they saw them? Would someone bury them, or would they believe they were really thieves and prostitutes? I felt as if I were riding a pendulum. Just as I would swing into the abyss of hopelessness, the pendulum would swing back with some small goodness.

One day, for example, just past Omsk, we stopped in the countryside. There was a small kiosk. Mother bribed a guard to let her out of the car. She came running back, her entire skirt bowed full and heavy. She knelt down in the car and released her skirt. Candy, toffees, lollipops, black licorice, mountains of gumdrops, and other treats spilled out onto the floor, unfolding like a rainbow in front of us. Bright colors everywhere—pink, yellow, green, red, and enough for everyone. The children squealed with delight and jumped up and down. I bit into a gumdrop. A burst of citrus exploded in my mouth. I laughed and Jonas laughed with me.

There were cigarettes, matches, and dark chocolate wafers for the adults.

"They didn't have bread or anything substantial," explained Mother as she divided the treasure amongst everyone. "There were no newspapers."

Children grabbed Mother's legs in glee, thanking her.

"Foolish woman. Why do you waste your money on us?" said the bald man.

"Because you are hungry and tired," Mother said, handing the man a cigarette. "And I know you would do the same for my children if they ever needed it."

"Bah," he scoffed and looked away.

Two days later, while on the bucket run, Andrius found an oval stone full of quartz and other minerals. Everyone passed it around, oohing and ahhing. Mrs. Arvydas joked and put it up to her finger as if it were a shimmering gemstone.

"Didn't you know?" she said. "I'm a train car princess."

We laughed. People smiled. I almost didn't recognize them. I looked over at Andrius. His face beamed with a grin that changed his appearance entirely. He was handsome when he smiled.

22

AFTER SIX WEEKS, and the third day without food, the train stopped. They did not open the door. The bald man, who had been charting our progress from the city markers called from the window slot, guessed we were somewhere in the Altai region, just north of China. I tried to peek through cracks in the wagon boards, but it was dark outside. We banged on the doors. No one came. I thought of the loaf of bread I had left on my windowsill, still warm and swollen from the oven. If only I could have a piece. Just one small pinch.

My stomach burned with hunger and my head throbbed. I missed drawing on real paper and longed for light to sketch properly. I was sick of being so close to people. I felt their sour breath all over me, elbows and knees constantly in my back. Sometimes I had the urge to start pushing people away from me, but it was no use. We were like matchsticks in a small box.

Late morning came and we heard clanking. The guards opened the door and said we would be getting out. Finally. My entire body trembled at the shock of daylight. I marked "Altai" on my handkerchief.

"Lina, Jonas, come here and comb your hair," Mother instructed. She smoothed out our clothes, a wasted effort, and helped me twist my hair into a crown. Twisting it made it itch even more.

"Remember, we must all stay together. Do not walk away or stray. Do you understand?" We nodded. Mother still clutched her coat tightly under her arm.

"Where are we?" asked Jonas. "Will they give us a bucket of water?"

"I don't know yet," said Mother, fixing her own hair. She pulled out a tube of lipstick and, with a weak hand, applied the melted color to her lips. Jonas smiled. She winked back at him.

The NKVD had bayoneted rifles at the ready. The sun reflected off the dagger-shaped blades. They could puncture us within a fraction of a second. Miss Grybas and Mrs. Rimas helped the small children out first, and we followed. Andrius and the gray-haired gentleman carried the bald man from the car.

We weren't at a train station. We were in a wide, deep valley, surrounded by forested hills. I saw mountains in the distance. The sky had never looked so blue, so beautiful. I had to shade my eyes from the intense sun. I breathed deeply and felt the crisp, clean air draft my polluted lungs. The NKVD directed the deportees from each train car to sit in groups on the grass, twenty feet from the tracks. We were given two buckets of slop and water. The children lunged for it.

It was the first time I had seen the other passengers. There were thousands of people. Did we look as pitiful as they did? Masses of Lithuanians with tattered suitcases and bulging bags poured out into the valley, dirty and gray with soiled clothing, as if they had lived in a gutter for years. Everyone moved in slow motion, some too weak to carry their belongings.

I didn't have control of my legs, nor did most others. Many buckled under their own weight onto the ground.

"We must stretch before sitting down, sweetheart," said Mother. "Our muscles have surely atrophied these past weeks."

Jonas stretched. He looked like a filthy street beggar. His golden hair stuck to his head in matted clumps, and his lips were dry and cracked. He looked at me, his eyes widened. I could only imagine the state I was in. We sat down and the grass felt heavenly, like a featherbed compared with the wagon floor. The chugging motion of the train, however, was still trapped in my body.

I looked at the people from our train car. They looked at me. Revealed by daylight, we saw the strangers we had shared a black closet with for six weeks. Ona was only a few years older than me. It had been dark when they put her on the truck in front of the hospital. Mrs. Arvydas was more attractive than her shadow. She had a very shapely figure, smooth brown hair, and full lips. Mrs. Rimas was a short woman with thick ankles, close to Mother's age.

People tried to communicate with the other groups, looking

for family members and loved ones. The man who wound his watch approached me.

"Do you have a handkerchief I could borrow?" he asked.

I nodded and quickly handed him the hankie, neatly folded to conceal my writing.

"Thank you," he said, dabbing his nose. He turned his back to me and walked amongst the crowd of people. I watched as he shook hands with a man he obviously recognized, passing the fabric within palms. The man patted his brow with the handkerchief before putting it in his pocket. Pass it along, I thought, imagining the hankie traveling hand to hand until it reached Papa.

"Elena, look," said Mrs. Rimas. "There are horse-drawn carts."

Mother stood up and looked down the row of groups. "There are men with the NKVD. They're walking amongst the people."

Andrius combed through his wavy hair with his fingers. He looked around constantly, watching the guards yet keeping his head down. He had to be nervous. His face had healed but was still sallow with remnants of yellow bruises. Would they recognize him? Would they haul him away or kill him right in front of us? I moved near him, trying to position my body to conceal his. But he was taller, his shoulders wide. I looked at the sharp blades of the bayonets and felt my stomach pitch with fear.

Ona began weeping loudly. "Pipe down," ordered the bald man. "You'll draw attention to us."

"Please, don't cry," said Andrius, shooting glances from Ona down to the guards.

A group near the front of the train was herded into two horse-drawn wagons. They drove away. I watched as the NKVD walked with men from cluster to cluster. The men looked strange, certainly not Lithuanian or Russian. They had darker skin and black hair, and their general appearance was disheveled, primitive. They stopped at the group of people next to us and began talking with the NKVD.

"Elena, what are they saying?" asked Mrs. Rimas.

Mother didn't answer.

"Elena?"

"They're . . ." She stopped.

"What?" said Mrs. Rimas.

"They're selling us," she whispered.

23

I WATCHED THE MEN walking amongst the groups, surveying the merchandise. They made people stand, turn around, and show them their hands.

"Mother, why are they selling us?" asked Jonas. "Where are we going?"

"Elena," said Mrs. Arvydas, "you must tell them that Andrius is a simpleton. Please. If not, they'll take him from me. Andrius, put your head down."

"They're selling us in groups," reported Mother.

I looked around our cluster. We were mostly women and children, with only two old men. But we had Andrius. Despite his injuries, he looked strong and able.

"Do we want to be bought?" asked Jonas. No one answered. A guard approached with a man. They stopped in front of our group. Everyone looked down, except me. I couldn't help myself. I stared at the guard, who appeared well rested, clean, and fed. I saw Mother cough into her hand and discreetly try to wipe off her lipstick. The disheveled man pointed at her and said something to the guard. The guard shook his head and waved a circular motion around our group. The man pointed at Mother once again and then made an obscene gesture. The guard laughed and began muttering. The man surveyed our group, and then, he pointed at Andrius.

The guard walked over to Andrius and barked a command. Andrius did not move. My stomach braided up into my throat.

"He's slow—leave him alone," said Mrs. Arvydas. "Elena, tell them."

Mother spoke one word in Russian. The guard grabbed Andrius by the hair and raised his face. Andrius stared blankly. Ona cried and rocked back and forth. Mr. Stalas moaned and grumbled. The man waved his hands in disgust at our group and walked away.

Other groups were purchased, loaded into wagons, and driven off through the valley to disappear through the V at the base of the hills. We finished the last drops of slop and water, debating whether we wanted to be bought.

Someone mentioned escaping. Running away was briefly discussed until a gunshot rang out, followed by screams near the front of the train. The little girl with the dolly began to cry.

"Elena," said Mrs. Rimas. "Ask one of the guards where they're taking the people."

Mother tried to speak with a guard, but he ignored her. For the moment, I didn't care what happened. The grass smelled like fresh chives, and the sunshine filled me with strength. I stood up and stretched.

The children spread out a bit, and the guards didn't seem to care. The NKVD inspected the train cars, stopping only to scream that we were filthy pigs who disrespected the train. The engine hissed, readying for departure.

"They're going back for more," said Andrius.

"You think so?" asked Jonas.

"They won't stop," said Andrius, "until they've gotten rid of all of us."

24

HOURS PASSED and the sun began to sink. Only two groups remained. The grouchy woman stomped around and yelled at us. She said Mother made our group appear weak and that now they would probably shoot everyone.

"Let them shoot us," said the bald man. "I'm telling you, we'll be better off."

"But they were going to make us slaves," argued Mrs. Arvydas.

"A little work wouldn't kill you," said the grouchy woman to Mrs. Arvydas. "They probably want some manual labor from us, that's all. That's why they took the other groups first, because most of you look so weak. I grew up on a farm. I'm not afraid to get my hands dirty."

"Then you're elected to go dig up some food," said Andrius. "Now leave our mothers alone."

Jonas and I were spread out on the grass, trying to stretch our stiff muscles. Andrius joined us, put his hands behind his head and stared up at the sky.

"Your forehead is getting red," I told him.

"A sunburn is the least of my worries," said Andrius. "I'm not turning my back to the guards. Maybe if we get a bit of color, we'll be bought and hauled off into Soviet slavery like the witch wants," he said.

Jonas rolled over onto his back like Andrius. "Just as long as we can stay together. Papa said that's important."

"I have no choice but to stay with my mother. I'm surprised she made it this far," said Andrius, looking over in her direction. Mrs. Arvydas was swatting flies away with her silk handkerchief and losing her balance in the process. "She's not exactly hardy."

"Do you have any sisters or brothers?" asked Jonas.

"No," said Andrius. "My mother didn't enjoy being pregnant. My father said that since he had a son, he didn't need any more children."

"My papa said that they're going to give us another brother or sister one day. I think I'd like a brother," said Jonas. "So, what do you think everyone at home is doing? Do you think they wonder what happened to us?"

"If they do, they're too scared to ask about it," said Andrius.

"But why? And why were we sent away?" asked Jonas.

"Because we were on the list," I said.

"But why were we on the list?" continued Jonas.

"Because Papa works at the university," I replied.

"But Mrs. Raskunas works at the university, and she wasn't taken," said Jonas.

Jonas was right. Mrs. Raskunas had peered out from behind her curtains as we were being hauled off in the night. I had seen her staring. Why wasn't her family taken? Why did they hide behind their curtains instead of trying to stop them from deporting us? Papa would never have done that.

"I can understand why the bald man is on the list," I said. "He's horrible."

"He's awfully eager to die, isn't he?" said Andrius, staring up at the sky.

"You know what?" said Jonas. "Looking at the sky, it's like I'm lying on the grass at home, in Lithuania."

That sounded like something Mother would say, throwing color onto a black-and-white picture.

"Look," continued Jonas, "that cloud looks like a cannon."

"Make it blow up the Soviets," I said, running my fingers over the blades of grass. "They deserve it."

Andrius turned his head to me. I felt awkward under his prolonged gaze.

"What?" I asked.

"You always seem to have a mouthful of opinions," he said.

"That's what Papa said. See, Lina, you better be careful," said Jonas.

~

My bedroom door swung open. "Lina, I want to see you in the living room," said Papa.

"Why?" I asked.

"In the living room, NOW!" Papa's nostrils flared. He walked out of the room.

"Mother, what's wrong?"

"You heard your father, Lina. Go to the living room."

We walked out into the hallway.

"Go to sleep, Jonas," said Mother without even looking in the direction of my brother's room. I looked over. Jonas was peeking out his bedroom door, his eyes wide.

Papa was steaming mad, and he was mad at me. What had I done? I walked into the living room.

"Is this what you waste your talent on?" He thrust a scrap of paper in my face.

"Papa, it was a joke," I explained.

"YOU think it's a joke. What if the Kremlin doesn't think it's a joke? They're perfect likenesses, for God's sake!" He dropped the paper into my lap.

I looked at my sketch. The likeness was perfect. Even in a clown suit, it was obviously Stalin. I drew him standing in our dining room, with Papa and his friends sitting around the table, launching paper airplanes at him. The men were laughing. Stalin had a sad clown face as airplanes hit his head. Papa and Dr. Seltzer were perfect likenesses. I hadn't quite mastered the journalist's chin yet.

"Are there others?" my father demanded, snapping the paper from me.

"It was for fun," said a small voice. Jonas stood in his pajamas in the hallway. "Please don't be mad, Papa."

"Were you in on this, too?" yelled my father.

"Oh, Jonas," said Mother.

"He wasn't in on it! I drew it myself. I showed it to him because I thought it was funny."

"Have you shown this to anyone else?" asked Papa.

"No. I just drew it this afternoon," I said.

"Lina," said Mother. "This is serious. The Soviets could arrest you if they saw your drawing."

"But how would they ever see it? I threw it away," I argued.

"What if someone found it in the trash like I did? A wind could have blown this to the foot of Stalin," said Papa. "You've drawn your father and his friends mocking the leader of the Soviet Union! Are there others?" he asked.

"No, that's the only one."

Papa tore up my drawing and threw the pieces into the fire.

~

Andrius continued to stare at me. "Is that what you want?" he finally asked. "To blow up the Soviets?"

I turned to look at him. "I just want to go home. I want to see my father," I said.

He nodded.

25

EVENING CAME and two groups were left. Most of the NKVD had departed with the train. Only five armed officers remained, with two trucks. Nearly seventy-five Lithuanians and only five Soviets, yet no one dared move. I think most of us were too tired and weak. The grass was a welcomed bed, the space a luxury. I made note of landmarks to draw for Papa.

The NKVD made a fire and cooked their dinner while we sat and stared. They had American canned goods, bread, and coffee. After dinner they drank vodka and smoked, the volume of their voices rising steadily.

"What are they saying?" I asked Mother.

"They're talking about their homes, where they're from. They're sharing stories of their friends and family," she said.

I didn't believe her. I listened to the Russian words. The tone of their voices and the cackling laughter didn't sound like talk of family. Ona began again. She had taken to chanting "No, no, no, no," over and over. One of the NKVD stood up and yelled, flipping his hand at our group.

"I better try to quiet her," said Mother, getting up, "before the guards become angry." Jonas was already asleep. I covered him with my blue raincoat and wiped his hair away from his eyes. The bald man snored. The gray-haired man wound his watch. Andrius sat at the edge of the group, one knee pulled to his chest, watching the guards.

He had a strong profile, an angular jaw. A piece of his disheveled hair fell perfectly against the side of his face. I'd need a soft pencil to draw it. He saw me staring. I turned away quickly.

"Hey," he whispered to me.

I looked up. Something rolled across the grass and hit my leg. It was the stone with the sparkles he had found that day when he jumped off the train.

"The crown jewel from the train car princess," I whispered, smiling.

He nodded with a laugh.

I picked it up to roll back to him.

"No, you keep it," said Andrius.

We woke at sunrise. A few hours later a wagon came, chose the other group, and took them away. The guards then loaded us into the back of two trucks and drove us across the valley beyond the notch in the hills where a road began. No one spoke. We were too frightened to discuss our possible destination.

Riding in the truck, I realized that trying to escape would have been ridiculous. There was nothing for miles. We didn't see a human being or pass another vehicle. I thought about the man who had my handkerchief, hoping it was passed along, moving closer to Papa. After two hours we saw huts dotting the sides of the road. We entered what appeared to be an inhabited area, and the truck pulled over in front of a wooden building. The guards jumped out, yelling, "Davai! Davai!" and other instructions.

"They say we should leave our luggage in the trucks," said Mother, clutching her coat tightly over her arm.

"I want to know where we're going before we get out," demanded Mrs. Arvydas.

Mother tried to talk to the guards. She turned and smiled. "It's a bathhouse."

We jumped off the truck. Mother folded her coat and put it in her suitcase. The guards split us into male and female groups.

"Boys, carry me," the bald man said to Andrius and Jonas. "You have to bathe me."

Jonas looked petrified, Andrius disgusted. I smiled, which seemed to annoy Andrius even more. The men went first. The guards called them up onto the porch and began yelling in their faces, pushing them. Jonas looked at Mother for translation.

"Take off your clothes, dear," Mother translated.

"Now? Right here?" Jonas asked, looking at all the women and girls.

"We'll all turn around, won't we, ladies?" said Mother. We all turned our backs to the porch.

"No use in being modest now," said Mr. Stalas. "We're nothing but skeletons. Now take off my pants, boy. Ow! Watch my leg."

I heard Mr. Stalas complaining and Jonas apologizing. A belt buckle knocked against the wood of the porch. I wondered if it was Andrius's. The guards yelled.

"He says you must leave your clothes there, that they will be deloused," Mother translated.

Something smelled funny. I couldn't tell if it came from our group of women or from the bathhouse. We heard the bald man yell from within the structure.

Mother turned around and clasped her hands together. "My sweet Jonas," she whispered.

26

WE WAITED. "What's going on in there?" I said. Mother shook her head. Three NKVD stood on the porch. One barked yet another command.

"Ten of us at a time," said Mother. "We must go to the porch and take off our clothes."

We were in the first group, along with Mrs. Arvydas, the grouchy woman, and her daughters. Mother helped Ona up onto the porch. I unbuttoned my dress and pulled it over my head, unbraided my hair, and took off my sandals. Mother stood in her brassiere and underwear, helping Ona. The guards stood on the porch, staring at us. I hesitated.

"It's okay, dear," said Mother. "Think of how nice it will be to feel clean again." Ona began to whimper.

A young blond guard lit a cigarette, turned his back, and looked off toward the truck. Another NKVD stared, grinning and biting his bottom lip.

I took off my bra and panties and stood on the porch, covering myself with my hands. Mrs. Arvydas stood next to me, her voluptuous breasts too large to conceal with her thin forearm. A guard with a gold tooth, who appeared to be a commander, walked down the porch stopping to look at each woman, scanning her up and down. He stopped at Mrs. Arvydas. She did not lift her head. He swirled a toothpick on his tongue and raised his brow, violating her with his stare.

I let out a breath in disgust. Mother's head snapped to me. The guard grabbed my arms and threw them down to my sides. He looked me up and down and grinned. He reached out and groped my breast. I felt his ragged fingernails scratch across my skin.

I had never been naked in front of a man before. His touch, the rough hand on me, made me feel sick, and dirtier on the inside than I was on the outside. I tried to cross my arms. Mother yelled something in Russian and pulled me behind Ona.

Ona's inner thighs and buttocks were caked with chunks of dried blood. The guard began to scream at Mother. She removed her remaining clothing and put her arm around me. They marched us into the bathhouse.

A GUARD STOOD AT a distance. He plunged a scoop in a bucket and threw some sort of white powder at us. The showers clicked on with an icy spray.

"We must hurry," said Mother. "We don't know how long they'll give us." She took a small chunk of soap and scrubbed at my scalp and face, ignoring her own body. I watched the brown rivers of dirt run down my legs, over my ankles, and into the drain. I wanted to be sucked down with it, away from the guards and the humiliation.

"Keep scrubbing, Lina, quickly," said Mother, turning to wash Ona.

I stood shivering under the stream of water, washing as well as I could, hoping the guards would not be waiting for us on the other side of the wall.

I washed Mother's back and tried to wash her hair. Mrs. Arvydas stood under the stream of water, her hands raised above her head gracefully, unaware, as if she were in her own private bath at home. The showers snapped off.

We retrieved our clothes on the other side of the wall. I quickly pulled my dress over my head and felt a knock against my thigh. The stone from Andrius. I put my hand in my pocket, my fingers searching for the smooth edge.

Mother combed through my hair with her fingers. I looked at her wet face. Water dripped from her blond waves onto her shoulders.

"I want to go home," I whispered, shivering. "Please."

She dropped her clothing and hugged me, long and hard. "We'll go home. Keep thinking of your father and of our house. We must keep it alive in our hearts." She let go and looked at me. "If we do, we'll get there."

The men were already in the first truck. Another group of women and children stood naked on the porch as we exited.

"Feel better, darling?" said Mother, smiling at Jonas as she climbed into the truck. She checked her suitcase for her coat. Jonas looked much improved, in appearance and disposition. So did Andrius. His wet hair was shiny, the color of dark cinnamon.

"Now we're clean dead men. So what of that?" said the bald man.

"If we were dead men, they wouldn't allow us to shower," said the gray-haired man, looking at his watch.

"Hey, there was blond hair under all that dirt," said Andrius, reaching out and grabbing a strand of my hair. I shrank back and looked away. Mother put her arm around me.

"What's wrong, Lina?" asked Jonas.

I ignored him. I thought of the guard who touched me and all the things I should have done—slapped him, kicked him, screamed in his face. I put my hand in my pocket and grabbed the stone from Andrius. I squeezed it and tried as hard as I could to break it.

"Do you suppose they'll take us for a four-course meal now that we've been to the sauna?" joked Mrs. Rimas.

"Oh, yes, a piece of black forest torte and a cognac or two," laughed Mrs. Arvydas.

"I'd love a nice hot coffee," said Mother.

"Strong coffee," added the bald man.

"Wow, I never thought it could feel so good to be clean!" exclaimed Jonas, looking at his hands.

Everyone's humor was much improved, except Ona's. She continued chanting. Despite the efforts of Mrs. Rimas, she could not be calmed. As the last group of women and children boarded the truck, the commander saw Ona standing up, sitting down, and pulling her hair. He yelled at her. The young blond guard appeared at the back of the truck.

"Leave her be," said Mrs. Rimas. "The poor dear is grieving."

Mother translated to the commander. Ona stood up and stamped her right foot. The commander stepped up and pulled Ona from the truck. She lost all control, screaming, clawing at him. She was no match for his height or strength. He threw her to the ground. His eyes narrowed and his square jaw tightened. Mother scrambled to jump off the truck to Ona. It was too late. The commander pulled out a pistol and shot Ona in the head.

I gasped, along with everyone else. Andrius grabbed Jonas's face and covered his eyes. Blood, the color of thick red wine, pooled under Ona's head. Her leg splayed out in an unnatural, bent angle. One of her feet was missing a shoe.

"Lina," said Andrius.

I turned my head to him, dazed.

"Don't look," he said.

My mouth opened, but nothing came out. I turned my head back. The young blond guard was staring at Ona's body.

"Lina, look at me," urged Andrius.

Mother slumped on her knees near the edge of the truck, looking down at Ona. I moved and sat down near my brother.

The engine rumbled and the truck began to roll. Mother sat down and put her face in her hands. Miss Grybas clucked her tongue, shaking her head.

Jonas pulled my head against his knees and patted my hair. "Please, don't say anything to the guards. Don't make them mad, Lina," he whispered.

Ona's body got smaller and smaller as we drove away. She lay dead in the dirt, murdered by the NKVD. Somewhere, hundreds of miles away, her daughter decomposed in the grass. How would her family ever know what happened to her? How would anyone know what was happening to *us*? I would continue to write and draw whenever I had the chance. I would draw the commander firing, Mother on her knees with her head in her hands, and our truck driving away, the tires spitting gravel onto Ona's dead body.

28

WE DROVE INTO A LARGE collective farming area. Clusters of decrepit one-room cabins formed a shanty village. The warm sun was clearly temporary. Buildings pitched at a slant, their warped roofs warning of extreme weather.

The guards ordered us off the truck. Andrius hung his head, standing close to his mother. They began directing us to what I thought were our own shacks, but when Miss Grybas and Mrs. Rimas entered one, a woman ran out and began arguing with the guards.

"There are people living in the cabins," whispered Jonas.

"Yes, we'll most likely have to share," said Mother, pulling us close.

Two women walked past us carrying large buckets of water. I didn't recognize them from our train.

We were assigned to a dingy hut near the back of the

settlement. The gray wood was bald, shaved by many seasons of wind and snow. The door had splits and cracks and sat crooked on the frame. A strong wind could whisk the shack up into the sky, scattering it in a burst of pieces. The blond guard pulled the door open, bellowed something in Russian and pushed us inside. A squat Altaian woman wrapped in layers ran to the door and began screaming after the guard. Mother moved us to the corner. The woman turned and began yelling at us. Her hair poked out of her kerchief like black straw. Wrinkles formed an atlas on her wide, weathered face.

"What's she saying?" asked Jonas.

"She says she has no room for filthy criminals," said Mother.

"We're *not* criminals," I said.

The woman continued her rant, throwing her arms in the air and spitting on the floor of the hut.

"Is she crazy?" asked Jonas.

"She says she barely has food enough for herself and she's not about to share it with criminals like us." Mother turned her back to the woman. "Well, now, we'll just set our things in this corner. Jonas, put your suitcase down."

The woman grabbed my hair and pulled it, yanking me toward the door to throw me out.

Mother yelled, blasting the woman in Russian. She ripped the woman's hand from my head, slapped her, and pushed her away. Jonas kicked her in the shin. The Altaian woman stared at us with angled black eyes. Mother returned the stare. The woman let out a hearty laugh. She asked a question.

"We're Lithuanian," said Mother, first speaking in Lithuanian and then in Russian. The woman jibbered.

"What's she saying?" I asked.

"She says feisty people make good workers and that we have to pay her rent." Mother continued asking questions.

"Pay her? For what? To live in this hole in the middle of nowhere?" I said.

"We're in Altai," said Mother. "They are farming potatoes and beets."

"So there are potatoes to eat?" asked Jonas.

"Food is rationed. She said the guards oversee the farm and the workers," said Mother.

I remembered Papa talking about Stalin confiscating peasants' land, tools, and animals. He told them what crops they would produce and how much they would be paid. I thought it was ridiculous. How could Stalin simply take something that didn't belong to him, something that a farmer and his family had worked their whole lives for? "That's communism, Lina," Papa had said.

The woman yelled at Mother, wagging her finger and shaking her head. She left the hut.

We were on a *kolkhoz*, a collective farm, and I was to become a beet farmer.

I hated beets.

maps and snakes

29

THE SHACK WAS approximately ten feet by twelve feet. Lodged in the corner was a small stove surrounded by a couple of pots and dirty tins. A pallet of straw sat next to the wall near the stove. There was no pillow, only a worn quilted coverlet. Two tiny windows were created out of bits of glass that had been puttied together.

"There's nothing here," I said. "There isn't a sink, a table, or a wardrobe. Is that where she sleeps?" I asked. "Where will we sleep? Where is the bathroom?"

"Where can we eat?" said Jonas.

"I'm not certain," said Mother, looking in the pots. "This is filthy. But nothing a little cleaning can't fix, right?"

"Well, it's nice to be off that train," said Jonas.

The young blond NKVD burst through the door. "Elena Vilkas," he said.

Mother looked up at the guard.

"Elena Vilkas!" he repeated, louder this time.

"Yes, that's me," said Mother. They began speaking in Russian, then arguing.

"What is it, Mother?" asked Jonas.

Mother gathered us into her arms. "Don't worry, love. We'll stay together."

The guard yelled, "Davai!" waving us out of the hut.

"Where are we going?" I asked.

"The commander wants to see me. I told him we all had to go together," said Mother.

The commander. My stomach rolled. "I'll stay here. I'll be fine," I said.

"No, we must all stay together," said Jonas.

We followed the blond guard between battered shacks until we reached a log building in much better condition than the others. A few NKVD gathered near the door smoking cigarettes. They leered at Mother. She surveyed the building and the guards.

"Stay here," she said. "I'll be right back."

"No," said Jonas. "We're coming in with you."

Mother looked toward the lusty guards, then at me.

A guard stepped down from the door. "Davai!" he yelled, pulling Mother by the elbow toward the building.

"I'll be right back," said Mother over her shoulder before she disappeared through the door.

~

"I'll be right back," said Mother.

"But what do you think?" I asked.

"I think you look lovely," said Mother, stepping back to admire the dress.

"Good," said the tailor, placing pins back into his small satin pin cushion. "All done, Lina. You can change now, but be careful, it's just pinned, not stitched."

"Meet me on the sidewalk," said Mother over her shoulder before she disappeared through the door.

"Your mother has excellent taste in dresses," said the tailor.

He was right. The dress was beautiful. The soft gray color made my eyes stand out.

I changed out of the dress and walked outside to meet Mother. She wasn't there. I peered down the row of brightly colored shops but didn't see her. Down the street, a door opened and Mother emerged. Her blue hat matched her dress, which fluttered around her legs as she walked toward me. She held up two ice cream cones and smiled, a shopping bag dangling from her arm.

"The boys are having their day and we'll have ours," said Mother, her red lipstick shining. She handed me a cone and steered us over to a bench. "Let's sit."

Papa and Jonas had gone to a soccer match, and Mother and I had spent the morning shopping. I licked the creamy vanilla ice cream and leaned back against the warm bench.

"It feels good to sit," sighed Mother. She looked over to me. "Okay, the dress is finished—what else did we have to do?"

"I need charcoal," I reminded her.

"Ah, that's right," said Mother. "Charcoal for my artist."

~

"We should have gone with her," said Jonas.

He was right. But I didn't want to be near the commander. Mother knew it. I should have gone in with her. Now she was alone with them, unprotected, and it was my fault. I tugged Jonas over to the side of the building near a dirty window.

"Stay here so the blond guard can see you," I told Jonas.

"What are you doing?" he said.

"I'm going to look in the window, to make sure Mother's all right."

"No, Lina!"

"Stay there," I told him.

The blond guard looked no more than twenty. He was the one who had turned away when we took our clothes off. He took out a pocketknife and began scraping underneath his fingernails. I edged over toward the window and stood on my toes. Mother sat in a chair and stared into her lap. The commander sat on the edge of a desk in front of her. He flipped through a file while speaking to Mother. He closed the file and balanced it on his thigh. I looked over at the guard, then stretched a bit higher for a better view.

"Stop it, Lina. Andrius says they'll shoot us if you make trouble," whispered Jonas.

"I'm not making trouble," I said, moving back to my brother. "I just wanted to make sure she was all right."

"Well, remember what happened to Ona," said Jonas.

What *had* happened to Ona? Was she in heaven with her daughter and my grandma? Or was she floating amongst the trains and masses of Lithuanians, searching for her husband?

Those were questions for Papa. He always listened intently

to my questions, nodding and then pausing carefully before answering. Who would answer my questions now?

The weather was warm, despite the cloudy sky. In the distance, beyond the shacks, I saw spruce and pine trees interspersed with farmlands. I looked around, memorizing the landscape to draw it for Papa. I wondered where Andrius and his mother were.

Some of the buildings were in better shape than ours. One had a log fence around it and another, a small garden. I'd draw them—sad and shriveled with barely a spot of color.

The door to the building opened and Mother emerged. The commander walked out and leaned against the door frame, watching her walk. Mother's jaw clenched. She nodded as she came toward us. The commander called something to her from the door. She ignored him and grabbed our hands.

"Take us back to the hut," she said, turning to the blond guard. He didn't move.

"I know the way," said Jonas, starting off through the dirt. "Follow me."

"Are you okay?" I asked Mother once we began walking.

"I'm fine," she said, her voice low.

My shoulders dropped as weight escaped them. "What did he want?"

"Not here," she said.

30

"THEY WANT ME to work with them," said Mother once Jonas had returned us to the shack.

"Work with them?" I said.

"Yes, well, they want me to work *for* them," she said. "Translating documents, and also speaking with the other Lithuanians who are here," she said.

I thought of the file that the commander held.

"What will you get for doing it?" asked Jonas.

"I'm not going to be their translator," said Mother. "I said no. They also asked me to listen to people's conversations and report them to the commander."

"To be a snitch?" said Jonas.

"Yes," said Mother.

"They want you to spy on everyone and report to them?" I asked.

Mother nodded. "They promised preferential treatment if I agreed."

"Pigs!" I shrieked.

"Lina! Lower your voice," said Mother.

"They think you would help them after what they've done to us?" I said.

"But Mother, maybe you will need the special treatment," said Jonas with concerned eyes.

"They don't mean it," I snapped. "They're all liars, Jonas. They wouldn't give her anything."

"Jonas," said Mother, stroking my brother's face. "I can't trust them. Stalin has told the NKVD that Lithuanians are the enemy. The commander and the guards look at us as beneath them. Do you understand?"

"Andrius already told me that," said Jonas.

"Andrius is a very smart boy. We must speak only to one another," said Mother, turning to me, "and please, Lina, be careful with anything you write or draw."

We dug through our suitcases and organized what we could sell if the need arose. I looked at my copy of *The Pickwick Papers*. Pages 6–11 were torn out. Page 12 had a smudge of dirt on it.

I grasped the gold picture frame and took it out of the suitcase, staring at my father's face. I wondered where the handkerchief was. I had to send more.

"Kostas," said Mother, looking over my shoulder. I handed her the frame. Her index finger lovingly traced my father's face and then her mother's. "It's wonderful that you brought this. You have no idea how it lifts my spirit. Please, keep it safe."

I opened the tablet of writing paper I had packed. *14 June, 1941. Dear Joana* stood alone on the first page, a title without a story. I had written that nearly two months ago, the night we were taken. Where was Joana, and where were the rest of our relatives? What would I write now if I were to finish it? Would I tell her that the Soviets had forced us into cattle cars and held us prisoner for six weeks with barely any food or water? Would I mention that they wanted Mother to spy for them? And what about the baby that died in our car and how the NKVD shot Ona in the head? I heard Mother's voice, warning me to be careful, but my hand began to move.

31

THE ALTAIAN WOMAN returned and clattered around. She put a pot on the stove. We watched as she boiled two potatoes and gnawed on a stump of bread.

"Mother," said Jonas, "will there be potatoes for us tonight?"

When we asked, we were told we had to work to earn food.

"If you worked for the NKVD, Mother, would they give you food?" asked Jonas.

"No, my dear. They would give me empty promises," she replied, "which is worse than an empty belly."

Mother paid the woman for a single potato, then again for the privilege to boil the potato. It was ridiculous.

"How much money do we have left?" I asked.

"Barely any," she said.

We tried to sleep, huddled against Mother on the floor of bare boards. The peasant woman slurped and snored, sunken in her bed of straw. Her sour breath filled the small room. Was she born here in Siberia? Had she ever known a life other than this? I stared into the dark and tried to paint images with my mind on the black canvas.

~

"Open it, darling!"

"I can't, I'm too nervous," I told Mother.

"She wanted to wait until you got home," Mother told Papa. "She's been holding that envelope for hours."

"Open it, Lina!" urged Jonas.

"What if they didn't accept me?" I said, my damp fingers clutching the envelope.

"Well, then you'll be accepted next year," said Mother.

"You won't know as long as the envelope is sealed," said Papa.

"Open it!" said Jonas, handing the letter opener to me.

I slid the silver blade under the flap on the back of the envelope. Ever since Mrs. Pranas had mailed my application, I had thought of little else. Studying with the best artists in Europe. It was such an opportunity. I sliced open the top of the envelope and removed a single sheet of folded paper. My eyes scanned quickly across the type.

"Dear Miss Vilkas,

"Thank you for your recent application for the summer arts program. Your samples are most impressive. It is with great pleasure that we offer you a place in our—"

"Yes! They said yes!" I screamed.

"I knew it!" said Papa.

"Congratulations, Lina," said Jonas, slinging his arm around me.

"I can't wait to tell Joana," I said.

"That's wonderful, darling!" said Mother. "We have to celebrate."

"We have a cake," said Jonas.

"Well, I was just certain we'd be celebrating." Mother winked.

Papa beamed. "You, my dear, are blessed with a gift," he said, taking my hands. "There are great things in store for you, Lina."

~

I turned my head toward a rustling sound. The Altaian woman waddled to the corner, grunted, and peed into a tin can.

32

IT WAS STILL DARK when the NKVD began yelling. They ordered us out of the shack, shouting at us to form a line. We scrambled to fall in with the others. My Russian vocabulary was growing. In addition to *davai*, I had learned other important words, such as *nyet*, which meant "no"; *sveenya*, which meant "pig"; and of course *fasheest*, "fascist." Miss Grybas and the grouchy woman were already in line. Mrs. Rimas waved to Mother. I looked around for Andrius and his mother. They weren't there. Neither was the bald man.

The commander walked up and down the line, chewing on his toothpick. He looked us over and made comments to the other guards.

"What's he saying, Elena?" asked Mrs. Rimas.

"He's dividing us up for work detail," said Mother.

The commander approached Mother and yelled in her

face. He pulled Mother, Mrs. Rimas, and the grouchy woman out of the line. The young blond guard pulled me out of line and pushed me toward Mother. He divided up the rest. Jonas was in a group with two elderly women.

"Davai!" The young blond guard handed Mother a belted piece of canvas and marched our group away.

"Meet us back at the shack," yelled Mother to Jonas. How would that be possible? Mother and I couldn't even find our way back from the NKVD building. It was Jonas who showed us the way. We would surely be lost.

My stomach turned with hunger. My legs dragged. Mother and Mrs. Rimas whispered back and forth in Lithuanian behind the blond guard. After walking a few kilometers we arrived at a clearing in the woods. The guard grabbed the canvas from Mother and threw it on the ground. He yelled a command.

"He says, 'dig,'" said Mother.

"Dig? Dig where?" asked Mrs. Rimas.

"Here, I guess," said Mother. "He says if we want to eat, we must dig. Our ration depends on our progress."

"What are we to dig with?" I asked.

Mother asked the blond guard. He kicked the heap of canvas. Mother unfolded it and found several rusty hand shovels, the kind used in a flower garden. The handles were missing.

Mother said something to the guard that prompted an irate "Davai" and the kicking of the shovels into our shins.

"Get out of my way," said the grouchy woman. "I'm going to get this over with. I need to eat and so do my girls." She got down on her hands and knees and started chipping away at the earth with the tiny shovel. We all followed. The guard sat under a tree and watched, smoking cigarettes.

"Where are the potatoes and the beets?" I asked Mother.

"Well, they are clearly punishing me," said Mother.

"Punishing you?" asked Mrs. Rimas. Mother whispered in her ear about the commander's offer to work for him.

"But Elena, you could have gotten preferential treatment," said Mrs. Rimas. "And most likely, extra food."

"A guilty conscience is not worth extra food," said Mother. "Think of the demands that could be made of me in that office. And think of what could happen to people. I don't need that on my soul. I'll persevere like everyone else."

"A woman said there's a town five kilometers away. There's a store, a post office, and a school," said Mrs. Rimas.

"Perhaps we could walk there," said Mother, "and send letters. Maybe someone has heard from the men."

"Be careful, Elena. Sending letters may endanger the people back home," said Mrs. Rimas. "Don't put anything in writing, ever."

I looked at my feet. I had been writing down everything and had already filled several pages with descriptions and drawings.

"No," whispered Mother. She looked to the grouchy woman pounding the dirt and leaned toward Mrs. Rimas. "I have a contact."

What did Mother mean, she had a "contact"? Who was her contact? And the war—now the Germans were in Lithuania.

What was Hitler doing? I wondered what had happened to our house and everything we left behind. And why were we digging this stupid hole?

"Well, at least your housemate talks to you," said Mother. "Ours is a beastly thing that grabbed Lina by the hair."

"The villagers are not happy," said Mrs. Rimas. "But they were expecting us. Apparently, several truckloads of Estonians were dumped in a nearby village a few days ago."

Mother's shovel paused. "Estonians?"

"Yes," whispered Mrs. Rimas. "They've deported people from Estonia and Latvia, too."

Mother sighed. "I feared that might happen. It's madness. How many will they deport?"

"Elena, there will be hundreds of thousands," said Mrs. Rimas.

"Quit your gossiping and get to work," barked the grouchy woman. "I want to eat."

33

WE HAD DUG a pit more than two feet deep when a truck brought a small bucket of water. The guard gave us a break. Blisters wept on my hands. Our fingers were caked with dirt. They wouldn't give us a ladle or cup. We bent like dogs, each taking turns lapping out of the bucket while the blond guard drank leisurely from a large canteen. The water smelled fishy, but I didn't care. My knees looked like raw meat, and my back ached from bending for hours.

We were digging in a small clearing, surrounded by woods. Mother asked permission to go to the bathroom and then pulled me, along with Mrs. Rimas, into the trees. We squatted, our dresses bunched around our waists, to relieve ourselves.

We faced each other, all on our haunches. "Elena, can you pass the talcum, please?" said Mrs. Rimas, wiping herself with a leaf.

We began to laugh. It was such a ridiculous sight, grabbing our knees in a circle. We actually laughed. Mother laughed so hard that her ringlets fell loose from the kerchief she had tied around her hair.

"Our sense of humor," said Mother, her eyes pooled with laughing tears. "They can't take that away from us, right?"

~

We roared with laughter. The lantern flames flickered in the dark. Joana's brother pumped a playful tune on the accordion. My uncle, who had indulged in blackberry liquor, danced a disjointed jig around the backyard of the cottage, trying to imitate our mothers. He pretended to hold a skirt and looped from side to side.

"Come," whispered Joana, grabbing my hand. "Let's take a walk."

We locked arms and walked between the dark cottages down to the beach. Sand crawled into my shoes. We stood on the shore, the water lapping near our feet. The Baltic Sea glistened in the moonlight.

"The way the moon is shining on the water, it's like it's beckoning us in," sighed Joana.

"It is. It's calling us," I said, memorizing the light and shadow to paint later. I kicked off my sandals. "Let's go."

"I don't have my bathing suit," said Joana.

"Neither do I. So what?"

"So what? Lina, we can't swim naked," she said.

"Who said anything about swimming naked?" I asked. I waded into the black water in my dress.

"Lina! For goodness' sake, what are you doing?" gasped Joana.

I held out my arms and traced the moon shadows on the water. My skirt lifted, weightless. "C'mon, it's lovely!" I dived under the surface.

Joana kicked off her shoes and waded into the water up to her ankles. The light reflected off of her long brown hair and tall frame.

"Come in, it's beautiful!" I said. She waded in slowly, too slowly. I jumped up and pulled her in. She screamed and laughed. Joana's laugh could be singled out in a crowd. It had a raw freedom that echoed around me.

"You're crazy!" she said.

"Why am I crazy? It looked so beautiful; I wanted to be part of it," I said.

"Will you paint us like this?" asked Joana.

"Yes, I'll call it . . . Two Heads, Bobbing in Black," I said, flicking water at her.

"I don't want to go home. It's just too perfect here," she said, swirling her arms through the water. "Shh, someone's coming."

"Where?" I said, spinning around.

"There, in the trees," she whispered. Two figures emerged from the trees in front of the beach. "Lina, it's him! The tall one. The one I told you about. The one I saw in town! What do we do?"

Two boys walked to shore, looking out at us.

"A bit late for a swim, isn't it?" said the tall boy.

"Not at all," I said.

"Oh, really, do you always go swimming after dark?" he asked.

"I go swimming whenever I feel like it," I said.

"And what about your older sister there? Does she always go swimming at night?"

"Why don't you ask her yourself?" I said. Joana kicked me underwater.

"You should be careful. You don't want someone to see you without clothes." He grinned.

"Really? You mean like this?" I jumped and stood up in the water. My wet dress clung to me like melted taffy to paper. I flung my arm in the water, trying to get them both wet.

"Crazy kid." He laughed, dodging the water.

"C'mon," said his friend. "We'll be late for the meeting."

"A meeting? What sort of meeting is going on at this hour?" I asked.

The boys dropped their heads for a moment. "We have to go. Good-bye, older sister," said the tall boy to Joana before turning to walk down the beach with his friend.

"Bye," said Joana.

We laughed so hard I thought surely our parents would hear us. We jumped out of the water, grabbed our sandals, and ran back through the sand onto the shadowy path. Frogs and crickets chirped and warbled all around us. Joana grabbed my arm, pulling me to a stop in the dark. "Don't tell our parents."

"Joana, we're soaking wet. They'll know we went swimming," I said.

"No, I mean about the boys . . . and what they said," she said.

"All right, older sister, I won't tell," I said, grinning. We ran through the dark, laughing all the way back to the cottage.

~

What did Joana know about the boys and their meeting that I didn't?

The laughter had died. "Lina, let's go, dear," said Mother.

I looked back to the hole. What if we were digging our own grave?

34

I FOUND A STICK and snapped it in half. I sat down and used it to draw in a patch of hard dirt. I drew our house, garden, and the trees before it was time to return to work. I pushed small stones into the earth with my thumb, creating a pathway to our front door, and lined the roof with twigs.

"We must prepare," said Mother. "The winter will be beyond anything we've experienced. Temperatures will be below freezing. There will be no food."

"Winter?" I said, leaning back on my heels. "Are you joking? You think we'll still be here when winter comes? Mother, no!" Winter was months away. I couldn't bear the thought of living in that shack, digging holes for months, and trying to avoid the commander. I glanced over to the blond guard. He was looking at my drawing in the dirt.

"I hope not," said Mother, lowering her voice. "But what

if we are? If we're not prepared, we'll surely freeze or starve." Mother had the grouchy woman's attention.

"The snowstorms in Siberia are treacherous," said Mrs. Rimas, nodding.

"I don't know how the shacks withstand it," said Mother.

"Why don't we build our own building?" I asked. "We can build a log house like the kolkhoz office, with a chimney and a stove. We can all live together."

"Stupid girl. They'll never give us time to build something of our own, and if we did build something, they'd take it for themselves," said the grouchy woman. "Keep digging."

It began to rain. Water plopped on our heads and shoulders. We opened our mouths to drink.

"This is insanity," said Mrs. Rimas.

Mother shouted over to the blond guard. The butt of his cigarette glowed under the shelter of the tree branches.

"He says we must dig faster," said Mother, raising her voice as the rain poured down in sheets. "That the soil will be soft now."

"Bastard," said Mrs. Rimas.

I looked over and saw our house melting in the dirt. My drawing stick rolled away, propelled by the wind and rain.

I put my head down and dug. I jabbed the small shovel into the earth, harder and harder, pretending the soil was the commander. My fingers cramped and my arms shook with exhaustion. The hem of my dress was ripped, and my face and neck were sunburned from the morning sun.

When the rain stopped, we marched back to the camp,

covered in mud up to our waists. My stomach convulsed with hunger. Mrs. Rimas slung the canvas over her shoulder and we dragged along, our hands cramped, still locked on to the shovel blades we had gripped for nearly twelve hours.

We entered the camp near the back. I recognized the bald man's shack with its brown door and was able to direct Mother toward ours. Jonas was inside waiting for us. Every pot was brimming with water.

"You're back!" he shouted. "I was worried you wouldn't find the hut."

Mother wrapped her arms around Jonas, kissing his hair.

"It was still raining when I got back," explained Jonas. "I dragged the pots outside so we could have water."

"Very smart, love. Have you had some to drink?" asked Mother.

"Plenty," he said, looking at me in my bedraggled state. "You can have a nice bath."

We drank from a large pot before washing our legs off. Mother insisted I drink more, even when I felt I couldn't.

Jonas sat cross-legged on the boards. One of Mother's scarves was spread out in front of him. In the center was a lonely piece of bread, with a small flower next to it.

Mother looked down at the bread and the wilted flower. "What sort of banquet do we have here?" she said.

"I received a ration coupon for my work today. I worked with two ladies making shoes," said Jonas, smiling. "Are you hungry? You look tired."

"I'm so hungry," I said, staring at the solitary piece of

bread. If Jonas received bread for working indoors on shoes, we must certainly be getting an entire turkey, I thought.

"We are each entitled to three hundred grams of bread for our work," explained Jonas. "You have to collect your ration coupon at the kolkhoz office."

"That's . . . that's all?" asked Mother.

Jonas nodded.

Three hundred grams of dry bread. I couldn't believe it. That's all we got after digging for hours. They were starving us and would probably dump us into the holes we dug. "It's not enough," I said.

"We'll find something more," said Mother.

Fortunately, the commander wasn't at the log building when we arrived. We were given our coupons without having to beg or dance. We followed the other workers into a nearby building. The bread was weighed and distributed to us. I could almost close my palm around the entire ration. On the way back, we saw Miss Grybas in back of her shack. She waved us over. Her arms and dress were filthy. She had been working in the beet fields all day. Her face twisted with revulsion when she saw us. "What are they doing to you?"

"Making us dig," said Mother, pushing her mud-encrusted hair away from her face. "In the rain."

"Quickly!" she said, pulling us toward her. Her hands trembled. "I could be in awful trouble taking risks like this for you. I hope you know that." She reached into her brassiere and pulled out a few small beets and passed them quickly to Mother. She then raised her dress and took two more from her underwear. "Now hurry, go!" she said. I heard the bald man yelling in the shack behind us.

We scurried back to our hut to begin our feast. I was too hungry to care that I hated beets. I didn't even care that they had been transported in someone's sweaty underwear.

35

"LINA, PUT THIS in your pocket and take it to Mr. Stalas," said Mother, handing me a beet.

The bald man. I couldn't. I just couldn't do it. "Mother, I'm too tired." I lay on the planks, my cheek flush to the wood.

"I brought some straw for us to sleep on," announced Jonas. "The women told me where I could find it. I'll bring more tomorrow," he said.

"Lina, hurry, before it gets too dark. Take it to Mr. Stalas," said Mother, organizing the straw with Jonas.

I walked into the bald man's shack. A woman and two wailing babies took up most of the gray space. Mr. Stalas was cramped in the corner, his broken leg splinted with a board.

"What took you so long?" he said. "Are you trying to starve me? Are you in cahoots with them? What torture. Crying day and night. I'd trade the rotting baby for this rubbish."

I dropped the beet onto his lap and turned to leave.

"What happened to your hands?" he said. "They're disgusting."

"I've been working all day," I snapped. "Unlike you."

"What do they have you doing?" he asked.

"Digging holes," I said.

"Digging, eh?" he mumbled. "Interesting, I thought they'd have pulled your mother."

"What do you mean?" I asked.

"Your mother is a smart woman. She studied in Moscow. The damn Soviets know everything about us. They know about our families. Don't think they won't take advantage of that."

I thought about Papa. "I need to get word to my father so he can find us."

"Find you? Don't be stupid," he scoffed.

"He will. He'll know how to find us. You don't know my father," I said.

The bald man looked down.

"Do you?"

"Have those guards gotten to you and your mother yet?" he asked. I looked at him. "Between your legs, have they gotten to you yet?"

I huffed in disgust. I couldn't take it anymore. I left him and walked out of the hut.

"Hey."

I turned toward the voice. Andrius was leaning up against the shack.

"Hi," I said, looking over to him.

"You look horrible," he said.

I was too exhausted to muster a clever reply. I nodded.

"What are they having you do?"

"We're digging holes," I said. "Jonas made shoes all day."

"I cut trees in the forest," he said. Andrius looked dirty, but untouched by the guards. His face and arms were tan, making his eyes appear very blue. I pulled a clump of dirt from my hair.

"Which shack are you in?" I asked.

"Somewhere over there," he said, without motioning in any particular direction. "Are you digging with that blond NKVD?"

"*With* him? That's a joke. He's not digging," I said. "He just stands around smoking and yelling at us."

"His name is Kretzsky," said Andrius. "The commander, he's Komorov. I'm trying to find out more."

"Where are you getting information? Is there any news of the men?" I asked, thinking of Papa. He shook his head.

"There's supposed to be a village nearby, with a post office," I said. "Have you heard that? I want to send a letter to my cousin."

"The Soviets will read everything you write. They've got people to translate. So be careful what you say."

I looked down, thinking of the NKVD asking Mother to be a translator. Our personal correspondence wasn't personal. Privacy was but a memory. It wasn't even rationed, like sleep or bread. I thought about telling Andrius that the NKVD had asked Mother to spy.

"Here," he said, holding out his hand. He opened his palm to reveal three cigarettes.

"You're giving me cigarettes?" I asked.

"Well, what did you think, that I had a roasted duck in my pocket?"

"No, I meant . . . Thank you."

"Sure. They're for your brother and your mother. Are they doing okay?"

I nodded, kicking at the dirt. "Where'd you get the cigarettes?" I asked.

"Around."

"How's your mom?"

"Fine," he said quickly. "Look, I gotta go. Tell Jonas I said hi. And try not to ruin the cigarettes with your blister juice," he teased.

I staggered back to our shack, trying to see which way Andrius went. Where was his hut?

I gave Mother the three cigarettes. "From Andrius," I said.

"How sweet of him," said Mother. "Where did he get them?"

"You saw Andrius?" said Jonas. "Is he okay?"

"He's okay. He chopped wood all day in the forest. He said to tell you hello."

The Altaian woman toddled over and thrust her hand out to Mother. They had a brief exchange interspersed with "nyets" and stomps from the Altaian woman's foot.

"Elena," said Mother, pointing to her own chest. "Lina, Jonas," she said, pointing to us.

"Ulyushka!" the woman said, thrusting her palm to Mother. Mother gave her a cigarette.

"Why are you giving her a cigarette?" asked Jonas.

"She says it's payment toward rent," said Mother. "Her name is Ulyushka."

"Is that her first or last name?" I asked.

"I don't know. But if we're to live here, we must be able to address one another properly."

I arranged my raincoat over some of the straw that Jonas had brought. I lay down. I hated the way Mother had said, "If we're to live here," like we were staying. I also heard Mother say *spaseeba*, which meant "thank you" in Russian. I looked over and saw her sharing a match with Ulyushka. Mother pulled two graceful puffs through her long fingers and then put it out quickly, rationing her own cigarette.

"Lina," whispered Jonas. "Did Andrius look okay?"

"He looked fine," I said, thinking of his tan face.

I was lying in bed, waiting for the sound. I heard soft footsteps outside. The curtain billowed up, revealing Joana's tanned face in the window.

"Come out," she said. "Let's sit on the porch."

I crept out of our bedroom and onto the porch of the cottage. Joana draped askew in the rocker, gliding back and forth. I sat in the chair next to her, pulling my knees up and tucking my bare feet under my cotton nightgown. The rocker croaked a steady rhythm while Joana stared off into the darkness.

"So? How was it?" I asked.

"He's wonderful," she sighed.

"Really?" I said. "Is he smart? He's not one of those dumb boys who drink beer at the beach all day, is he?"

"Oh no," she breathed. "He's in his first year at university. He wants to study engineering."

"Hmph. And he doesn't have a girlfriend?" I asked.

"Lina, stop trying to find something wrong with him."

"I'm not. I'm just asking," I said.

"One day, someone will catch your eye, Lina, and hopefully when it happens, you won't be so critical."

"I'm not critical," I said. "I just want to make sure he's good enough for you."

"He has a younger brother," said Joana, grinning at me.

"Really?" I crinkled my nose.

"See? You're already critical and you haven't even met him."

"I'm not being critical! So where is this younger brother?"

"He'll be here next week. Do you want to meet him?"

"I don't know, maybe. It depends what he's like," I said.

"Well, you won't know until you meet him, will you?" teased Joana.

36

WE WERE ASLEEP WHEN it happened. I had rinsed off my blisters and started a letter to Joana. But I was too tired. I fell asleep. The next thing I knew, the NKVD was yelling at me, pushing me to get outside.

"Mother, what's happening?" said Jonas.

"They say we must report to the kolkhoz office immediately."

"Davai!" shouted a guard holding a lantern. They became impatient. One drew a pistol.

"*Da!* Yes!" said Mother. "Hurry, children! Move!" We scrambled out of our straw. Ulyushka rolled over, turning her back to us. I looked over to my suitcase, grateful I had hidden my drawings.

Others were also herded from their huts. We walked in a line down the dirt path toward the kolkhoz office. I heard the bald man yelling somewhere behind us.

They packed us into the main room of the log building.

The gray-haired man who wound his watch stood in the corner. The little girl with the dolly waved excitedly to me, as if reunited with a long-lost friend. A wide bruise blossomed across her cheek. We were instructed to wait quietly until the others arrived.

The log walls were chinked with gray paste. At the head of the room, a desk with a black chair took up much of the floor. Portraits of Marx, Engels, Lenin, and Stalin hung above the desk.

Iosif Vissarionovich Dzhugashvili. He called himself Josef Stalin, which meant "Man of Steel." I stared at the picture. He seemed to stare back. His right eyebrow arched, challenging me. I looked at his bushy mustache and dark, stony eyes. The portrait showed him almost smirking. Was that intentional? I wondered about the artists who painted Stalin. Were they grateful to be in his presence, or terrified of the outcome if he found their portraits unbecoming? The picture of Stalin was crooked.

The door opened. The bald man hobbled in on his broken leg.

"And not one of you thought to help me!" he yelled.

Komorov, the commander, marched in, followed by several NKVD carrying rifles. The blond guard, Kretzsky, was at the end of the line carrying a stack of papers. How did Andrius learn their names? I looked around for Andrius and his mother. They weren't there.

Komorov began speaking. Everyone turned toward Mother. The commander paused and raised his eyebrow at her, twirling the ever-present toothpick on his tongue.

Mother's face tightened. "He says we've been brought here for paperwork."

"Paperwork?" said Mrs. Rimas. "At this hour?"

Komorov continued speaking. Kretzsky held up a typewritten document.

"We are all to sign that document," said Mother.

"What does it say?" the crowd demanded.

"It says three things," said Mother, staring at Komorov. He continued speaking, with Mother translating in between for the group.

"First, we sign that we agree to join this collective farm." There were rumbles within the room. People turned back to the commander as he spoke. His arm casually moved his uniform aside, displaying the gun at his hip. The crowd shifted.

"Second," said Mother, "we sign that we agree to pay a war tax of two hundred rubles per person, children included."

"Where are we to get two hundred rubles?" said the bald man. "They've already stolen all that we had."

Chattering ensued. An NKVD pounded the butt of his rifle on the desk. The room quieted.

I looked at Komorov as he spoke. He stared straight at Mother, as if he were deeply enjoying what he was saying to her. Mother paused. Her mouth sagged.

"Well, what is it? What's the third, Elena?" said Mrs. Rimas.

"We agree that we are criminals." Mother paused. "And that our sentence shall be . . . twenty-five years' hard labor."

Shouts and wails erupted in the small room. Someone

began to hyperventilate. The crowd pushed forward toward the desk, arguing. The NKVD lifted their rifles, pointing them at us. My jaw unlatched. Twenty-five years? We were going to be imprisoned for twenty-five years? That meant I would be older than Mother when we were released. I reached out to Jonas to steady myself. He wasn't there. He had collapsed at my feet.

I couldn't pull a deep breath. The room began to fold in around me. I was sliding, tangled in panic's undertow.

"SILENCE!" yelled a male voice. Everyone turned. It was the gray-haired man who wound his watch.

"Calm yourselves," he said slowly. "We do no good by becoming hysterical. We can't think clearly if we panic. It's scaring the children."

I looked at the little girl with the dolly. She clung to her mother's dress, tears spilling onto her bruised face.

The man lowered his voice and spoke calmly. "We are intelligent, dignified people. That is why they have deported us. For those of you who don't know me, my name is Alexandras Lukas. I am an attorney from Kaunas." The crowd quieted. Mother and I helped Jonas to his feet.

The commander, Komorov, yelled from the desk at the front of the room.

"Mrs. Vilkas, please tell the commander that I am explaining the situation to our friends," said Mr. Lukas. Mother translated. Kretzsky, the young blond guard, chewed his thumbnail.

"I'm not signing any document," said Miss Grybas. "They made us sign a registration document at the teachers' conference. Look where it got me. That's how they collected the names of all the teachers to deport."

"They'll kill us if we don't sign," said the grouchy woman.

"I don't believe so," said the gray-haired man. "Not before winter. We are in the first week of August. There is much work to be done. We are good, strong workers. We are farming for them, building structures for them. It is to their benefit to use us, at least until winter comes."

"He's right," said the bald man. "First they'll grind us from grain to flour, then they'll kill us. Who wants to wait around for that? Not me."

"They shot the girl who had the baby," huffed the grouchy woman.

"They shot Ona because she lost her senses," said Mr. Lukas. "She was out of control. We are not out of control. We are intelligent, rational people."

"So we shouldn't sign?" someone asked.

"No. I believe we should sit down in an orderly manner. Mrs. Vilkas will explain that we are not ready to sign paperwork."

"Not ready?" said Mrs. Rimas.

"I agree," said Mother. "We must not completely refuse. And we must show that we are not hysterical. Form three lines."

The NKVD held up their rifles, unsure what we might do. We sat down in straight lines in front of the desk, under portraits of Russia's leaders. The guards looked at one another, dumbfounded. We sat calmly. We had regained a slice of dignity. I put my arm around Jonas.

"Mrs. Vilkas, please ask Commander Komorov what the charges are," said the gray-haired man. Mother translated. Komorov sat on the edge of the desk, swinging his boot.

"He says we are charged under Article 58 of the Soviet Penal Code for counterrevolutionary activities against the USSR," said Mother.

"That doesn't carry a twenty-five-year sentence," muttered the bald man.

"Tell him we will work for them and we will provide good labor, but we are not yet ready to sign," said Mr. Lukas.

Mother translated. "He says we must sign now."

"I am not signing a paper condemning me to twenty-five years," said Miss Grybas.

"Nor am I," I said.

"So what do we do?" asked Mrs. Rimas.

"We wait here quietly until we are dismissed," said Mr. Lukas, winding his watch.

And so we waited.

"Where's Andrius?" whispered Jonas.

"I don't know," I said. I had heard the bald man ask the same question.

We sat on the floor of the kolkhoz office. Every few minutes, Komorov would slap or kick someone, trying to bully them into signing. No one did. I winced with his every step. Sweat trickled across the nape of my neck and along my spine. I tried to keep my head down, afraid that Komorov would notice me. Those who fell asleep were beaten.

Hours passed. We sat obediently, like schoolchildren in

front of the principal. Finally, Komorov spoke to Kretzsky.

"He's telling the young guard to take over," Mother translated.

Komorov marched over to Mother. He grabbed her by the arm and spit something that resembled an oyster onto her face. Then he left.

Mother quickly wiped off the slime, as if it didn't bother her at all. It bothered me. I wanted to roll the hate up into my mouth and spit it back in his face.

37

AT SUNRISE THEY TOLD us it was time to go back to work. Tired but relieved, we dragged ourselves to our shack. Ulyushka was already gone. The hut smelled of rotten eggs. We drank some of the rainwater and ate a stub of bread Mother had saved. Despite my washing efforts, my dress was still stiff with mud. My hands looked like a small animal had chewed on them. Yellow pus leaked from the blisters.

I tried my best to clean the sores with the rainwater. It didn't help. Mother said I needed to form calluses.

"Just do the best you can, dear," said Mother. "Move your arm as if you're digging, but don't press. I'll do the work." We set off out of the hut, walking toward the lineup for work detail.

Mrs. Rimas walked toward us, her face covered in fear. Then I saw it, the body of a man with a stake driven through his chest into the side of the kolkhoz office. His arms and legs dangled like a limp marionette. Blood soaked through his shirt and dripped to form a stain beneath him. Buzzards feasted on his fleshy bullet wounds. One pecked at his empty eye socket.

"Who is he?" I asked.

Mother gasped, grabbed me, and tried to cover my eyes.

"He wrote a letter," whispered Mrs. Rimas.

I moved past Mother, looking at the piece of paper tacked up, fluttering next to the dead man. I saw handwriting and a very crude diagram.

"He wrote a letter to the partisans—the Lithuanian freedom fighters. The NKVD found it," said Mrs. Rimas.

"Who translated it for them?" whispered Mother. Mrs. Rimas shrugged.

My stomach dropped, thinking of my drawings. I felt nauseous and put my hand to my mouth.

The blond guard, Kretzsky, stared at me. He looked tired and angry. Our standoff had deprived him of sleep. He marched us out to the clearing at a faster pace than normal, yelling and pushing at us.

We arrived at the large pit we had dug the day before. Looking at it, I estimated that four men lying down could fit inside. Kretzsky instructed us to dig another pit next to the first. I couldn't erase the image of the dead man from my mind. His diagram was nothing more than a few crude lines. I thought of my drawings, lifelike and full of pain, sitting in my suitcase. I had to hide them.

I yawned and hacked away at the dirt. Mother said the

time went faster if we talked about things that made us happy. She said it gave us strength.

"I want to find that village," I said. "Maybe we can buy food or send letters."

"How can we go anywhere, when all we do is work?" said the grouchy woman. "And if we don't work, we don't eat."

"I'll try to ask the woman I live with," said Mrs. Rimas.

"Be careful who you ask," said Mother. "We don't know who we can trust."

I missed Papa. He would know who we could ask and who we should stay away from.

We dug and dug until the water arrived. Commander Komorov was on the truck. He walked around the holes, inspecting them. I eyed the bucket of water. My hair stuck to my face. I wanted to submerge my head and drink. Komorov barked a command. Kretzsky shifted his feet. Komorov repeated the command.

Mother's face was suddenly the color of chalk. "He says . . . we must get in the first hole," she said, clenching her dress.

"For what?" I asked.

Komorov yelled and pulled a pistol from his belt. He pointed it at Mother. She jumped down into the first hole. The pistol moved to my head. I jumped in. He continued until all four of us were in the hole. He laughed and gave another instruction.

"We must put our hands on our heads," said Mother.

"No, dear God," said Mrs. Rimas, shaking.

Komorov walked around the hole, looking at us, pointing the pistol. He told us to lie down. We lay next to each other. Mother grasped my hand. I stared up. The sky was blue behind the silhouette of his large, square frame. He circled the hole again.

"I love you, Lina," whispered Mother.

"Our Father, who art in heaven," began Mrs. Rimas.

BANG!

He shot into the hole. Dirt crumbled down from above our heads. Mrs. Rimas screamed. Komorov told us to shut up. He circled around and around, muttering that we were disgusting pigs. Suddenly, he began kicking dirt from the large pile into the hole. He laughed and kicked faster and faster. The soil landed on my feet, then on my dress, then on my chest. He kicked furiously, covering us in dirt, still pointing the gun at our faces. If I sat up, I'd be shot. If I didn't sit up, I'd be buried alive. I closed my eyes. A heavy load of dirt sat on my body. Then finally, dirt fell onto my face.

BANG!

More dirt crumbled above our heads. Komorov laughed wildly, kicking dirt onto our faces. Dirt covered my nose. I opened my mouth to breathe and choked on the soil.

I heard Komorov cackling and then hacking. He laughed and coughed, trying to regain composure, as if he had outdone himself. Kretzsky said something.

BANG!

Then it was quiet. We lay there, buried in our own efforts. I heard a muffled rumble of the truck driving away. I couldn't open my eyes. I felt Mother squeezing my hand. She was still alive. I squeezed back. Then I heard Kretzsky's voice above us. Mother sat up and frantically began wiping dirt from my face. She pulled me up. I hugged her, not wanting to let go. Mrs. Rimas dug the grouchy woman out. She wheezed and coughed up dirt.

"It's okay, darling," said Mother, rocking me into her. "He's just trying to scare us. He wants us to sign those documents."

I couldn't cry. I couldn't even speak.

"Davai," said Kretzsky softly. He reached out his hand.

I looked up at his outstretched arm. I hesitated. He reached down farther. I grabbed his forearm. He grasped mine. I dug my toe into the dirt and let him pull me out. I stood at the side of the hole, face-to-face with Kretzsky. We stared at each other.

"Get me out of here!" yelled the grouchy woman. I looked away, where the truck had driven off. Kretzsky sent us back to digging. No one spoke for the rest of the day.

38

"WHAT'S WRONG?" asked Jonas when we arrived back at the shack.

"Nothing, dear," said Mother.

Jonas looked from Mother to me, searching our faces for answers.

"We're just tired." Mother smiled.

"Just tired," I told Jonas.

Jonas motioned us over to his pallet of straw. Inside his small cap were three large potatoes. He put his finger to his lips so our gasps wouldn't be audible. He didn't want Ulyushka to take the potatoes for rent.

"Where did you get them?" I whispered.

"Darling, thank you!" said Mother. "And I think we have just enough rainwater left. We'll make a nice potato soup."

Mother grabbed the coat out of her suitcase. "I'll be right back."

"Where are you going?" I asked.

"To take food to Mr. Stalas," she said.

I checked my suitcase, thinking of the dead man knifed up against the kolkhoz office. My drawings were undisturbed. The lining on the bottom of my suitcase was held down by snaps. I tore each drawing and page of writing from my tablet, slid it under the lining, and snapped it back in place. I would hide my messages to Papa until I found a way to send something.

I helped Jonas set the water to boil. Then it occurred to me. Miss Grybas wasn't able to give us beets today. Mother didn't take a potato. So what was she feeding the bald man?

I walked through the huts and quickly ducked out of sight. Mother was talking to Andrius in front of the bald man's shack. She was no longer holding her coat. I couldn't hear their conversation. Andrius looked concerned. He discreetly handed a bundle to Mother. She reached out and patted his shoulder. Andrius turned to leave. I ducked behind the shack. Once Mother passed, I peeked out and began to follow him.

Andrius walked down the row of barracks. I stayed well behind, just close enough to see where he was going. He made his way to the edge of the camp, then continued on to a large log building with windows. He stopped and looked around. I ducked behind the edge of a shack. It looked like Andrius entered the building from the rear. I crept closer and hid behind a bush.

I squinted to peer in the window. A group of NKVD sat around a table. I looked to the back of the building. No, Andrius couldn't have gone inside an NKVD building. I was just about to follow him farther. Then I saw her. Mrs. Arvydas appeared in the window carrying a tray of glasses. Her hair was clean and styled. Her clothes were pressed. She was wearing makeup. She smiled and distributed the drinks to the NKVD.

Andrius and his mother were working with the Soviets.

39

I SHOULD HAVE BEEN grateful for the potato soup that night. But all I could think about was Andrius. How could he do it? How could he work with them? Did he live in that building? I thought about lying in that hole while Andrius lay in a bed, a Soviet bed. I kicked at my itchy straw, staring at the rusted ceiling.

"Mother, do you think they'll let us sleep tonight? Or will they insist we go to the office to sign the papers?" asked Jonas.

"I don't know," said Mother. She turned her head to me. "Andrius gave me that nice bread we had with our soup. It's very courageous of him to take risks like that for us."

"Oh, he's courageous, isn't he?"

"What do you mean by that?" said Jonas. "He is courageous. He gets us food nearly every day."

"He sure looks like he's eating well, doesn't he? I think he's actually gained weight," I said.

"And be glad of that," said Mother. "Be glad that not everyone is desperate for food like we are."

"Yes, I'm very glad the NKVD aren't hungry. If they were hungry, how would they have the strength to bury us alive?" I said.

"What?" said Jonas.

Ulyushka yelled at us to be quiet.

"Hush, Lina. Let's say our prayers and give thanks for that wonderful meal. Let's pray that your father is just as well."

We slept through the night. The next morning, Officer Kretzsky told Mother that we were to join the other women in the beet fields. I was thrilled. We bent and thrashed amongst the long green rows of sugar beets, using hoes without handles. Miss Grybas lectured us on the pace of our work. She told us that on the first day, someone leaned on the handle a moment to wipe their brow. The Soviets made them saw the handles off. I realized how difficult it was for Miss Grybas to steal beets for us. Armed guards stood watch. Although they seemed more interested in smoking and telling jokes, slipping a beet into my underwear unnoticed was no easy task. It poked out like an extra limb.

That evening, I refused to take food to Mr. Stalas. I told Mother I felt too sick to walk. I couldn't stand to see Andrius. He was a traitor. He was plump on Soviet food, eating from the hand that strangled us each and every day.

"I'll take Mr. Stalas his food," said Jonas after a few days.

"Lina, go with him," said Mother. "I don't want him to go alone." I walked with Jonas to the bald man's shack. Andrius was waiting outside.

"Hi," he said. I ignored him, left Jonas outside, and walked in to give Mr. Stalas his beets. He was standing up.

"There you are. Where have you been?" he said, leaning up against the wall. I noticed Mother's coat tucked into his bed of straw.

"Disappointed I'm not dead?" I said, handing him the beets.

"That's a sour mood," he said.

"Are you the only one who's allowed to be angry? I'm sick of this. I'm tired of the NKVD hounding us."

"Bah. They don't care if we sign," said the bald man. "Do you really think they need our permission, our signatures, to do what they're doing to us? Stalin needs to break our will. Don't you understand? He knows if we sign some stupid papers, we'll give up. He'll break us."

"How do you know?" I asked.

He waved me away. "It doesn't look good on you—anger," he said. "Now get out."

I walked out of the shack. "Let's go, Jonas."

"Wait," whispered Jonas, leaning in to me. "He brought us salami."

I folded my arms across my chest.

"I guess she's allergic to kindness," said Andrius.

"That's not what I'm allergic to. Where did you get your salami?" I said.

Andrius stared at me. "Jonas, can you leave us for a minute?" he said.

"No, he can't leave us. My mother doesn't want him to be alone. That's the only reason I came," I said.

"I'm fine," said Jonas. He turned and walked away.

"So, is that what you're eating these days?" I asked. "Soviet salami?"

"When I can get it," he said. He took out a cigarette and lit it. Andrius looked stronger, his arms muscular. He drew in a breath and blew a plume of smoke over our heads.

"And cigarettes, too," I commented. "Are you sleeping in a nice bed in that Soviet building?"

"You have no idea," he said.

"I don't? Well, you don't look tired or hungry. You weren't dragged to the kolkhoz office in the middle of the night and condemned to twenty-five years. So, are you reporting all of our conversations to them?"

"You think I'm spying?"

"Komorov asked Mother to spy and report to him. She said no."

"You don't know what you're talking about," said Andrius, the crimson in his face rising.

"I don't?"

"No, you have no idea," he said.

"I don't see your mother working in the dirt—"

"No," said Andrius, leaning in, an inch from my face. "You know why?" A vein in his temple bulged. I felt his breath on my forehead.

"Yes, because—"

"Because they threatened to kill me unless she slept with them. And if they get tired of her, they still might kill me. So how would you feel, Lina, if your mother felt she had to prostitute herself to save your life?"

My jaw dropped.

The words flew out of his mouth. "How do you think my father would feel if he knew? How does my mother feel, lying with the men who murdered her husband? No, your mother might not translate for them, but what do you think she'd do if they held a knife to your brother's neck?"

"Andrius, I—"

"No, you have no idea. You have no idea how much I hate myself for putting my mother through this, how every day I think of ending my life so she can be free. But instead, my mother and I are using our misfortune to keep others alive. But you wouldn't understand that, would you? You're too selfish and self-centered. Poor you, digging all day long. You're just a spoiled kid." He turned and walked away.

40

THE STRAW PRICKLED AGAINST my face. Jonas had fallen asleep a long time ago. A soft whistle blew each time he exhaled. I tossed and turned.

"He's trying, Lina," said Mother.

"He's sleeping," I said.

"Andrius. He's trying and you're blocking him at every pass. Men aren't always graceful, you know."

"Mother, you don't understand," I said.

She ignored me and continued. "Well, I can see you're upset. Jonas said that you were nasty to Andrius. That's unfair. Sometimes kindness can be delivered in a clumsy way. But it's far more sincere in its clumsiness than those distinguished men you read about in books. Your father was very clumsy."

A tear rolled down my cheek.

She chuckled in the darkness. "He says I bewitched him the very instant he saw me. But do you know what really happened?

He tried to talk to me and fell out of a tree. He fell out of an oak tree and broke his arm."

"Mother, it's not like that," I said.

"Kostas," she sighed. "He was so clumsy, but he was so sincere. Sometimes there is such beauty in awkwardness. There's love and emotion trying to express itself, but at the time, it just ends up being awkward. Does that make sense?"

"Mmm, hmm," I said, trying to muffle my tears.

"Good men are often more practical than pretty," said Mother. "Andrius just happens to be both."

~

I couldn't sleep. Each time I closed my eyes I saw him winking at me, his beautiful face coming toward mine. The smell of his hair lingered around me.

"Are you awake?" I whispered.

Joana rolled over. "Yes, it's too hot to sleep," she said.

"I feel like I'm spinning. He's so . . . handsome," I told her.

She giggled, tucking her arms under her pillow. "And he dances even better than his older brother."

"How did we look together?" I asked.

"Like you were having a great time," she said. "Everyone could see that."

"I can't wait to see him tomorrow," I sighed. "He's just perfect."

The next day after lunch we ran back to the cottage to brush our hair. I nearly ran over Jonas on my way out.

"Where are you going?" he asked.

"For a walk," I said, rushing after Joana.

I walked as fast as I could without breaking into a jog.

I tried not to crumple the drawing rolled in my hand. I had decided to draw him when I couldn't sleep. The portrait came out so well that Joana suggested I give it to him. She assured me he'd be impressed with my talent.

His brother rushed up to Joana, meeting her in the street.

"Hey, stranger," he said, smiling at Joana.

"Hi!" said Joana.

"Hi, Lina. What do you have there?" he said, motioning to the paper in my hand.

Joana looked over toward the ice cream shop. I moved around her to find him.

"Lina," she said, reaching out to hold me back.

It was too late. I had already seen. My prince had his arm around a girl with red hair. They were cozy, laughing, sharing an ice cream cone. My stomach plunged and twisted.

"I forgot something," I said, backing away. My fingers wrenched the portrait in my sweaty hand. "I'll be right back."

"I'll come with you," said Joana.

"No, that's all right," I said, hoping the blotches of heat I felt on my neck weren't visible. I attempted a smile. The sides of my mouth trembled. I turned and walked away, trying to keep my composure until I reached a safe distance.

Clenching my jaw didn't stop the tears. I stopped and leaned against a trash can on the street.

"Lina!" Joana caught up to me. "Are you all right?"

I nodded. I opened the crinkled portrait of his handsome face. I ripped it up and threw it away. Stray pieces escaped my grip and blew across the street. Boys were idiots. They were all idiots.

AUTUMN APPROACHED. The NKVD pushed us harder. If we so much as stumbled, they reduced our bread rations. Mother could close her thumb and middle finger around my forearm. I had no tears. The sensation of crying would fill me, but my eyes would only dry-heave and burn.

It was hard to imagine that war raged somewhere in Europe. We had a war of our own, waiting for the NKVD to choose the next victim, to throw us in the next hole. They enjoyed hitting and kicking us in the fields. One morning, they caught an old man eating a beet. A guard ripped out his front teeth with pliers. They made us watch. Every other night they woke us to sign the documents sentencing us to twenty-five years. We learned to sit in front of Komorov's desk and rest with our eyes open. I managed to escape the NKVD while sitting right in front of them.

My art teacher had said that if you breathed deeply and

imagined something, you could be there. You could see it, feel it. During our standoffs with the NKVD, I learned to do that. I clung to my rusted dreams during the times of silence. It was at gunpoint that I fell into every hope and allowed myself to wish from the deepest part of my heart. Komorov thought he was torturing us. But we were escaping into a stillness within ourselves. We found strength there.

Not everyone could sit still. People became restless, exhausted. Finally, some gave in.

"Traitors!" spit Miss Grybas under her breath, clucking her tongue. People argued about those who signed. The first night someone signed, I was furious. Mother told me to feel sorry for the person, that they had been pushed over the edge of their identity. I couldn't feel sorry for them. I couldn't understand.

Walking to the fields each morning, I could predict who would be the next to sign. Their faces sang songs of defeat. Mother saw it, too. She would chat with the person and work next to them in the field, trying to bolster their spirit. Sometimes it worked. Many times it didn't. At night I drew portraits of those who had signed and wrote about how the NKVD broke them down.

The NKVD's hostilities strengthened my defiance. Why would I give in to people who spit in my face and tormented me each and every day? What would I have left if I gave them my self-respect? I wondered what would happen if we were the only ones left who wouldn't sign.

The bald man moaned that we could believe no one. He accused everyone of being a spy. Trust crumbled. People began to question each other's motives and planted seeds of doubt. I thought of Papa, telling me to be careful with my drawing.

Two nights later, the grouchy woman signed the papers. She bent over the desk. The pen trembled in her knobby hand. I thought she might change her mind, but suddenly she scribbled something and threw the pen down, committing herself and her little girls to twenty-five years. We stared at her. Mother bit her bottom lip and looked down. The grouchy woman began screaming, telling us we were imbeciles, that we were all going to die, so why didn't we eat well until then? One of her daughters began to cry. That night, I drew her face. Her mouth sagged, forlorn. The lines of her brow plunged with both anger and confusion.

Mother and Mrs. Rimas scavenged for news of the men or the war. Andrius passed information to Jonas. He ignored me. Mother wrote letters to Papa, even though she had no idea where to send them.

"If only we could get to that village, Elena," said Mrs. Rimas one night in the ration line. "We could mail our letters."

People who signed the twenty-five-year sentence were able to go to the village. We were not.

"Yes, we need to get to the village," I said, thinking of getting something to Papa.

"Send the whore, that Arvydas woman," said the bald man. "She'll hustle the best deals. Her Russian is probably pretty good by now."

"How dare you!" said Mrs. Rimas.

"You disgusting old man. Do you think she wants to sleep

with them?" I yelled. "Her son's life depends on it!" Jonas hung his head.

"You should feel sorry for Mrs. Arvydas," said Mother, "just as we feel sorry for you. Andrius and Mrs. Arvydas have put extra food in your mouth many a night. How can you be so ungrateful?"

"Well, then you'll have to bribe that cranky cow who signed," said the bald man. "You can buy her off to mail your letters."

We had all written letters that Mother planned to mail to her "contact," a distant relative who lived in the countryside. The hope was that Papa had done the same thing. We weren't able to sign our names or write anything specific. We knew the Soviets would read the notes. We wrote that we were all well, having a lovely time, learning good trade skills. I drew a picture of Grandma and wrote "Love from Grandma Altai" underneath with my scribbled signature. Surely Papa would recognize the face, my signature, and the word *Altai*. Hopefully the NKVD wouldn't.

MOTHER HELD THREE sterling silver serving pieces she had sewn into the coat. She had carried them since we were deported.

"Wedding gifts," she said, holding the silver, "from my parents." Mother offered one piece to the grouchy woman in exchange for mailing letters and picking up sundries and news when she went to the village. She accepted.

Everyone longed for news. The bald man told Mother of a secret pact between Russia and Germany. Lithuania, Latvia, Estonia, Poland, and others were divided between Hitler and Stalin. I drew the two of them, dividing countries like children dividing toys. Poland for you. Lithuania for me. Was it a game to them? The bald man said Hitler broke his agreement with Stalin, because Germany invaded Russia a week after we were deported. When I asked Mother how the bald man knew about the pact, she said she didn't know.

What had happened to our house and everything we owned since we were deported? Did Joana and my other relatives know what had happened? Maybe they were looking for us.

I was glad that Hitler had pushed Stalin out of Lithuania, but what was he doing there?

~

"Nothing could be worse than Stalin," said one of the men at the dining room table. "He is the epitome of evil."

"There is no better or worse," said Papa, his voice low. I leaned farther around the corner to listen.

"But Hitler won't uproot us," said the man.

"Maybe not you, but what about us Jews?" said Dr. Seltzer, my father's close friend. "You heard the circulation. Hitler made the Jews wear armbands."

"Martin's right," said my father. "And Hitler's setting up a system of ghettos in Poland."

"A system? Is that what you call it, Kostas? He's locked up hundreds of thousands of Jews in Lodz and sealed off even more in Warsaw," said Dr. Seltzer, his voice soaked with desperation.

"It was a bad choice of words. I'm sorry, Martin," said Papa. "My point is that we're dealing with two devils who both want to rule hell."

"But Kostas, to remain neutral or independent will be impossible," said a man.

"Lina!" whispered Mother, grabbing me by my collar. "Go to your room."

I didn't mind. The constant talk of politics bored me. I was only listening for my drawing game. I tried to draw their expressions simply by hearing the conversation but not seeing their faces. I had heard enough to draw Dr. Seltzer.

~

Jonas continued to work with the two Siberian women making shoes. They liked him. Everyone loved Jonas and his sweet disposition. The women advised that he'd best make boots for winter. They looked the other way when he set aside scraps of materials. Jonas was learning Russian much quicker than I was. He could understand a fair amount of conversation and could even use slang. I constantly asked him to translate. I hated the sound of the Russian language.

43

I THRASHED NEXT to Mother in the beet field. Black boots appeared near my feet. I looked up. Kretzsky. His yellow hair parted on the side and cascaded across his forehead. I wondered how old he was. He didn't look much older than Andrius.

"Vilkas," he said.

Mother looked up. He rattled off something in Russian, too quickly for me to understand. Mother looked down and then back at Kretzsky. She raised her voice and yelled out to the field. "They're looking for someone who can draw."

I froze. They had found my drawings.

"Do any of you draw?" she said, shading her eyes and looking across the field. What was Mother doing? No one responded.

Kretzsky's eyes narrowed, looking at me.

"They'll pay two cigarettes for someone to copy a map and a photograph—"

"I'll do it," I said quickly, dropping my hoe.

"No, Lina!" said Mother, grabbing my arm.

"Mother, a map," I whispered. "Maybe it will bring us news of the war or the men. And I won't have to be in this field." I thought about giving a cigarette to Andrius. I wanted to apologize.

"I'll go with her," said Mother in Russian.

"NYET!" yelled Kretzsky. He grabbed me by the arm. "Davai!" he yelled, pulling me away.

Kretzsky dragged me from the beet field. My arm ached under his grip. As soon as we disappeared from view, he let go of me. We walked in silence toward the kolkhoz office. Two NKVD approached down the row of shacks. One caught sight of us and shouted to Kretzsky.

He looked over to them, then back at me. His posture changed. "Davai!" yelled Kretzsky. He slapped me across the face. My cheek stung. My neck twisted from the unexpected blow.

The two NKVD drew near, watching. Kretzsky called me a fascist pig. They laughed. One of them asked for a match. Kretzsky lit the guard's cigarette. The NKVD brought his face an inch from mine. He muttered something in Russian, then blew a long stream of smoke in my face. I coughed. He took the burning cigarette and pointed the glowing tip at my cheek. Brown tar stains filled a crack between his front teeth. His lips were chapped and crusty. He stepped back, looking me over, nodding.

My heart hammered. Kretzsky laughed and slapped the

guard on the shoulder. The other NKVD raised his eyebrows and made obscene gestures with his fingers before laughing and walking away with his friend. My cheek throbbed.

Kretzsky's shoulders dropped. He stepped back and lit a cigarette. "Vilkas," he said, shaking his head and blowing smoke out of the corner of his mouth. He laughed, grabbed my arm, and dragged me toward the kolkhoz office.

What had I just agreed to?

I SAT AT A TABLE in the kolkhoz office. I shook out my hands, hoping to stop them from quivering. A map was placed to my upper left, and a photograph to my upper right. The map was of Siberia, the photo of a family. In the photograph, a black box had been drawn around the man's head.

An NKVD brought paper and a box with a nice selection of pens, pencils, and drafting supplies. I ran my fingers over the writing utensils, longing to use them for my own drawings. Kretzsky pointed to the map.

I had seen maps in school, but they had never interested me as this one did. I looked at the map of Siberia, shocked by its enormity. Where were we on the map? And where was Papa? I surveyed the details of the plot. Kretzsky pounded his fist on the table, impatient.

Several officers hovered around while I drew. They flipped

through files and pointed to locations on the map. The files had papers and photographs affixed to them. I stared at the cities on the map as I was drawing, trying to commit them to memory. I would re-create it on my own later.

Most of the officers left as soon as the map was finished. Kretzsky flipped through files, drinking coffee while I drew the man in the photograph. I closed my eyes and inhaled. The coffee smelled incredible. The room was warm like our kitchen at home. When I opened my eyes, Kretzsky was staring at me.

He set his coffee cup down on the table, examining the drawing. I looked at the man's face as it came to life on my page. He had bright eyes and a warm smile. His mouth was relaxed and calm, not pinched like Miss Grybas' or the bald man's. I wondered who he was and whether he was Lithuanian. I thought about creating something his wife and children would like to look at. Where was this gentleman, and why was he important? The ink from the pen flowed smoothly. I wanted that pen. When Kretzsky turned, I dropped it in my lap and leaned closer to the table.

I needed texture to capture the man's hair. I dipped my finger into Kretzsky's coffee cup, lifting grounds onto my finger. I dabbed them on top of my other hand and swished the brown around on my skin. I used the coffee grounds to blot texture into the hair. *Almost.* I leaned forward and brushed a bit of the grit with my pinky. It curved softly in a gentle sweep. *Perfect.* I heard footsteps. Two cigarettes appeared in front of me. I turned, startled. The commander stood behind me. My skin prickled at the sight of him, bristling on my arms and the back of my neck. I pushed myself against the table, trying to conceal the pen in my lap. He raised his eyebrows at me, flashing the gold tooth under his lip.

"Finished," I said, sliding the drawing toward him.

"Da," he said, nodding. He stared at me, his toothpick bobbing on his tongue.

I WALKED BETWEEN the huts in the dark, making my way toward the NKVD building at the back of the camp. I heard voices mumbling behind the brittle walls. I hurried along the tree line, cradling the cigarettes and the pen in my pocket. I stopped behind a tree. The NKVD barracks looked like a hotel compared with our shacks. Kerosene lamps burned brightly. A group of NKVD sat on the porch playing cards and passing a flask.

I crept in the shadows to the back of the building. I heard something—crying, and whispers in Lithuanian. I turned the corner. Mrs. Arvydas sat on a crate, her shoulders rising and falling in rhythm with muffled sobs. Andrius knelt down in front of her, his hands clasping hers. I inched closer. His head snapped up.

"What do you want, Lina?" said Andrius.

"I . . . Mrs. Arvydas, are you all right?" She turned her head away from me.

"Leave, Lina," said Andrius.

"Can I help somehow?" I asked.

"No."

"Is there anything I can do?" I pressed.

"I said, leave!" Andrius stood up to face me.

I hung motionless. "I came to give you—" I reached in my pocket for the cigarettes.

Mrs. Arvydas turned her head to me. Her eye makeup ran down over a bloody welt that blazed across her cheek.

What had they done to her? I felt the cigarettes crush between my fingers. Andrius stared at me.

"I'm sorry." My voice caught and broke. "I'm really so sorry." I turned quickly and began to run. Images streaked and bled together, contorted by my speed—Ulyushka, grinning with yellow teeth; Ona in the dirt, her one dead eye open; the guard moving toward me, smoke blowing from his pursed lips—*Stop it, Lina*—Papa's battered face looking down at me from the hole; dead bodies lying next to the train tracks; the commander reaching for my breast. *STOP IT!* I couldn't.

I ran back to our shack.

"Lina, what's wrong?" asked Jonas.

"Nothing!"

I paced the floor. I hated this labor camp. Why were we here? I hated the commander. I hated Kretzsky. Ulyushka complained and stomped for me to sit down.

"SHUT UP, YOU WITCH!" I screamed.

I rifled through my suitcase. My hand knocked the stone from Andrius. I grabbed it. I thought about throwing it at Ulyushka. Instead, I tried to crush it. I didn't have the strength. I put it in my pocket and snatched my paper.

I found a sliver of light outside in back of our hut. I held the stolen pen above the paper. My hand began to move in short, scratchy strokes. I took a breath. Fluid strokes. Mrs. Arvydas slowly appeared on the page. Her long neck, her full lips. I thought of Munch as I sketched, his theory that pain, love, and despair were links in an endless chain.

My breathing slowed. I shaded her thick chestnut hair resting in a smooth curve against her face, a large bruise blazing across her cheek. I paused, looking over my shoulder to make certain I was alone. I drew her eye makeup, smudged by tears. In her watery eyes I drew the reflection of the commander, standing in front of her, his fist clenched. I continued to sketch, exhaled, and shook out my hands.

I returned to our shack and hid the pen and drawing in my suitcase. Jonas sat on the floor, bobbing his knee nervously. Ulyushka was asleep on her pallet, snoring.

"Where's Mother?" I asked.

"The grouchy woman went to the village today," said Jonas. "Mother walked down the road to meet her on the way back."

"It's late," I said. "She's not back?" I had given the grouchy woman a wood carving to pass along for Papa.

I walked outside and saw Mother coming toward the shack. She carried coats and boots. She smiled her huge smile when she saw me. Miss Grybas came scurrying toward us.

"Hurry!" she said. "Put those things out of sight. The NKVD is rounding everyone up to sign papers."

I didn't have a chance to tell Mother about Mrs. Arvydas. We put everything in the bald man's shack. Mother put her arms around me. Her dress hung on her thin frame, her hip bones protruding at the belted waistline.

"She mailed our letters!" whispered Mother, beaming. I nodded, hoping the handkerchief had passed across hundreds of miles already, ahead of the letters.

It wasn't five minutes before the NKVD burst into our hut, yelling for us to report to the office. Jonas and I marched along with Mother.

"And drawing the map this afternoon?" she asked.

"Easy," I said, thinking of the stolen pen hidden in my suitcase.

"I wasn't sure it was safe," said Mother. "But I guess I was wrong." She put her arms around us.

Sure, we were safe. Safe in the arms of hell.

~

"Tadas was sent to the principal today," announced Jonas at dinner. He wedged a huge piece of sausage into his small mouth.

"Why?" I asked.

"Because he talked about hell," sputtered Jonas, juice from the plump sausage dribbling down his chin.

"Jonas, don't speak with your mouth full. Take smaller pieces," scolded Mother.

"Sorry," said Jonas with his mouth stuffed. "It's good." He

finished chewing. I took a bite of sausage. It was warm and the skin was deliciously salty.

"Tadas told one of the girls that hell is the worst place ever and there's no escape for all eternity."

"Now why would Tadas be talking of hell?" asked Papa, reaching for the vegetables.

"Because his father told him that if Stalin comes to Lithuania, we'll all end up there."

"IT'S CALLED TURACIAK," Mother told us the next day. "It's up in the hills. It's not large, but there's a post office and even a small schoolhouse."

"There's a school?" said Miss Grybas excitedly.

Jonas shot me a look. He had been asking about school since the beginning of September.

"Elena, you must tell them I'm a teacher," said Miss Grybas. "The children in the camp must go to school. We have to create some sort of school here."

"Did she mail the letters?" asked the bald man.

"Yes," said Mother. "And she wrote the post office address on the return."

"But how will we know if any letters arrive for us?" said Mrs. Rimas.

"Well, we'll have to continue to bribe someone who signed,"

said Miss Grybas with a grimace. "They'll check for our mail when they take their trips to the village."

"She said she met a Latvian woman whose husband is in a prison near Tomsk," said Mother.

"Oh, Elena, could our husbands be in Tomsk?" asked Mrs. Rimas, bringing her hand to her chest.

"Her husband wrote that he is spending time with many Lithuanian friends." Mother smiled. "But she said the letters were cryptic and arrived with markings."

"Of course they did," said the bald man. "They're censored. That Latvian woman better be careful what she writes. And you better be careful, too, unless you want to be shot in the head."

"Will you never stop?" I said.

"It's the truth. Your love letters could get them killed. And what of the war?" asked the bald man.

"The Germans have taken Kiev," said Mother.

"What are they doing there?" asked Jonas.

"What do you think they're doing? They're killing people. This is war!" said the bald man.

"Are the Germans killing people in Lithuania?" said Jonas.

"Stupid boy, don't you know?" said the bald man. "Hitler, he's killing the Jews. Lithuanians could be helping him!"

"What?" I said.

"What do you mean? Hitler pushed Stalin out of Lithuania," said Jonas.

"That doesn't make him a hero. Our country is doomed, don't you see? Our fate is death, no matter whose hands we fall into," said the bald man.

"Stop it!" yelled Miss Grybas. "I can't bear to hear about it."

"That's enough, Mr. Stalas," said Mother.

"What about America or Britain?" asked Mrs. Rimas. "Surely they'll help us."

"Nothing yet," said Mother. "But soon, I hope."

And that was the first news of Lithuania in months. Mother's spirits soared. Despite her hunger and blisters from hard work, she was effervescent. She walked with a bounce. Hope, like oxygen, kept her moving. I thought about Papa. Was he really in prison somewhere in Siberia? I recalled the map I had drawn for the NKVD, and then Stalin and Hitler dividing up Europe. Suddenly, a thought hit me. If Hitler was killing the Jews in Lithuania, what had happened to Dr. Seltzer?

The possibility of letters en route made for endless conversation. We learned the names of everyone's relatives, neighbors, coworkers—anyone who could possibly send a letter. Miss Grybas was sure the young man who had lived next door to her would send a letter.

"No, he won't. He probably never noticed you lived there," said the bald man. "You're not exactly the noticeable type."

Miss Grybas was not amused. Jonas and I laughed about it later. At night, we'd lie in our straw creating ridiculous scenarios of Miss Grybas romancing her young neighbor. Mother told us to stop, but sometimes I heard her giggling right along with us.

Temperatures dipped and the NKVD pushed us harder.

They even gave us an extra ration at one point because they wanted another barrack built before the snow came. We still refused to sign the papers. Andrius still refused to speak to me. We planted potatoes for spring, even though no one wanted to believe we might still be in Siberia when the cold broke.

The Soviets forced Mother to teach school to a mixed class of Altaian and Lithuanian children. Only the children whose parents signed were allowed to attend school. They forced her to teach in Russian, even though many children did not yet fully understand the language. The NKVD would not let Miss Grybas teach. It pained her. They told her if she signed, they would allow her to assist Mother. She wouldn't sign, but helped Mother with lesson plans in the evenings.

I was happy that Mother was able to teach in a covered shack. Jonas had been reassigned to chopping logs for firewood. The snow had arrived, and he came back each night wet and freezing. The tips of his frozen hair would simply break off. My joints became stiff from the cold. I was sure the insides of my bones were full of ice. They made a cracking, snapping sound when I stretched. Before we could get warm, we'd feel a horrible stinging sensation in our hands, feet, and face. The NKVD grew more irritable when the cold came. So did Ulyushka. She demanded rent whenever she felt like it. I literally wrestled my bread ration out of her hand on several occasions.

Jonas paid Ulyushka our rent with splinters and logs he stole from the cutting. Thankfully, he had made sturdy boots and shoes for us while working with the two Siberian women.

His Russian was quickly improving. I drew my little brother taller, his face somber.

I was assigned to hauling sixty-pound bags of grain on my back through the snow. Mrs. Rimas taught me how to pilfer some by moving the weave of the bag aside with a needle and then moving it back, undetected. We were quickly perfecting the art of scavenging. Jonas sneaked out each night to retrieve scraps of food from the NKVD's trash. Bugs and maggots didn't deter anyone. A couple of flicks of the finger and we stuffed it in our mouths. Sometimes, Jonas would return with care packages that Andrius and Mrs. Arvydas would hide in the trash. But aside from the occasional bounty from Andrius, we had become bottom-feeders, living off filth and rot.

AS THE BALD MAN predicted, we were able to continually bribe the grouchy woman into visiting the post office for us when she went to the village. For two months, our bribes returned nothing. We shivered in our shacks, warmed only by the promise of an eventual envelope carrying news from home. Temperatures lived well below zero. Jonas slept near the little stove, waking every few hours to add more wood. My toes were numb, the skin cracked.

Mrs. Rimas was the first to receive a letter. It was from a distant cousin and arrived mid-November. News traveled fast around the camp that a letter had arrived. Nearly twenty people pushed inside her shack to hear the news from Lithuania. Mrs. Rimas hadn't returned from the ration line. We waited. Andrius arrived. He squeezed in next to me. He produced stolen crackers from his pockets for everyone. We tried to keep our voices down, but excitement percolated through the packed crowd.

I turned, accidentally elbowing Andrius. "Sorry," I said. He nodded.

"How are you?" I asked.

"Fine," he replied. The bald man entered the shack and complained there was no room. People pushed forward. I was smashed against the front of Andrius's coat.

"How's your mother?" I asked, glancing up at him.

"As well as can be expected," he said.

"What do they have you doing these days?" My chin was practically against his chest.

"Chopping down trees in the forest." He shifted his weight, looking down at me. "You?" he asked. I could feel a wisp of his breath on the top of my hair.

"Hauling bags of grain," I said. He nodded.

The envelope was handed around. Some people kissed it. It came to us. Andrius ran his finger over the Lithuanian stamp and postmark.

"Have you written to anyone?" I asked Andrius.

He shook his head. "We're not sure it's safe yet," he said.

Mrs. Rimas arrived. The group tried to part, but it was too crowded. I was shoved onto Andrius again. He grabbed me, trying to keep us from pushing the crowd like a line of dominoes. We steadied ourselves. He quickly let go.

Mrs. Rimas said a prayer before opening the envelope. As expected, some lines of the letter were crossed out with thick black ink. But enough was legible.

"'I have had two letters from our friend in Jonava,'" read Mrs. Rimas. "That has to be my husband," she cried. "He was born in Jonava. He's alive!" The women hugged.

"Keep reading!" yelled the bald man.

"'He said that he and some friends decided to visit a summer camp,'" said Mrs. Rimas.

"'He finds it to be beautiful,'" she continued. "'Just as described in Psalm 102.'"

"Someone get their Bible. Look up Psalm 102," said Miss Grybas. "There's some sort of message in that."

We helped decode the rest of the letter with Mrs. Rimas. Someone joked that the crowd was better than a stove for warmth. I stole glances at Andrius. His bone structure and eyes were strong, perfectly proportioned. It appeared he was able to shave from time to time. His skin was wind-burned like the rest of us, but his lips weren't thin or cracked like the NKVD. His wavy brown hair was clean compared with mine. He looked down. I looked away. I couldn't imagine how filthy I must have looked, or what he saw in my hair.

Jonas returned with Mother's Bible.

"Hurry!" someone said. "Psalm 102."

"I have it," said Jonas.

"Shh, let him read."

> *"Hear my prayer, O Lord, and let my cry come unto thee.*
>
> *"Hide not thy face from me in the day when I am in trouble; incline thine ear unto me: in the day when I call, answer me speedily.*

"For my days are consumed like smoke, and my bones are burned as a firebrand.

"My heart is stricken, and withered like grass; I forget to eat my bread.

"By reason of the voice of my groaning, my bones cleave to my flesh . . ."

Someone gasped. Jonas's voice trailed off. I clutched Andrius's arm.

"Keep going," said Mrs. Rimas. She wrung her hands.

The wind whistled and the walls of the hut shuddered. Jonas's voice grew faint.

"I am like a pelican of the wilderness: I am like an owl in the desert.

"I watch, and am as a sparrow alone upon the housetop.

"Mine enemies reproach me all the day; and they that are mad against me are sworn against me.

"For I have eaten ashes like bread, and mingled my drink with weeping.

"My days are like a shadow that declineth; and I am withered like grass."

"Make him stop," I whispered to Andrius, dropping my head against his coat. "Please." But he didn't stop.

Jonas finally finished. A gust of wind clattered against the roof.

"Amen," said Mrs. Rimas.

"Amen," echoed the others.

"He's starving," I said.

"So what? We're starving. I'm withered like grass, too," said the bald man. "He's no worse off than me."

"He's alive," said Andrius quietly.

I looked up at him. Of course. He wished his father was alive, even if he was starving.

"Yes, Andrius is right," said Mother. "He's alive! And your cousin has probably sent him word that you're alive, too!"

Mrs. Rimas read the letter again. Some people left the shack. Andrius was one of them. Jonas followed.

IT HAPPENED A WEEK later. Mother said she had seen signs. I saw nothing.

Miss Grybas waved frantically to me. She was trying to run through the snow.

"Lina, you must hurry! It's Jonas," she whispered.

Mother said she had noticed that his color had turned. Everyone's color had turned. Gray had crept beneath our skin, settling in dark trenches under our eyes.

Kretzsky wouldn't let me leave my work. "Please," I begged. "Jonas is sick." Couldn't he help, just this once?

He pointed back to the stack of grain sacks. The commander walked around, yelling and kicking at us to hurry. A snowstorm was coming. "Davai!" yelled Kretzsky.

By the time I returned to our shack, Mother was already there. Jonas was lying on her pallet of straw, nearly unconscious.

"What is it?" I asked, kneeling beside her.

"I don't know." She pulled up Jonas's pant leg. His shin was covered in spots. "It may be some sort of infection. He has a fever," she said, putting her hand on my brother's forehead. "Did you notice how irritable and tired he has become?"

"Honestly, no. We're all irritable and tired," I said. I looked at Jonas. How could I not have noticed? Sores lined his bottom lip, and his gums looked purple. Red spots dotted his hands and fingers.

"Lina, go get our bread rations. Your brother will need nourishment to fight this off. And see if you can find Mrs. Rimas."

I fought my way through the swirling snow in the dark, the wind stabbing at my face. The NKVD wouldn't give me three rations. Because Jonas collapsed on the job, they said, he had forfeited his ration. I tried to explain that he was ill. They waved me away.

Mrs. Rimas didn't know what it was, nor Miss Grybas. Jonas seemed to slip further from consciousness.

The bald man arrived. He loomed over Jonas. "Is it contagious? Does anyone else have spots? The boy could be the angel of death for us all. A girl died of dysentery a few days ago. Maybe that's what it is. I think they threw her in that hole you dug," he said. Mother ordered him out of the shack.

Ulyushka yelled at us to take Jonas outside in the snow. Mother yelled back and told her to sleep somewhere else if she was worried about contagion. Ulyushka stomped out. I sat next to Jonas, holding a snow-cooled cloth to his forehead. Mother knelt down and spoke softly, kissing his face and hands.

"Not my children," whispered Mother. "Please, God, spare him. He is so young. He's seen so little of life. Please . . . take me instead." Mother raised her head. Her face contorted with pain. "Kostas?"

It was late when the man who wound his watch arrived with a kerosene lamp. "Scurvy," he announced after looking at Jonas's gums. "It's advanced. His teeth are turning blue. Don't worry; it's not contagious. But you'd best find this boy something with vitamins before his organs shut down completely. He's malnourished. He could turn at any point."

My brother was a rendering from Psalm 102, "weak and withered like grass." Mother rushed out into the snow to beg, leaving me with Jonas. I laid compresses on his forehead. I tucked the stone from Andrius under his hand and told him that the sparkles inside would heal him. I recounted stories from our childhood and described our house, room by room. I took Mother's Bible and prayed for God to spare my brother. My worry made me nauseous. I grabbed my paper and began to sketch something for Jonas, something that would make him feel better. I had started a drawing of his bedroom when Andrius arrived.

"How long has he been like this?" he said, kneeling by Jonas.

"Since this afternoon," I replied.

"Can he hear me?"

"I don't know," I said.

"Jonas. You're going to be all right. We just need to find you something to eat and drink. Hang on, friend, do you hear me?" Jonas lay motionless.

Andrius took a cloth bundle from inside his coat. He unwrapped a small silver can and pulled a pocketknife from his pants. He punctured the top of the can.

"What is it?" I asked.

"He has to eat this," said Andrius, leaning toward my brother's face. "Jonas, if you can hear me, open your mouth."

Jonas didn't move.

"Jonas," I said. "Open your mouth. We have something that's going to help you."

His lips parted.

"That's good," said Andrius. He dipped the blade of the knife into the can. It reappeared with a juicy stewed tomato on it. The back of my jaws cramped. Tomatoes. I began to salivate. As soon as the tomato touched Jonas's mouth, his lips began to quiver. "Yes, chew it and swallow," said Andrius. He turned to me. "Do you have any water?"

"Yes, rainwater," I said.

"Give it to him," said Andrius. "He has to eat all of this."

I eyed the can of tomatoes. Juice spilled off of Andrius's knife and onto his fingers. "Where did you get them?" I asked.

He looked at me, disgusted. "I got them at the corner market. Haven't you been there?" He stared, then turned away. "Where do you think I got them? I stole them." He heaped the last of the tomatoes into my brother's mouth. Jonas drank the juice from the can. Andrius wiped the blade and juice from his fingers on his trousers. I felt my body surge forward toward the juice.

Mother arrived with one of the Siberian shoemakers. Snow was piled atop their heads and shoulders. The woman ran to my brother, speaking quickly in Russian.

"I tried to explain what was wrong," said Mother, "but she insisted on seeing for herself."

"Andrius brought a can of tomatoes. He fed them to Jonas," I said.

"Tomatoes?" gasped Mother. "Oh, thank you! Thank you, dear, and please thank your mother for me."

The Siberian woman began speaking to Mother.

"There's a tea she thinks will heal him," translated Andrius. "She's asking your mother to help her collect the ingredients." I nodded.

"Andrius, could you stay a bit longer?" asked Mother. "I know Jonas would feel so much better with you here. Lina, boil some water for the tea." Mother leaned over my brother. "Jonas, I'll be right back, darling. I'm going for a tea that will help you."

WE SAT IN SILENCE. Andrius stared at my brother, his fists clenched. What was he thinking? Was he mad that Jonas was sick? Was he mad that his mother was sleeping with the NKVD? Was he mad that his father was dead? Maybe he was just mad at me.

"Andrius."

He didn't look at me.

"Andrius, I'm a complete idiot."

He turned his head.

"You're so good to us, and I'm . . . I'm just an idiot." I looked down.

He said nothing.

"I jumped to a conclusion. I was stupid. I'm sorry I accused you of spying. I've felt horrible." He remained silent. "Andrius?"

"Okay, you're sorry," he said. He looked back to my brother.

"And . . . I'm sorry about your mother!" I blurted.

I grabbed my writing tablet. I sat down to finish the drawing of Jonas's room. At first, I was conscious of the silence. It hung heavy, awkward. As I continued to sketch, I slipped into my drawing. I became absorbed with capturing the folds of the blanket perfectly, softly. The desk and the books had to be just right. Jonas loved his desk and his books. I loved books. How I missed my books.

~

I held my schoolbag, protecting the books. I couldn't let it slap and bang in the usual way. After all, Edvard Munch was in my bag. I had waited nearly two months for my teacher to receive the books. They had finally arrived, from Oslo.

I knew my parents wouldn't appreciate Munch or his style. Some called it "degenerate art." But as soon as I saw photos of Anxiety, Despair, *and* The Scream, *I had to see more. His works wrenched and distorted, as if painted through neurosis. I was fascinated.*

I opened our front door. I saw the solitary envelope and raced toward the foyer table. I tore it open.

Dear Lina,

Happy New Year. I'm sorry I haven't written. Now that the Christmas holiday is passed, life seems on a more serious course. Mother and Father have been arguing. Father is constantly ill-tempered and rarely sleeps. He paces the house through all hours of the night and comes home at lunchtime to get the mail. He's boxed up most of his books, saying they take up too much space. He even tried to box up some of my medical books. Has he gone mad? Things have changed since the annexation.

Lina, please draw a picture of the cottage in Nida for me. The warm and sunny memories of the summer will help push me through the cold to spring.

Please send me your news and let me know where your thoughts and drawings take you these days.

Your loving cousin,
Joana

~

"He told me about his airplane," said Andrius, pointing over my shoulder to the drawing. I had forgotten he was there.

I nodded. "He loves them."

"Can I see?"

"Sure," I said, handing him my tablet.

"It's good," said Andrius. His thumb was pressed against the edge of the tablet. "Can I look at the others?"

"Yes," I said, thankful there were only a few sketches I hadn't yet torn from the pad.

Andrius turned the page. I took the compress from Jonas's head and went to cool it in the snow. When I returned, Andrius was looking at a picture I had drawn of him. It was from the day Mrs. Rimas received the letter.

"It's a strange angle," he said, laughing quietly.

I sat down. "You're taller than me. That's how I saw it. And we were all packed pretty tight."

"So, you had a good angle of my nostrils," he said.

"Well, I was looking up at you. This angle would be different," I said, observing him.

He turned to me.

"See, you look different from this perspective," I said.

"Better or worse?" he asked.

Mother and the Siberian woman returned.

"Thank you, Andrius," said Mother.

He nodded. He leaned over and whispered something to Jonas. He left.

We steeped the leaves in the water I had boiled. Jonas drank it. Mother stayed propped at his side. I lay down but couldn't sleep. Each time I closed my eyes, I saw the painting of *The Scream* in my head, but the face was my face.

50

IT TOOK TWO WEEKS for Jonas to improve. His legs trembled when he walked. His voice was barely more than a whisper. In the meantime, Mother and I became weaker. We had to split our two bread rations to feed Jonas. At first, when we asked, people contributed a portion of what they had. But as the cold crept deeper into our shacks, it began to chill generosity. One day, I saw Miss Grybas turn her back and shove her entire bread ration into her mouth the moment it was handed to her. I couldn't blame her. I had often thought of doing the same thing. Mother and I didn't ask for contributions after that.

Despite our pleadings, the NKVD refused to give us food for Jonas. Mother even tried speaking to the commander. He laughed at her. He said something that upset her for days. We had nothing left to sell. We had bartered practically everything we owned with the Altaians for warm clothing. The lining of Mother's coat hung thin, like fluttering cheesecloth.

The approach of Christmas bolstered spirits. We gathered in each other's shacks to reminisce about the holidays in Lithuania. We talked endlessly about *Kucios*, our Christmas Eve celebration. It was decided that Kucios would be held in the bald man's shack. He grudgingly agreed.

We closed our eyes when listening to the descriptions of the twelve delicious dishes representing the twelve apostles. People rocked back and forth, nodding. Mother talked of the delicious poppy seed soup and cranberry pudding. Mrs. Rimas cried at the mention of the wafer and the traditional Christmas blessing, "God grant that we are all together again next year."

The guards warmed themselves with drink after work. They often forgot to check on us or didn't want to venture out into the biting, frosty winds. We gathered each night to hear about someone's holiday celebration. We grew to know each other through our longings and cherished memories. Mother insisted that we invite the grouchy woman to our meetings. She said that just because she had signed didn't mean she wasn't homesick. Snow fell and the temperatures plummeted, but work and the cold felt tolerable. We had something to look forward to—a small ritual that brought relief to our gray days and dark nights.

I had begun to steal logs to keep the stove fired. Mother constantly worried, but I assured her I was careful and that the NKVD were too lazy to come out into the cold. One night, I left the bald man's shack to get a log for the stove. I crept around his shack. I heard movement and froze. Someone was standing in the shadows. Was it Kretzsky? My heart stopped . . . Was it the commander?

"It's just me, Lina."

I heard Andrius's voice in the darkness. He struck a match and lit a cigarette, briefly illuminating his face.

"You scared me," I said. "Why are you standing out here?"

"I listen from out here."

"Why don't you come inside? It's freezing," I said.

"They wouldn't want me inside. It's not fair. Everyone is so hungry."

"That's not true. We'd be happy to have you. We're just talking about Christmas."

"I know. I've heard. My mother begs me to bring her the stories each night."

"Really? If I hear about cranberry pudding one more time, I'll go crazy," I said, smiling. "I just need to get some wood."

"You mean steal some?" he said.

"Well, yes, I guess," I said.

He shook his head, chuckling. "You're really not scared, are you?"

"No," I said. "I'm cold." He laughed.

"Do you want to walk with me?" I asked.

"Nah, I better get back," he said. "Be careful. Good night."

Three days later Mrs. Arvydas and Andrius arrived with a bottle of vodka. The crowd fell silent when they walked through the door. Mrs. Arvydas wore stockings. Her hair was clean and curled. Andrius looked down. He stuffed his hands in his pockets. I didn't care that she wore a clean dress and wasn't hungry. No one wanted to trade places with her.

"A toast," said Mother, lifting the bottle of vodka to Mrs. Arvydas. "To good friends."

Mrs. Arvydas smiled and nodded. Mother took a small sip from the bottle and then shimmied at the hips, delighted. We all joined in, taking small sips and laughing together, savoring the moment. Andrius leaned back against the wall, watching us and grinning.

That night, I fantasized about Papa joining us for the holiday. I imagined him trudging through the falling snow toward Altai, arriving in time for Christmas with my handkerchief in his breast pocket. *Hurry, Papa*, I urged. *Please hurry.*

~

"Don't worry, Lina, he'll be here soon," said Mother. "He's getting the hay for the table."

I stood at the window, looking out into the snow.

Jonas helped Mother in the dining room. "So we'll have twelve courses tomorrow. We'll be eating all day." He smacked his lips.

Mother smoothed the white tablecloth over the dining room table.

"Can I sit next to Grandma?" asked Jonas.

Papa's dark silhouette emerged on the street before I could protest and argue that I wanted to sit next to Grandma.

"He's coming!" I shouted. I grabbed my coat. I ran down the front steps and stood in the middle of the street. The small dark figure grew taller as it approached through the low light

of dusk and the curtain of falling snow. A tinkling of bells from a horse's harness floated from the street over.

I heard his voice before I could make out his face. "Now, what sort of sensible girl stands in the middle of the road when it's snowing?"

"Only one whose father is late," I teased.

Papa's face appeared, frosty and red. He carried a small bundle of hay.

"I'm not late," he said, putting his arm around me. "I'm right on time."

51

CHRISTMAS EVE ARRIVED. I worked all day chopping wood. Moisture from my nose froze, encrusted around my nostrils. I kept my mind busy trying to remember details about each Christmas at home. No one swallowed their bread ration in line that night. We greeted each other kindly and made our way back to our shacks. Jonas looked somewhat like himself again. We washed our hair in melted snow and scrubbed at our fingernails. Mother pinned her hair up and dotted lipstick on her lips. She rubbed a bit of the red into my cheeks for color.

"It's not perfect, but we do the best we can," said Mother, adjusting our clothes and hair.

"Get the family picture," said Jonas.

The others had the same idea. Photographs of families and loved ones were plentiful in the bald man's shack. I saw a photo of Mrs. Rimas and her husband. He was short, like her. She was laughing in the photo. She looked so different, strong. Now she drooped, like someone had sucked air out of her. The bald man was particularly quiet.

We sat on the floor as if around a table. There was a white cloth in the center with hay and fir boughs in front of each person. One spot was left empty. A stub of tallow burned in front of it. Lithuanian tradition called for an empty place to be left at the table for family members who were gone or deceased. People placed photographs of their family and friends around the empty seat. I gently set our family photo at the empty setting.

I took out the bundle of food I had been saving and placed it on the table. Some people had small surprises—a potato they had saved or something they had pilfered. The grouchy woman displayed some biscuits she must have bought in the village. Mother thanked her and made a fuss.

"The Arvydas boy and his mother sent this," said the bald man. "For after dinner." He tossed something out. It landed with a thud. People gasped. I couldn't believe it. I was so shocked I started to laugh. It was chocolate. Real chocolate! And the bald man hadn't eaten it.

Jonas whooped.

"Shh . . . Jonas. Not too loud," said Mother. She looked at the package on the table. "Chocolate! How wonderful. Our cup runneth over."

The bald man put the bottle of vodka on the table.

"Now, you know better," scolded Miss Grybas. "Not for Kucios."

"How the hell should I know?" snapped the bald man.

"Maybe after dinner." Mother winked.

"I don't want any part of it," said the bald man. "I'm Jewish."

Everyone looked up.

"But . . . Mr. Stalas, why didn't you tell us?" asked Mother.

"Because it's none of your business," he snapped.

"But for days we've been meeting about Christmas. And you've been so kind to let us use your hut. If you had told us, we could have included a Hanukkah celebration," said Mother.

"Don't assume I haven't celebrated the Maccabees," said the bald man, pointing his finger. "I just don't blather on about it like you fools." The room fell quiet. "I don't wax on about my worship. It's personal. And honestly, poppy seed soup, bah."

People shifted uncomfortably. Jonas started to laugh. He hated poppy seed soup. The bald man joined in. Soon we were all laughing hysterically.

We sat for hours at our meal and makeshift table. We sang songs and carols. After much pressing, Mother persuaded the bald man to recite the Hebrew prayer *Ma'oz Tzur*. His voice lacked its usual pinched tone. He closed his eyes. The words quivered with emotion.

I stared at our family picture, sitting at the empty seat. We had always spent Christmas at home, with bells tinkling in the streets, and warm smells wafting from the kitchen. I pictured the dining room dark, the chandelier laced in cobwebs, and the table covered in a fine layer of dust. I thought of Papa.

What was he doing for Christmas? Did he have a tiny piece of chocolate to melt on his tongue?

The door to the shack blew open. The NKVD pushed inside, pointing guns at us.

"Davai!" yelled a guard, grabbing the man who wound his watch. People began to protest.

"Please, it's Christmas Eve," pleaded Mother. "Don't try to make us sign on Christmas Eve."

The guards yelled and began pushing people out of the shack. I wasn't leaving without Papa. I scrambled over to the other side of the table. I grabbed our family photo and stuffed it up my dress. I would hide it on the way to the kolkhoz office. Kretzsky didn't notice. He stood motionless, holding his rifle, staring at all the photographs.

52

THEY WORKED US hard on Christmas Day. I stumbled from fatigue, having had no sleep the night before. When I returned to the shack, I could barely walk. Mother had given Ulyushka a whole package of cigarettes for Christmas. She sat, with her feet propped up near the stove, smoking. Where had Mother gotten the cigarettes? I couldn't understand why Mother gave anything to Ulyushka.

Jonas arrived with Andrius.

"Merry Christmas," he said.

"Thank you for the chocolate," said Mother. "We were beside ourselves."

"Andrius, wait a minute," said Jonas. "I have something for you."

"I have something for you, too," I said. I reached into my suitcase and pulled out a sheet of paper. I handed it to Andrius.

"It's not very good," I said, "but it's a better angle. Smaller nostrils."

"It's great," said Andrius, looking at my drawing.

"Really?"

His eyes flashed up, locking on mine. "Thank you."

I opened my mouth. Nothing came out. "Merry Christmas," I finally said.

"Here," said Jonas, holding out his hand. "It was yours, then you gave it to Lina. She gave it to me when I was sick. I survived, so I figure it must be pretty lucky. I think it's your turn to have it." Jonas opened his fingers to reveal the stone with the sparkles inside. He handed it to Andrius.

"Thanks. I guess this thing is lucky," said Andrius, looking at the stone.

"Merry Christmas," said Jonas. "And thanks for the tomatoes."

"I'll walk back with you," said Mother. "I'd like to wish your mother a Merry Christmas, if she can steal away for a moment."

Jonas and I lay on our straw, bundled in our coats and boots.

"Remember when we used to sleep in pajamas?" asked Jonas.

"Yes, with goose-down covers," I said. My body sank into the straw and into the quiet. I felt the chill of the hard ground slowly creeping onto my back and up over my shoulders.

"I hope Papa has a goose-down blanket tonight," said Jonas.

"Me, too," I said. "Merry Christmas, Jonas."

"Merry Christmas, Lina."

"Merry Christmas, Papa," I whispered.

53

"LINA!" SAID ANDRIUS, running into our shack. "Hurry, they're coming for you."

"Who?" I asked, startled. I had just returned from work.

"The commander and Kretzsky are on their way now."

"What? Why?" gasped Mother.

I thought of the stolen ink pen, hidden in my suitcase. "It's . . . I . . . stole a pen," I said.

"You did what?" said Mother. "How could you be so foolish! Stealing from the NKVD?"

"It's not about a pen," said Andrius. "The commander wants you to draw his portrait."

I stopped and turned to Andrius. "What?"

"He's an egomaniac," said Andrius. "He went on about needing a portrait for the kolkhoz office, a portrait for his wife—"

"His wife?" said Jonas.

"I can't do it," I said. "I can't concentrate around him." I looked at Andrius. "He makes me uncomfortable."

"I'm going with you," said Mother.

"He won't allow it," said Andrius.

"I'll break my hands if I have to. I can't do it," I said.

"Lina, you will do nothing of the sort," said Mother.

"If you break your hands, you won't be able to work," said Andrius. "And if you can't work, you'll starve to death."

"Do they know she has other drawings?" Jonas said quietly. Andrius shook his head.

"Lina." Andrius lowered his voice. "You have to make the picture . . . flattering."

"You're telling me how to draw?" I said.

He sighed. "I like your drawings. Some are very realistic, but some, they're, well, twisted."

"But I draw what I see," I said.

"You know what I mean," said Andrius.

"And what am I going to get for this?" I asked. "I'm not doing this for a piece of bread or a couple of bent cigarettes."

We argued about what to ask for. Mother wanted postage stamps and seeds. Jonas wanted potatoes. I wanted our own shack and a goose-down blanket. I thought about what Andrius said and struggled to decide what was "flattering." Broad shoulders would signify power. His head turned slightly would accentuate his strong jawline. The uniform would be easy. I could draw it very accurately. It was his face that concerned me. When I imagined sketching the commander, I had no problem, until I got to his head. My mind saw a clean and pressed uniform, with a nest of wicked snakes sprouting out of his neck, or a skull with hollow black eyes, smoking a cigarette. The impressions were strong. I longed to draw them. I needed to draw them. But I couldn't, not in front of the commander.

A FIRE CRACKLED in the kolkhoz office. The room smelled of burning timber. I took off my mittens and warmed my hands on the fire.

The commander marched in. He wore a spotless green uniform with blue piping. A black pullover strap cradled his pistol holder. I tried to make note quickly so I wouldn't have to look at him. Blue pants, a blue hat with a raspberry band above the brim. Two shiny gold medals hung on the left side of the uniform. And of course, the ever-present toothpick danced back and forth from each side of his mouth.

I dragged a chair near his desk and sat, motioning for the commander to be seated. He pulled his chair out and sat down in front of me, his knees nearly touching mine. I moved my chair back, pretending I was searching for the right angle.

"Coat," he said.

I looked up at him.

"Take it off."

I didn't move.

He nodded, his deep-set eyes glaring through me. He wrapped his tongue around the toothpick, swirling it from side to side.

I shook my head and rubbed my arms. "Cold," I said.

The commander rolled his eyes.

I took a deep breath and looked up at the commander. He stared at me.

"How old are you?" he asked, his eyes running over my body.

It started. Snakes slithered out of his collar and wrapped themselves around his face, hissing at me. I blinked. A gray skull sat on his neck, its jaws flapping, laughing.

I rubbed my eyes. There are no snakes. Don't draw the snakes. I now knew how Edvard Munch felt. "Paint it as you see it," he had said during his lifetime. "Even if it's a sunny day but you see darkness and shadows. Paint it as you see it." I blinked again. I can't, I thought. I can't draw it as I see it.

"I don't understand," I lied. I motioned for him to turn his head to the left.

I drew a loose outline. I'd have to start with the uniform. I couldn't look at his face. I tried to work quickly. I didn't want to spend a minute longer than necessary near the man. Sitting in front of him felt like a shiver that would never go away.

How can I do this in an hour? Focus, Lina. No snakes.

The commander was not a good sitter. He insisted on

frequent breaks to smoke. I found I could get him to sit longer if I showed him my progress from time to time. He was enchanted with himself, lost in his own ego.

After another fifteen minutes, the commander wanted a break. He reclaimed his toothpick from the desk and walked outside.

I looked at the drawing. He looked powerful, strong.

The commander returned. He had Kretzsky with him. He snapped the pad from my hands. He showed it to Kretzsky, swatting him on the shoulder with the back of his hand.

Kretzsky's face was turned to the drawing, but I could feel he was staring at me. The commander said something to Kretzsky. He replied. Kretzsky's speaking voice was very different from his commands. His tone was calm, young. I kept my head down.

The commander handed the pad back to me. He circled me, his black boots taking slow, even steps around my chair. He looked at my face and then barked a command at Kretzsky.

I started sketching his hat. That was the last piece. Kretzsky returned and handed the commander a file. Komorov opened the file and flipped through papers. He looked at me. What did it say in that file? What did he know about us? Did it say something about Papa?

I began sketching furiously. Hurry, davai, I told myself. The commander began asking questions. I could understand bits and pieces.

"Been drawing since child?"

Why did he want to know? I nodded, motioning for him to turn his head slightly. He obliged and posed.

"What you like to draw?" he asked.

Was he making conversation with me? I shrugged.

"Who is favorite artist?"

I stopped and looked up. "Munch," I told him.

"Munch, hmm." He nodded. "Don't know Munch."

The red stripe above his brim needed more detail. I didn't want to spend the time. I just shaded it all in quickly. I carefully tore the sheet from the pad. I handed the paper to the commander.

He dropped the file on the desk and grabbed the portrait. He walked around the office, admiring himself.

I stared at the file.

It was just sitting there, lying on the desk. There had to be something about Papa in that file, something that could help me get a drawing to him.

The commander gave Kretzsky an order. Bread. He told Kretzsky to give me bread. I was supposed to get more than bread.

The commander left the room. I began to protest.

Kretzsky pointed to the front door. "Davai!" he yelled, waving for me to leave. I saw Jonas waiting outside.

"But—" I started.

Kretzsky shouted something and exited behind the desk.

Jonas opened the door and peeked in. "He told us to go to the kitchen door. I heard him. We can get our bread there," he whispered.

"But we're supposed to get potatoes," I argued. The commander was a liar. I should have drawn the snakes. I turned to pick up my drawing pad. I saw the file on the desk.

"C'mon, Lina, I'm hungry," said Jonas.

"Okay," I said, pretending to gather my paper. I grabbed the file and shoved it in my coat.

"Yes, let's go," I said, rushing through the door. Jonas had no idea what I had done.

55

WE WALKED TO the NKVD barracks. I felt my heartbeat thump in my ears. I tried to calm myself, act normal. I looked over my shoulder. I saw Kretzsky exit the rear door of the kolkhoz office. He walked in the shadows to the barracks, his long wool coat swaying around his feet. We waited in back near the kitchen, as instructed.

"He may not come," I said, eager to run back to the shack.

"He has to come," said Jonas. "They owe us food for your drawing."

Kretzsky appeared at the back door. A loaf of bread sailed into the dirt. Couldn't he hand the bread to us? Would that be so difficult for him? I hated Kretzsky.

"C'mon, Jonas. Let's go," I said. Suddenly, potatoes rocketed at us. I heard laughter from inside the kitchen.

"Do you have to throw them?" I said, moving toward the dark doorway. The door closed.

"Look, there are several!" said Jonas, running to pick them up.

The door opened. A tin can smacked against my forehead. I heard clapping and felt a warm dripping above my eyebrow. Cans and garbage rained down around us. The NKVD amused themselves by pelting helpless children with garbage.

"They're drunk. Hurry, let's go! Before they start shooting," I said, not wanting to drop the file.

"Wait, some of it is food!" said Jonas, frantically collecting things off the ground. A sack flew out and hit Jonas in the shoulder, knocking him over. A cheer erupted from behind the door.

"Jonas!" I ran to him. Something wet hit me in the face.

Kretzsky appeared at the door and said something.

"Hurry," said Jonas. "He says we're stealing food and he's going to report us."

We scurried around, like hens in a yard, craning our necks for anything that touched the ground. I reached up to clear the smelly slop from my eyes. Rotten potato peels. I put my head down and ate them.

"Fasheest sveenya!" yelled Kretzsky. He slammed the door.

I gathered things in my skirt, holding my arm against my coat and the file. I took all I could carry, even empty cans for residue. The left side of my forehead throbbed. I reached up and felt a big, wet goose egg.

Andrius emerged from the side of the building. He looked

around. "I see you got something for your drawing," he said.

I ignored him and quickly began snatching the potatoes with my free hand. I stuffed them into my pockets and skirt, desperate to get each one.

Andrius moved to lift the sack I was straddling. He put his hand on my shoulder. "Don't worry," he said gently. "We'll get it all."

I looked up at him.

"You're bleeding."

"It's nothing. I'm fine," I said, pulling potato rot from my hair.

Jonas scooped up the bread. Andrius picked up the big sack.

"What's in that?" asked Jonas.

"Flour," said Andrius. "I'll carry it back for you."

"Did you hurt your arm?" asked Andrius, watching me clutch my coat.

I shook my head.

We trudged through the snow in silence.

56

"HURRY, JONAS," I said as soon as we were a safe distance from the NKVD building. "Mother will be worried. Run ahead and let her know we're okay."

Jonas ran toward our shack. I slowed my pace. "They have a file on us," I said, watching my brother shrink in the distance.

"They have files on everyone," said Andrius. He tossed the sack of flour up, readjusting it on his shoulder.

"Maybe you could help me with something," I said.

Andrius shook his head, almost laughing. "I can't steal a file, Lina. That's a lot different from wood or a can of tomatoes. It's one thing to get in the kitchen, but—"

"I don't need you to take the file," I said, stopping short of our shack.

"What?" Andrius stopped.

"I don't need you to steal the file." I looked around and opened my coat slightly. "I already have it," I whispered. "It was on the commander's desk. I need you to put it back once I've read it."

Shock flooded Andrius's face. His head snapped from side to side, to see if we were alone. He pulled me behind a shack. "What's wrong with you! Do you want to get yourself killed?" he whispered.

"The bald man said it's all in our files, where we were sent, perhaps what happened to the rest of our family. It's all right here." I crouched down, letting go of the potatoes and other items I had been carrying. I reached into my coat.

"Lina, you can't do this. Give me the file. I'm taking it back."

Footsteps approached. Andrius stood in front of me. Someone passed.

He dropped the sack and reached for the file. I moved away from him and opened it. My hands trembled. There were photos of our family, and papers attached to the folder. My heart sank. It was all in Russian. I turned to Andrius. He grabbed the file from my hand.

"Please," I begged. "Tell me what it says."

"Are you really that selfish? Or are you just stupid? They'll kill you and your family," he said.

"No." I grabbed his arm. "Please, Andrius. It might help me find my father. You heard him on the train. I can help him find us. I can send him my drawings. I just need to know where he is. I . . . I know you can understand."

He stared at me and then opened the file. "I don't read Russian that well." His eyes quickly scanned the papers.

"What does it say?"

"Students at the Academy," he said, looking over his shoulder. "This word is 'artist.' That's you. Your father," he said, putting his finger under a word.

"Yes, what?" I said.

"Location."

I huddled near Andrius. "What does it say?"

"Krasnoyarsk. Prison."

"Papa's in Krasnoyarsk?" I remembered drawing Krasnoyarsk on the map for the NKVD.

"I think this word means 'offense' or 'charge,'" he said, pointing to some writing. "It says your father is—"

"Is what?"

"I don't know this word," whispered Andrius. He snapped the file shut and stuffed it in his coat.

"What else does it say?"

"That's all it says."

"Can you find out what the word is? The one about Papa?"

"What if I get caught with this?" said Andrius, suddenly full of anger.

What if he did get caught? What would they do to him? He turned to walk away. I grabbed him. "Thank you," I said. "Thank you so much."

He nodded, pulling away from me.

MOTHER WAS DELIGHTED with the food. We decided to eat most of it immediately, just in case the NKVD tried to take it back. The canned sardines were delicious, well worth the tender gash on my head. Their oil felt silky against my tongue.

Mother gave Ulyushka a potato. She invited her to share our meal. She knew Ulyushka was less likely to report that we had food if she ate some herself. I hated that Mother shared with Ulyushka. She had tried to throw Jonas out into the snow when he was sick. She didn't think twice about stealing from us. She never shared her food. She ate egg after egg, right in front of us. Yet Mother insisted on sharing with her.

I worried about Andrius, hoping he was able to return the file unnoticed. And what was the word that he had pointed to, the one he thought was "offense" or "charge"? I refused to believe that Papa had done something wrong. I turned it over in my head. Mrs. Raskunas worked at the university with Papa. She wasn't deported. I saw her peeking out of her window the night we were taken away. So not everyone from the university was deported. Why Papa? I wanted to tell Mother that Papa was sent to Krasnoyarsk, but I couldn't. She'd be too worried about him being in prison, and she'd be angry that I had stolen the file. She would also worry about Andrius having it. I worried about Andrius.

That night, I tore more drawings from my tablet and hid them with the others under my suitcase lining. I had two pages left. My pencil hovered around the edge of the paper. I looked up. Mother and Jonas spoke quietly. I rolled the pencil between my fingers. I drew a collar. A snake began to draw itself, coiling upward. I quickly scratched it out.

The next afternoon I saw Andrius on my way back from work. I scanned his face for news of the file. He nodded. My shoulders relaxed. He had returned it. But had he found the meaning of the word? I smiled at him. He shook his head, annoyed, but kind of smiled, too.

I found a thin, flat piece of birch and brought it back to our hut. At night, I decorated the edges with Lithuanian embroidery patterns. I drew a picture of our house in Kaunas on it, along with other symbols of Lithuania. On the bottom I wrote, "Deliver to Krasnoyarsk Prison. With love from Miss Altai." I included my scribble signature, along with the date.

"What am I supposed to do with it?" asked the grouchy woman when I approached her.

"Just give it to a Lithuanian you see in the village," I said. "Tell them to pass it on. It has to get to Krasnoyarsk."

The grouchy woman looked at my drawings of the Lithuanian coat of arms, Trakai Castle, our patron saint, Casimir, and the stork, the national bird of Lithuania.

"Here," I said, extending a tattered piece of clothing bunched in my hand. "Maybe one of your girls can use this underskirt. I know it's not much, but—"

"Keep your slip," said the grouchy woman, still looking at my drawings. "I'll pass it along."

58

MARCH 22. MY SIXTEENTH birthday. My forgotten birthday. Mother and Jonas left the shack for work. Neither acknowledged my birthday. What did I expect, a celebration? We barely had a scrap to eat. Mother traded what she could for stamps to mail letters to Papa. I wouldn't say anything about it to Mother. She would feel horrible for having forgotten. The month before, I had reminded her it was Grandma's birthday. She felt guilty for days. After all, how could she forget her own mother's birthday?

I spent the day piling wood, imagining the party I'd have if we were still in Lithuania. People in school would wish me a happy birthday. Our family would dress in some of our finest clothes. Papa's friend would take photographs. We'd go to an expensive restaurant in Kaunas. The day would feel special, different. Joana would send a present.

I thought of my last birthday. Papa was late coming to the

restaurant. I told him I had received nothing from Joana. I noticed that he stiffened at the mention of my cousin. "She's probably just busy," he had said.

Stalin had taken my home and my father. Now he had taken my birthday. My feet dragged as I walked through the snow after work. I stopped for my ration. Jonas was in line.

"Hurry!" he said. "Mrs. Rimas received a letter from Lithuania. It's a thick one!"

"Today?" I asked.

"Yes!" he said. "Hurry! Meet me at the bald man's shack."

The line moved slowly. I thought about the last time Mrs. Rimas had received a letter. It was warm in her crowded shack. I wondered if Andrius would be there.

I got my ration and ran through the snow to the bald man's shack. Everyone huddled in a ball. I saw Jonas. I walked up behind him.

"What did I miss?" I whispered.

"Just this," he said.

The crowd parted. I saw Mother.

"Happy birthday!" everyone yelled.

A lump bobbed in my throat.

"Happy birthday, darling!" said Mother, throwing her arms around me.

"Happy birthday, Lina," said Jonas. "Did you think we forgot?"

"I did. I thought you forgot."

"We didn't forget," said Mother with a squeeze.

I looked around for Andrius. He wasn't there.

They sang a birthday song. We sat and ate our bread

together. The man who wound his watch told the story of his sixteenth birthday. Mrs. Rimas told of the buttercream frosting she made for cakes. She stood and demonstrated how she'd position the bowl on her hip and whip the spatula. Frosting. I remembered the creamy consistency and sweetness.

"We have a present for you," said Jonas.

"A present?" I asked.

"Well, it's not wrapped, but yes, it's a present," said Mother.

Mrs. Rimas handed me a bundle. It was a pad of paper and a stub of a pencil.

"Thank you! Where did you get it?" I asked.

"We can't tell our secrets," said Mother. "The paper is ruled, but it's all we could find."

"Oh, it's wonderful!" I said. "It doesn't matter that it has lines."

"You'll draw straighter." Jonas smiled.

"You must draw something to remember your birthday. This will be a unique one. Soon this will all be a memory," said Mother.

"A memory, bah. Enough celebration. Get out. I'm tired," complained the bald man.

"Thank you for hosting my party," I said.

He grimaced and flapped his hands, pushing us out the door.

We linked arms and started toward Ulyushka's. I looked up at the frosty gray sky. More snow was on the way.

"Lina." Andrius stepped out from behind the bald man's shack.

Mother and Jonas waved and continued on without me.

"Happy birthday," he said.

I moved toward him. "How did you know?"

"Jonas told me."

The tip of his nose was red. "You can come inside, you know," I told him.

"I know."

"Have you figured out the word in the file?" I asked.

"No, I didn't come for that. I came . . . to give you this." Andrius revealed something from behind his back. It was wrapped in a cloth. "Happy birthday."

"You brought me something? Thank you! I don't even know when your birthday is."

I took the package. Andrius turned to leave.

"Wait. Sit down," I said, motioning to a log in front of a shack.

We sat next to each other. Andrius's brow creased with uncertainty. I pulled the cloth back. I looked at him.

"I . . . I don't know what to say," I stuttered.

"Say you like it."

"I do like it!"

I loved it. It was a book. Dickens.

"It's not *The Pickwick Papers.* That's the one I smoked, right?" He laughed. "This one's *Dombey and Son.* It was the only Dickens I could find." He blew into his gloved hands and rubbed them together. His warm breath swirled like smoke in the cold air.

"It's perfect," I said. I opened the book. It was printed in Russian.

"So now you have to learn Russian or you won't be able to

read your present," he said.

I mocked a scowl. "Where did you get it?"

He pulled in a breath, shaking his head.

"Uh-oh. Should we smoke it right away?"

"Maybe," he said. "I tried to read a bit of it." He faked a yawn.

I laughed. "Well, Dickens can be a little slow at first." I stared at the book in my lap. The burgundy binding felt smooth and tight. The title was etched deep in gold print. It was beautiful, a real present, the perfect present. Suddenly, it felt like my birthday.

I looked at Andrius. "Thank you," I said. I put my mittens on his cheeks. I pulled his face to mine and kissed him. His nose was cold. His lips were warm and his skin smelled clean. My stomach fluttered. I pulled back, looking at his handsome face, and tried to remember how to breathe. "Really, thank you. It's a wonderful present."

Andrius sat on the log, stunned. I stood up.

"It's November twentieth," he said.

"What?"

"My birthday."

"I'll remember that. Good night." I turned and walked away. Snow began to fall.

"Don't smoke it all at once," I heard behind me.

"I won't," I called over my shoulder, hugging my treasure.

59

WE DUG THROUGH the snow and slosh for the sun to reach our little potato patch. The temperatures inched just above freezing according to a thermometer outside the kolkhoz office. I could unbutton my coat.

Mother ran into the hut, her face flushed, gripping an envelope. Her hand trembled. She had received a letter from our housekeeper's cousin, telling her through coded words that Papa was alive. She held me tight, saying "Yes" and "Thank you" over and over.

The letter made no mention of his location. I looked at the crease within her brow, newly carved since we had been deported. It was unfair to keep it from her. I told Mother that I had seen the file and that Papa was in Krasnoyarsk. Her first reaction was of anger, shocked at the risk I took, but over the following days her posture improved and her voice carried a lilt of happiness. "He'll find us, Mother, he will!" I told her, thinking of the piece of birch already en route to Papa.

Activity increased in the camp. Deliveries came from Moscow. Andrius said some contained boxes of files. Guards left. New ones arrived. I wished Kretzsky would leave. I hated the constant fear, wondering if he would throw something at me. He did not leave. I noticed he and Andrius spoke from time to time. One day, while I walked to chop wood, trucks arrived with officers. I didn't recognize them. Their uniforms had different coloring. They walked with a tight gait.

After being forced to draw the commander, I drew whatever I saw or felt. Some drawings, like Munch's, were full of pain, others hopeful, longing. All were an accurate portrayal and would certainly be considered anti-Soviet. At night I would read half a page of *Dombey and Son.* I labored over each word. I constantly asked Mother to translate.

"It's old, very proper Russian," said Mother. "If you learn to speak from this book, you'll sound like a scholar."

Andrius began to meet me in the ration line. I chopped a little harder, hoping the day would move faster. I washed my face at night in the snow. I tried to brush my teeth and comb through my tangled hair.

"So, how many pages have you smoked so far?" his voice whispered behind me.

"Almost ten," I said over my shoulder.

"You must be nearly fluent in Russian by now," he teased, pulling on my hat.

"Peerestan," I said, smiling.

"Stop? Ah, very good. So you really did learn something. What about this word—*krasivaya*?"

I turned around. "What does that mean?"

"You'll have to learn it," said Andrius.

"Okay," I said. "I will."

"Without asking your mother," he said. "Promise?"

"All right," I said. "Say it again."

"Krasivaya. Really, you have to learn it on your own."

"I will."

"We'll see," he said, smiling as he walked away.

IT WAS THE FIRST WARM DAY of spring. Andrius met me in the ration line.

"I got through two pages last night, all by myself," I boasted, taking my chunk of bread.

Andrius wasn't smiling. "Lina," he said, taking my arm.

"What?"

"Not here." We walked away from the line. Andrius didn't speak. He gently steered me behind a nearby shack.

"What is it?" I asked.

He looked over his shoulder.

"What's going on?"

"They're moving people," he whispered.

"The NKVD?"

"Yes."

"Where?" I asked.

"I don't know yet." The light that had bounced through his eyes the day before had disappeared.

"Why are they moving people? How did you find out?"

"Lina," he said, holding on to my arm. His expression frightened me.

"What is it?"

He took my hand. "You're on the list."

"What list?"

"The list of people who are being moved. Jonas and your mother are on it, too."

"Do they know I took the file?" I asked. He shook his head. "Who told you?"

"That's all I know," he said. He looked down. His hand squeezed mine.

I looked at our clasped hands. "Andrius," I said slowly, "are you on the list?"

He looked up. He shook his head.

I dropped his hand. I ran past the tattered shacks. Mother. I had to tell Mother. Where were they taking us? Was it because we hadn't signed? Who else was on the list?

"Lina, calm yourself!" said Mother. "Slow down."

"They're taking us away. Andrius said so," I panted.

"Maybe we're going home," said Jonas.

"Exactly!" said Mother. "Maybe we're going someplace better."

"Maybe we're going to be with Papa," said Jonas.

"Mother, we haven't signed. You didn't see the look on Andrius's face," I said.

"Where is Andrius?" asked Jonas.

"I don't know," I said. "He's not on the list."

Mother left the shack to find Andrius and Mrs. Rimas. I paced the floor.

~

The floorboards creaked, complaining of Papa's pacing.

"Sweden is preferable," said Mother.

"It's not possible," explained Papa. "Germany is their only choice."

"Kostas, we have to help," said Mother.

"We are helping. They'll take a train to Poland, and we'll arrange passage to Germany from there."

"And the papers?" asked Mother.

"Arranged."

"I would feel better if it were Sweden," said Mother.

"It cannot be. It's Germany."

"Who's going to Germany?" I yelled from the dining room.

Silence.

"Lina, I didn't know you were in here," said Mother, coming out of the kitchen.

"I'm doing my homework."

"A colleague of your father's is going to Germany," said Mother.

"I'll be back for dinner." Papa kissed Mother on the cheek and rushed out the back door.

~

News of the impending move burned through the camp like a spark riding gasoline. People dashed in and out of huts. Speculations flew. Stories changed each minute. Others cropped up the next. Someone claimed additional NKVD had arrived in camp. Someone else said they saw a group of NKVD loading their rifles. No one knew the truth.

Ulyushka threw open the door of the shack. She spoke to Jonas and quickly exited.

"She's looking for Mother," said Jonas.

"Does she know something?" I asked.

Miss Grybas ran into our shack. "Where is your mother?" she asked.

"She went to find Andrius and Mrs. Rimas," I said.

"Mrs. Rimas is with us. Bring your mother to the bald man's shack."

We waited. I didn't know what to do. Should I put everything in my suitcase? Were we really leaving? Could Jonas be right? Could we be going home? We hadn't signed. I couldn't shake the image of concern on Andrius's face when he told me we were on the list. How did he know we were on it? How did he know he wasn't?

Mother returned. People stood elbow-to-elbow in the bald man's shack. The volume grew as we entered.

"Shh," said the man who wound his watch. "Everyone, please sit down. Let's hear from Elena."

"It's true," said Mother. "There is a list and there is word of moving people."

"How did Andrius find out about it?" asked Jonas.

"Mrs. Arvydas received some information." Mother looked away. "I don't know how she came by it. I am on the list. So are my children. Mrs. Rimas is on the list. Miss Grybas, you are not on the list. That's all I know."

People quickly began asking if they were on the list.

"Stop your yapping. She said that's all she knows," said the bald man.

"Interesting," said the man who wound his watch. "Miss Grybas is not on the list. She hasn't signed. So it's not just those who refuse to sign."

"Please," choked Miss Grybas, "don't leave me here."

"Quit blubbering. We don't know what's happening yet," said the bald man.

I tried to find the pattern. How were they sorting us for the impending move? But there wasn't a pattern. Stalin's psychology of terror seemed to rely on never knowing what to expect.

"We must be prepared," said Mr. Lukas, winding his watch. "Think of the journey we had in coming here. We're not nearly as strong. If we are to face that journey again, we must be prepared."

"You don't think they'll put us back in the train cars, do you?" gasped Mrs. Rimas. A wave of cries rippled through the group.

How could we be prepared? None of us had food. We were malnourished, weak. We had sold nearly all of our valuables.

"If it is true, and I am not leaving, I will sign the papers," announced Miss Grybas.

"No! You mustn't!" I said.

"Stop," said Mrs. Rimas. "You're not thinking clearly."

"I'm thinking very clearly," said Miss Grybas, sniffing back tears. "If you and Elena are gone, I will be nearly alone. If I sign, they will allow me to teach the children in the camp. Even if my Russian is poor, I can still teach. And if I'm alone, I'll need to have access to the village. They'll grant access only if I sign. That way, I can continue writing letters for all of us. It must be done."

"Let's not make any decisions yet," said Mother, patting Miss Grybas's hands.

"Maybe it's all a mistake," said Mrs. Rimas.

Mother looked down and closed her eyes.

ANDRIUS CAME TO OUR shack late that night and spoke to Mother outside.

"Andrius would like to speak with you," said Mother. Ulyushka said something to her in Russian. Mother nodded.

I walked outside. Andrius stood with his hands in his pockets.

"Hi." He chipped at the dirt with his shoe.

"Hi."

I stared down the row of shacks. A breeze lifted the ends of my hair. "It's getting warm," I finally said.

"Yeah," said Andrius, looking up at the sky. "Let's walk."

The snow had melted and the mud had firmed. Neither one of us spoke until we passed the bald man's shack.

"Do you know where they're taking us?" I asked.

"I think they're transferring you to another camp. It seems that some of the NKVD are going, too. They're packing up."

"I can't stop thinking of my father and what it said in the file."

"Lina, I figured out what the word in the file means," said Andrius.

I stopped, looking to him for the answer.

He reached out and gently moved my hair away from my eyes. "It means 'accessory,'" said Andrius.

"Accessory?"

"It probably means that he tried to help people who were in danger," said Andrius.

"Well, of course he'd do that. But you don't think he actually committed some kind of crime, do you?"

"Of course not! We're not criminals," he said. "Well, maybe you are—stealing logs, pens, and files." He looked over at me, suppressing a grin.

"Oh, you should talk—tomatoes, chocolate, vodka."

"Yeah, and who knows what else," said Andrius.

He took my hand and kissed it.

We walked hand in hand, neither one of us speaking. My pace slowed. "Andrius, I'm . . . scared."

He stopped and turned to me. "No. Don't be scared. Don't give them anything, Lina, not even your fear."

"I can't help it. I'm not even used to this camp. I miss home, I miss my father, I miss school, I miss my cousin." My breathing quickened.

"Shh," said Andrius. He pulled me to his chest. "Be careful

who you talk to. Don't let your guard down, okay?" he whispered. His arms tightened around me.

"I don't want to go," I said. We stood, quiet.

How did I get here? How did I end up in the arms of a boy I barely knew, but knew I didn't want to lose? I wondered what I would have thought of Andrius in Lithuania. Would I have liked him? Would he have liked me?

"I don't want you to go," he finally whispered, barely audible.

I closed my eyes. "Andrius, we have to get back home."

"I know," he said. "We will." He took my hand and we started back.

"I'll write to you. I'll send letters to the village," I said.

He nodded.

We arrived back at our shack. "Wait a minute," I told him. I went inside. I gathered all of my drawings, even the ones on small scraps, from underneath the lining in my suitcase. I tore papers out of my sketchbook. I walked outside and handed the stack to Andrius. The drawing of his mother, her face bruised, slipped out and wafted to the ground. Her eyes stared up at us from the dirt.

"What are you doing?" he asked, quickly picking up the drawing.

"Hide them. Keep them safe for me," I said, putting my hands on top of his. "I don't know where we're going. I don't want them to be destroyed. There's so much of me, of all of us, in these drawings. Can you find a safe place for them?"

He nodded. "There's a loose floorboard under my bunk.

It's where I hid *Dombey and Son*. Lina," he said slowly, looking down at the drawings. "You have to keep drawing. My mother says the world has no idea what the Soviets are doing to us. No one knows what our fathers have sacrificed. If other countries knew, they might help."

"I will," I said. "And I've been writing it all down. That's why you have to keep these safe for me. Hide them."

He nodded. "Just promise me you'll be careful," he said. "Don't be stupid and go looking for files or running under any trains."

We stared at each other.

"So, don't smoke any books without me, okay?" he said.

I smiled. "I won't. How long do you think we have?"

"I don't know. It could be any day."

I stood on my toes and kissed him.

"Krasivaya," he said into my ear, his nose tracing along my cheek. "Have you learned it yet?" He kissed my neck.

"Not yet," I said, closing my eyes.

Andrius exhaled and stepped back slowly. "Tell Jonas I'll come by to see him in the morning, okay?"

I nodded, the touch of his lips still warm against my neck.

He walked away in the dark, clutching my drawings under his coat. He turned and looked over his shoulder. I waved. He waved back. His silhouette became smaller and smaller and then finally, faded into the darkness.

THEY CAME BEFORE sunrise. They burst into our shack waving rifles, just as they had burst into our home ten months before. We had only minutes. This time I was ready.

Ulyushka rose from her pallet. She barked at Mother.

"Stop yelling. We're leaving," I told her.

She began handing Mother potatoes, beets, and other food she had stored. She handed Jonas a thick animal hide to put in his suitcase. She gave me a pencil. I couldn't believe it. Why was she giving us food? Mother tried to hug her. They barely embraced. Ulyushka pushed her away and stomped out.

The NKVD told us to stand and wait outside our shack. The man who wound his watch came walking toward us, suitcase in hand. He was on the list. Mrs. Rimas was behind him, followed by the girl with the dolly, her mother, and a stream of other people. We began a slow procession toward the kolkhoz office, dragging our belongings. Faces looked years older than when we had arrived ten months before. Did I look older, too? Miss Grybas ran to us, crying.

"They've sent for you. You're going to America. I just know it. Please don't forget about me," she begged. "Please don't let me waste away here. I want to go home."

Mother and Mrs. Rimas hugged Miss Grybas. They assured her they would not forget her. I would never forget her, or the beets she hid under her dress.

We trudged on. I heard Miss Grybas's crying fade behind us. The grouchy woman walked out of her shack. She held up a withered hand and nodded. Her daughters clung to her legs. I remembered her, hiding the bathroom hole on the train with her girth. She had lost so much weight. My eyes scanned for Andrius. I had *Dombey and Son* tucked safely in my suitcase, next to our family picture.

A large truck sat near the kolkhoz office. Kretzsky smoked with two NKVD nearby. The commander stood on the porch with an officer I didn't recognize. They began calling names alphabetically. People climbed into the back of the truck.

"Take care, Jonas," said Andrius's voice behind us. "Good-bye, Mrs. Vilkas."

"Good-bye, Andrius," said Mother, grasping his hands and kissing his cheeks. "Take care of your mother, dear."

"She wanted to come but . . ."

"I understand. Give her my love," said Mother.

The NKVD continued reading names off the list.

"Write to me, okay, Jonas?" said Andrius.

"I will," said Jonas. He extended his small hand for a handshake.

"Take care of these two, okay? Your father and I are counting on you," said Andrius.

Jonas nodded.

Andrius turned. His eyes found mine. "I'll see you," he said.

My face didn't wrinkle. I didn't utter a sound. But for the first time in months, I cried. Tears popped from their dry sockets and sailed down my cheeks in one quick stream. I looked away.

The NKVD called the bald man's name.

"Look at me," whispered Andrius, moving close. "I'll see you," he said. "Just think about that. Just think about me bringing you your drawings. Picture it, because I'll be there."

I nodded.

"Vilkas," the NKVD called.

We walked toward the truck and climbed inside. I looked down at Andrius. He raked through his hair with his fingers. The engine turned and roared. I raised my hand in a wave good-bye.

His lips formed the words "I'll see you." He nodded in confirmation.

I nodded back. The back gate slammed and I sat down. The truck lurched forward. Wind began to blow against my face. I pulled my coat closed and put my hands in my pockets. That's when I felt it. The stone. Andrius had slipped it into my pocket. I stood up to let him know I had found it. He was gone.

ice and

ashes

63

WE TRAVELED ALL morning in the truck. The road squirreled a thin line, hidden in the trees. Like Mother, I tried to think of the positive. I thought of Andrius. I could still hear his voice. At least we had left the commander and Kretzsky behind. I hoped we would be somewhere near Krasnoyarsk, closer to Papa.

The truck stopped next to a field. We were allowed to jump off and relieve ourselves in the grass. The NKVD began yelling within a matter of seconds.

"Davai!"

I knew that voice. I looked over. Kretzsky.

Late that afternoon, we reached a train station. A faded sign creaked in the wind. Biysk. Trucks littered the train yard. The scene was unlike the train station when we were deported. In Kaunas, back in June, we were frantic. Panic rose everywhere. People ran and screamed. Now, masses of tired, gray people made their way slowly toward the train cars, like a group of exhausted ants marching toward a hill.

"Everyone stand at the front of the door opening," instructed the bald man. "Look uncomfortable. Maybe they won't put more people in here and we'll have room to breathe."

I stepped up into the train car. It was different from the previous car, longer. A lamp hung from above. The carriage smelled of sour body odor and urine. I missed the fresh air and the scent of wood from the labor camp. We did as the bald man suggested and crowded near the door. It worked. Two groups of people were steered toward other cars.

"This is filthy," said Mrs. Rimas.

"What did you expect? A luxury sleeper car?" said the bald man.

They shoved a few more people into our car before slamming the door. A woman with two boys and an older man climbed in. A tall man stepped in and looked around nervously. A woman and her daughter were hoisted up. Jonas nudged my arm. The girl looked as yellow as a lemon, her eyes nothing more than swollen slits. Where had she been? The mother spoke in Lithuanian to her daughter.

"Just another short trip and we'll be home, dear," said the girl's mother. Mother helped the woman with her luggage. The girl hacked and coughed.

We were lucky. We had only thirty-three people in our car. We had room and light this time. We gave the lemon girl a plank to sleep on. Mother insisted that Jonas have one as well. I sat on the floor, next to the girl with the dolly, whose hands were now empty.

"Where's your doll?" I asked.

"Dead," said the girl, with a hollow look in her eyes.

"Oh."

"The NKVD killed her. Remember how they shot the woman with the baby? That's what they did to Liale, except they threw her in the air and shot her head off. Kind of like a pigeon."

"You must miss her a lot," I said.

"Well, I missed her at first. I kept crying and crying. A guard told me to stop crying. I tried, but I couldn't. He clobbered me in the head. See my scar?" she said, pointing to a thick red fold on her forehead.

Bastards. She was only a child.

"You couldn't stop crying either?" she asked.

"What?"

She pointed to the scar above my eyebrow.

"No, they hit me with a can of sardines," I said.

"Because you were crying?" she said.

"No, just for fun," I answered.

She curled her finger toward me, beckoning me closer. "Want to know a big secret?" she asked.

"What's that?"

She leaned over and whispered in my ear. "Mama says the NKVD are going to hell." She leaned back. "But you can't tell anyone. It's a secret, okay? You see, Liale, my dolly, she's up in heaven. She talks to me. She tells me things. So that's a secret, but Liale said I could tell you."

"I won't tell anyone," I said.

"What's your name?" she asked.

"Lina," I said.

"And your brother?"

"Jonas."

"My name is Janina," she said, continuing to chatter. "Your mama, she looks old now. My mama does, too. And you like the boy who was waiting near the truck."

"What?"

"The one who put something into your pocket. I saw. What did he give you?"

I showed her the stone.

"It's so sparkly. I think Liale would like it. Maybe you could give it to me."

"No, it was a present. I think I better hold on to it for a while," I said.

Mother sat down next to me.

"Did you see the present Lina's boyfriend gave her?" asked Janina.

"He's not my boyfriend."

Was he my boyfriend? I wanted him to be my boyfriend. I showed Mother the stone.

"I see it made its way back to you," she said. "That's good luck."

"My dolly's dead," announced Janina. "She's in heaven."

Mother nodded and patted Janina's arm.

"Someone shut that kid up," said the bald man. "You, the tall one. What do you know of the war?"

"The Japanese bombed Pearl Harbor, they bombed," said the man.

"Pearl Harbor? They bombed America?" said Mrs. Rimas.

"When?" asked the bald man.

"Months ago. Around Christmas, yes, Christmas." He repeated his words, a nervous tic.

"So the United States has declared war on Japan?" asked Mother.

"Yes, along with Britain. Britain has also declared war."

"Where did you come from?" asked the bald man.

"Lithuania," said the man.

"I know that, idiot. Where did you come from today?"

"Kalmanka," said the man. "Yes, Kalmanka."

"Kalmanka, eh? Was it a prison or a camp?" asked the bald man.

"A camp, hmm, a camp. A potato farm. You?"

"A beet farm near Turaciak," replied Mother. "Were there all Lithuanians in your camp?"

"No, mostly Latvians," said the man. "And Finns. Yes, Finns."

Finns. I had forgotten about Finland. I remembered the night Dr. Seltzer came to the house looking for Papa. The Soviets had invaded Finland.

"It's only thirty kilometers from Leningrad, Elena," Dr. Seltzer had told Mother. "Stalin wants to protect himself from the West."

"Will the Finns negotiate?" asked Mother.

"The Finns are strong people. They'll fight," said Dr. Seltzer.

THE TRAIN CHURNED forward. The rhythm of the rails tormented me, screeching and banging. They pulled me away from Andrius, further into an unknown. The metal lamp swayed above like a pendulum, illuminating hollow faces, throwing shadows throughout the carriage. Janina whispered to the ghost of her dead doll, giggling.

The yellow girl hacked and wheezed next to Jonas. She spit up blood all over his back. Mother snatched Jonas off the plank. She tore off his shirt and threw it down the bathroom hole. It didn't seem necessary. We were all breathing the same air as the yellow girl. Phlegm and blood on a shirt couldn't be any more contagious.

"I'm so sorry," sobbed the girl. "I've ruined your shirt."

"It's okay," said Jonas, hugging his naked torso. His scurvy spots hadn't entirely disappeared. Pink blotches dotted his emaciated rib cage.

The tall man, the repeater, spoke sprightly, convinced of America, America. I wasn't convinced of anything, except my yearning to see Papa, Andrius, and home.

On the third night, I woke up. Something tapped on my chest. I opened my eyes. Janina's face hovered above mine, her eyes wide. The light swung back and forth behind her head.

"Janina? What is it?"

"It's Liale."

"Tell Liale it's time to sleep," I said, closing my eyes.

"She can't sleep. She says the yellow girl is dead."

"What?"

"Liale says she's dead. Can you check if her eyes are open? I'm scared to look."

I pulled Janina against me, laying her head on my chest. "Shh. Go to sleep." She trembled in my arms. I listened. The coughing had stopped. "Shh. Time to sleep, Janina." I rocked her gently.

I thought of Andrius. What was he doing back at the camp? Had he looked at my drawings? I reached into my pocket and wrapped my fingers around the stone. I saw him smiling, tugging my hat in the ration line.

The yellow girl was dead. Streaks of dried blood ran from the corners of her mouth to her chin. The next day, the guards dragged her stiff body out of the train. Her mother jumped down after her, crying. A gunshot fired. A thud hit the dirt. A grieving mother was an annoyance.

Ulyushka, the woman I despised, kept us alive on the train. We lived off the food she had given Mother. We shared it with others. I drew Ulyushka's wide face and stalks of black hair, trying to steady my hand through the train's vibration.

No one refused the water or gray slop in the buckets. We ate greedily, licking our palms and sucking under our dirty fingernails. Janina's mother slept often. I could barely sleep even though I was exhausted. The noise and movement from the train kept me awake. I sat, wondering where they were taking us and how I would let Papa know.

Janina tapped the bald man on the shoulder. "I heard you're a Jew," she said.

"That's what you heard, eh?" said the bald man.

"Is it true?" asked Janina.

"Yes. I heard you're a little brat, is that true?"

Janina paused, thinking. "No, I don't think so. Did you know Hitler and the Nazis might kill the Jews? My mama said that."

"Your mother's wrong. Hitler *is* killing the Jews."

"But why?" asked Jonas.

"The Jews are the scapegoat for all of Germany's problems," said the bald man. "Hitler's convinced racial purity is the answer. It's too complicated for children to understand."

"So you're here with us, rather than with the Nazis?" asked Jonas.

"You think I'd choose this? Under Hitler or Stalin, this war will end us all. Lithuania is caught in the middle. You heard the man. The Japanese have bombed Pearl Harbor. The United States may already be allied with the Soviets. Enough talk. Be quiet," said the bald man.

"We're going to America," said the repeater. "America."

AFTER A WEEK, the train stopped late at night. Mrs. Rimas said she saw a sign that said Makarov. They herded us out of the carriages. The open air swirled around my face, clean, fresh. I breathed in through my nose and exhaled through my dry lips. The guards directed us toward a large building four hundred yards away. We dragged our filthy belongings from the train. Mother collapsed in the dirt.

"Lift her, quickly," said Mrs. Rimas, looking around for the guards. "If they would shoot a grieving mother, they might shoot a woman with loose legs."

"I'll be fine. I'm just tired," said Mother. Mrs. Rimas and I helped Mother walk. Jonas dragged our suitcases. Mother stumbled again near the building.

"Davai!" Two NKVD approached, clutching rifles. Mother wasn't moving fast enough.

They marched toward us. Mother straightened up. One of the NKVD spit in the dirt. The other looked at her. My stomach dropped. Kretzsky. He had traveled with us.

"Nikolai," Mother said weakly.

Kretzsky pointed in another direction. He marched away toward a group of people.

The building felt large, like an enormous barn. There must have been a thousand of us. We were too tired to speak. We fell to the ground on our belongings. My muscles released their clench. The stillness of the ground felt wonderful, as if a hand had stopped a metronome. The screeching of the rails had finally ended. I put my arm around my suitcase, hugging *Dombey and Son*. It was quiet. We lay in our rags and slept.

Morning broke. I felt Janina breathing, nestled against my back. Jonas sat on top of his suitcase. He nodded at me. I looked at Mother. She slept soundly, her face and arms on her suitcase.

"She called him Nikolai," said Jonas.

"What?" I asked.

Jonas began pacing. "Kretzsky. Did you hear her? Last night, she called him Nikolai."

"Is that his first name?" I asked.

"Exactly. I don't know. How does she know?" snapped Jonas. "Why did he come with us?" Jonas kicked at the dirt.

The NKVD arrived with bread and buckets of mushroom soup. We woke Mother and dug in our bags for a cup or a dish.

"They are preparing us, preparing," said the repeater. "We shall feast every day in America. Every day."

"Why are they feeding us?" I asked.

"To strengthen us for work," said Jonas.

"Eat every last bit," instructed Mother.

After the meal, the guards began rounding up groups. Mother strained to hear.

She laughed weakly. "We're going to bathe. We'll be able to bathe!"

We scurried toward a large wooden bathhouse. Mother's stride had steadied. We were divided at the gate into male and female groups.

"Wait for us," Mother told Jonas.

We were instructed to take off our clothes and give them to Siberian men working at the door. All modesty dissolved. The women quickly undressed. They wanted to be clean. I looked down, hesitating.

"Hurry, Lina!"

I didn't want them to touch me, to look at me. My arms folded over my breasts.

Mother spoke to one of the men. "He says we must hurry, that this is a travel stop. A large group is coming later today. He says that Latvians, Estonians, and Ukranians have already passed through," said Mother. "It's okay, darling, really."

The men didn't seem to be paying any attention. Of course not. Our shrunken bodies appeared almost androgynous. I hadn't had a period in months. Nothing about me felt feminine. A piece of pork or a foamy beer would be more alluring to men.

After our showers, we were put on a truck with our belongings. They drove us several kilometers through the woods until we arrived at the bank of the Angara River.

"Why are we here?" asked Jonas.

Large wooden sheds dotted the bank. Tucked near the trees was a large NKVD building.

"They're putting us on boats. Don't you see? We're going to America. America!" said the repeater. "We're traveling up the Angara to the Lena and then across the sea to the Bering Strait. The Bering Strait."

"That journey would take months," said the man who wound his watch.

America? How could we leave Papa behind in a prison in Krasnoyarsk? How would I get my drawings to him? And what about the war? What if other countries became allies with Stalin? I saw Andrius's face, when he told me we were on the list. Something about his expression told me we weren't going to America.

66

THE BOATS WERE delayed. We waited on the stony banks of the Angara River for more than a week. They fed us barley porridge. I couldn't figure out why they were feeding us more than bread. It was not out of kindness. Our strength would be needed, but what for? We sat in the sun, as if on vacation. I drew for Papa and wrote to Andrius every day. I drew on small scraps of paper so as not to be noticed and hid them between the pages of *Dombey and Son*. An Estonian woman noticed me drawing and gave me additional paper.

We hauled logs, but only for our nightly bonfires. We sat around the crackling fires and sang Lithuanian songs. The entire forest echoed in song from the people of the Baltics singing of their homeland. Two women were chosen to travel to Tcheremchov by train to help carry supplies back for the NKVD. They mailed our letters for us.

"Please, could you take this to Tcheremchov and pass it along to someone?" I handed a slat of wood to the woman.

"It's lovely. The flowers—you've done a beautiful job. I had rue flowers in my backyard at home," she said, sighing. She looked up at me. "Your father is in Krasnoyarsk?"

I nodded.

"Lina, please don't get your hopes up. Krasnoyarsk is a long way from here," said Mother.

One day, after sitting in the sun, Mother and I waded into the Angara. We ran out of the water, laughing. Our clothes clung tightly to our thin bodies.

"Cover yourself!" said Jonas, looking around.

"What do you mean?" said Mother, pulling at the wet fabric clinging to her.

"They're watching," said Jonas, motioning with his head to the NKVD.

"Jonas, they have no interest. Look at us. We're hardly glamorous," said Mother, wringing water from her hair. I wrapped my arms around my torso.

"They found Mrs. Arvydas interesting. Maybe he finds you interesting," said Jonas.

Mother's hands dropped. "What are you talking of? Who?"

"Nikolai," said Jonas.

"Kretzsky?" I said. "What about him?"

"Ask Mother," said Jonas.

"Stop it, Jonas. We don't know Nikolai," said Mother.

I faced Mother. "Why do you call him Nikolai? How do you know his name?"

Mother looked from me to Jonas. "I asked him his name," she said.

My stomach dropped. Was Jonas right? "But Mother, he's a monster," I said, wiping water from the scar on my forehead.

She moved in closer, wringing out her skirt. "We don't know what he is."

I snorted. "He's a—"

Mother grabbed my arm. Pain shot up into my shoulder. She spoke through clenched teeth. "We don't know. Do you hear me? We don't know what he is. He's a boy. He's just a boy." Mother let go of my arm. "And I'm not lying with him," she spat at Jonas. "How dare you imply such a thing."

"Mother . . . ," stammered Jonas.

She walked away, leaving me rubbing my arm.

Jonas stood, shocked by Mother's outburst.

67

FOR WEEKS, THE BARGES crept farther north up the Angara. We disembarked and rode for days in the back of black trucks through dense forests. We passed enormous fallen trees, with trunks so large the truck could have driven inside them. I saw no human beings. The dark forest seemed to surround us, impenetrable. Where were they taking us? We broiled each day and shivered at night. Blisters healed. We ate everything given to us, thankful we weren't put to work.

The trucks arrived at Ust Kut, on the River Lena. We waited once again for barges. The bank of the Lena was blanketed with tiny pebbles. It poured rain. The makeshift tents on the bank did nothing to shelter us. I lay on top of my suitcase, protecting *Dombey and Son*, the stone, my drawings, and our family photo. Janina stood in the rain. She stared at the sky, carrying on conversations with no one. Kretzsky's boots crunched up and down the bank. He yelled at us to stay in groups. At night, he'd stand staring at the silvery ribbon of moonlight on the Lena, moving only to bring his glowing cigarette to his lips.

My Russian improved. Jonas was still far ahead of me.

After two weeks, the barges arrived and the NKVD once again boarded us to float north.

We left Ust Kut and passed Kirensk.

"We're traveling north," said Jonas. "Maybe we really will sail for America."

"And leave Papa behind?" I asked.

Jonas looked out at the water. He said nothing.

The repeater spoke of nothing but America. He tried to draw maps of the United States, discussing details he had heard from friends or relatives. He needed to believe it was possible.

~

"In America there are excellent universities in an area they call New England. They say New York is quite fashionable," said Joana.

"Who says New York is fashionable?" I asked.

"My parents."

"What do they know of America?" I asked.

"Mother has an uncle there," said Joana.

"I thought all of Auntie's family was in Germany," I said.

"Apparently she has a relative in America. She gets letters from him. He's in Pennsylvania."

"Hmph. I don't much care for America. They certainly lack for art. I can't name a single American artist who is accomplished."

"You better not be drawing me," said the bald man. "I don't want any pictures drawn of me."

"Actually, I'm almost finished," I said, shading in the gray area of his spotted cheeks.

"Tear it up," he insisted.

"No," I said. "Don't worry, I won't show it to anyone."

"You won't, if you know what's good for you."

I looked down at my drawing. I had captured his curled lip and the surly expression he always wore. He wasn't ugly. The deep lines above his brow just made him look cranky.

"Why were you deported?" I asked him. "You said you were a stamp collector. But why would they deport you for collecting stamps?"

"Mind your own business," he said.

"Where is your family?" I pressed.

"I said it's none of your business," he snapped, pointing his crooked finger at me. "And if you know what's best for you, you'll keep your drawings out of sight, you hear me?"

Janina sat down next to me.

"You'll never be a famous artist," said the bald man.

"Yes, she will," argued Janina.

"No, she won't. You know why? Because she's not dead. But maybe there's still hope for that. America, bah."

I stared at him.

"My dolly's dead," said Janina.

68

WE APPROACHED JAKUTSK.

"Now we shall see. We shall see," said the repeater, fidgeting. "If we disembark here, we will not go to America. We will not go."

"Where would we go?" asked Jonas.

"To the Kolyma region," said the bald man. "To the prisons, maybe Magadan."

"We're not going to Magadan," said Mother. "Stop such talk, Mr. Stalas."

"Not Kolyma, no, not Kolyma," said the repeater.

The barges slowed. We were coming to a stop.

"No, please, no," whispered Jonas.

Mrs. Rimas began to cry. "I can't be in prison this far from my husband."

Janina tugged at my sleeve. "Liale says we're not going to

Kolyma."

"What?" I said.

"She says we're not going." She shrugged.

We crowded near the edge of the barge. Some of the NKVD disembarked. Kretzsky was among them. He carried a rucksack. A commander met the guards on the shore. We watched as they checked assignments.

"Look," said Jonas. "Some of the NKVD are loading supplies onto the boat."

"So we're not getting off here?" I asked.

Suddenly, voices rose from the bank. It was Kretzsky. He was arguing with a commander. I understood the commander. He told Kretzsky to get back on the barge.

"Kretzsky wants to stay," said Jonas.

"Good, let him stay," I said.

Kretzsky flailed his arms at the commander, who pointed back at the boat.

Mother sighed and looked down. Kretzsky turned back toward the barge. He wasn't leaving. He was coming with us, wherever we were going.

The passengers cheered and embraced as the barge pulled away from Jakutsk.

A week later spirits were still buoyant. People sang on the deck of the barge. Someone played an accordion. Kretzsky stormed through the crowd, shoving people aside. "What's wrong with you? Are you all imbeciles? You cheer as if you're going to America. Fools!" he yelled.

The elation collapsed to murmurs.

"America. America?" said the repeater quietly.

Where were they taking us? It was already August. Temperatures dropped as we sailed northward. It felt like late October, not summer. The forests along the bank of the Lena thinned.

"We've crossed into the Arctic Circle," announced the man who wound his watch.

"What?" gasped Jonas. "How can that be? Where are they taking us?"

"That is correct," said the repeater. "We'll go to the mouth of the Lena and get on huge steamships to America. Steamships."

The barges stopped in Bulun and Stolbai in the Arctic. We watched as large groups were herded off the barge and simply left standing on the deserted shore as we pulled away. We sailed on.

In late August we reached the mouth of the River Lena. The temperature was just above freezing. The icy waves of the Laptev Sea crashed against the barge as it was moored to the shore.

"Davai!" yelled the guards, jabbing us with the butts of their rifles.

"They're going to drown us," said the bald man. "They've brought us all this way to drown us and get rid of us here."

"Dear God, no," said Mrs. Rimas.

The NKVD threw a wooden plank against the side of the barge. They pushed the children down the plank, screaming for them to hurry.

"Hurry, where? There's nothing here," said Mother.

She was right. It was completely uninhabited, not a single bush or tree, just barren dirt to a shore of endless water. We were surrounded by nothing but polar tundra and the Laptev Sea. The wind whipped. Sand blew into my mouth and stung my eyes. I clutched my suitcase and looked around. The NKVD made their way to two brick buildings. How would we all fit? There were more than three hundred of us.

Kretzsky argued with some of the NKVD, repeating that he had to go to Jakutsk. An NKVD with greasy hair and brown crooked teeth stopped us.

"Where do you think you're going?" he demanded.

"To the buildings," said Mother.

"Those are for the officers," he snapped.

"And where are we supposed to stay?" asked Mother. "Where is the village?"

The guard waved his arms wide. "*This* is the village. You have the whole village for yourself." The other NKVD laughed.

"Excuse me?" said Mother.

"What, you don't like it? You think you're too good for this? Fascist pig. Pigs sleep in the mud. Didn't you know that? But before you sleep, you have to finish the bakery and build a fish factory." He moved closer to Mother. His corroded teeth protruded from under his top lip. "You fascists like fish, don't you? You pigs disgust me." He spit on her chest and walked away. "You don't even deserve the mud," he yelled over his shoulder.

They made us carry bricks and wood from the barge. We filed in and out of the barge's deep hold, carrying as many bricks as we could. It took ten hours to unload the barges. In addition to bricks and wood, we carried barrels of kerosene, flour, and even small fishing boats, all for the NKVD. My arms trembled with fatigue.

"Liale says we're not going to America," announced Janina.

"No kidding. Did your ghost doll tell you we'd be here?" demanded the bald man. He pointed to a sign, crisped and faded from the weather.

Trofimovsk. The very top of the Arctic Circle, near the North Pole.

69

WE HUDDLED TOGETHER and pulled our coats tight for warmth. I longed for the labor camp, for Ulyushka's hut, for Andrius. The steamer's whistle shrieked and pulled the barges back down the Lena. Were they going to pick up more people?

"How will you mail letters to Papa from here?" asked Jonas.

"There has to be a village close by," said Mother.

I thought of the piece of wood, handed off in Tcheremchov. Something had to have made its way to Papa by now.

"So this is their plan," said the bald man, looking around. "This is how Stalin will end us? He'll let us freeze to death. He'll let the foxes eat us."

"Foxes?" said Mrs. Rimas. Janina's mother snapped a glance at the bald man.

"If there are foxes, we can eat them," said Jonas.

"Have you ever caught a fox, boy?" asked the bald man.

"No, but I'm sure it can be done," said Jonas.

"He said we have to build a factory for them," I said.

"This can't be our destination," said Mother. "Surely they're going to transport us somewhere else."

"Don't be so sure, Elena," said the man who wound his watch. "To the Soviets, there is no more Lithuania, Latvia, or Estonia. Stalin must completely get rid of us to see his vision unlittered."

Litter. Is that what we were to Stalin?

"It's nearly September," said the man who wound his watch. "Soon the polar night will be upon us."

Nearly September. We were freezing. We had learned about the polar night in school. In the polar region, the sun falls below the horizon for 180 days. Darkness for nearly half a year. I hadn't paid much attention to the lecture in school. I had sketched the sun sinking over the horizon. Now my heart sank into my stomach where the bile began to chew it.

"We haven't much time," continued the man who wound his watch. "I think—"

"STOP IT! Stop talking!" shrieked Janina's mother.

"What's wrong, dear?" asked Mother.

"Shh . . . Don't draw the attention of the guards," said Mrs. Rimas.

"Mama, what's wrong?" asked Janina. Her mother continued shrieking.

The woman had barely spoken during the entire voyage and suddenly we couldn't make her stop.

"I can't do this! I won't die here. I will not let a fox eat us!"

Suddenly the woman grabbed Janina by the throat. A thick gurgle came from Janina's windpipe.

Mother threw herself on Janina's mother and pried her fingers from her daughter's neck. Janina caught her breath and began to sob.

"I'm so sorry," cried her mother. She turned her back to us, placed her hands on her own throat, and tried to strangle herself.

Mrs. Rimas slapped the woman across the face. The man who wound his watch restrained her arms.

"What's wrong with you? If you want to kill yourself, do it in private," said the bald man.

"It's your fault," I said. "You told her she'd be eaten by a fox."

"Stop it, Lina," said Jonas.

"Mama," sobbed Janina.

"She already talks to her dead doll. Do we really want to hear about her dead mother?" said the bald man.

"Mama!" shrieked Janina.

"You're going to be fine," said Mother, stroking the woman's filthy hair. "We're all going to be fine. We mustn't lose our senses. It's going to be all right. Really."

AT DAYBREAK, the NKVD shouted at us to get to work. My neck hurt from sleeping on my suitcase. Jonas and Mother had slept under a fishing boat to protect themselves from the wind. I had slept only a few hours. After everyone was asleep, I drew by moonlight. I sketched Janina's mother, her hands squeezing tight around her daughter's neck, Janina's eyes bulging. I wrote a letter to Andrius, telling him we were in Trofimovsk. How would I ever mail the letter? Would Andrius think I had forgotten about him? *I'll find you*, he had said. How could he ever find us here? Papa, I thought. You're coming for us. Hurry.

The NKVD divided us into twenty-five groups, fifteen people per group. We were group number eleven. They took the men with any strength and sent them to work finishing the NKVD barracks. The boys were sent to fish in the Laptev Sea. The remainder of the women and elderly were instructed to build a *jurta,* a hut, for their group. We could not, however, use any of the bricks or wood near the NKVD building. Those were reserved for the NKVD barracks. After all, winter was coming and the NKVD needed warm housing, said Ivanov, the brown-toothed guard. We could use scraps or pieces of logs that might have floated ashore.

"Before we even think of building something, we'll need supplies," said Mrs. Rimas. "Hurry, scatter and pick up anything and everything you can find before the others take it all. Bring it back here."

I picked up large stones, sticks, and chips of brick. Were we really going to build a house from sticks and stones? Mother and Mrs. Rimas found logs that had washed ashore. They dragged them all the way back to our site and went back for more. I saw a woman digging up moss with her hands and using it as mortar between the rocks. Janina and I ripped up pieces of moss and piled it near our supplies. My stomach churned with hunger. I couldn't wait for Jonas to return with the fish.

He returned, wet and shivering. His hands were empty.

"Where are the fish?" I asked. My teeth chattered.

"The guards say we're not allowed fish. All of the fish we catch is stored for the NKVD."

"What will we eat?" I asked.

"Bread rations," he replied.

It took us a week to collect enough logs to create a framework for our jurta. The men discussed the design. I drew the sketches.

"These logs don't look very strong," commented Jonas. "They're just driftwood."

"It's all we have," said the man who wound his watch. "We must hurry. We must finish before the first snow comes. If we don't, we won't survive."

"Hurry. Hurry," said the repeater.

I dug deep notches in the hard dirt with a flat stone. The ground was frozen. As I dug deeper, I had to hack at ice. Mother, Mrs. Rimas and I stood the logs vertically in the notches. We packed dirt around them.

"It doesn't look big enough for fifteen people," I said, looking at the framing. The wind whipped, stinging my face.

"We'll be warmer if we're close together," said Mother.

Ivanov approached with Kretzsky. I understood most of the conversation.

"The slowest pigs in Trofimovsk!" said Ivanov through his rotten teeth.

"You need a roof," said Kretzsky, motioning with his cigarette.

"Yes, I know. And heat?" I said. We had enough logs for a roof, but what would we do for heat?

"We'll need a stove," Mother said in Russian.

Ivanov found that particularly funny. "You'd like a stove? What else? A hot bath? A glass of cognac? Shut up and get to work." He walked away.

Mother looked at Kretzsky.

He looked down and then walked off.

"See, he won't help," I said.

We worked for another week, building from scratch. It wasn't a house. It was a dung heap, a bunch of logs covered in mud, sand, and moss. It looked like something a child would make in the dirt. And we had to live in it.

The men finished building the barracks and a bakery for the NKVD. They were proper brick buildings with stoves or fireplaces in each room. The man who wound his watch said it was well outfitted. And we were expected to endure an arctic winter in a mud hut? No, they expected us not to endure at all.

THE DAY AFTER we finished our jurta, Janina came running to me. "Lina, there's a ship! There's a ship coming!"

Within seconds, the NKVD was upon us, pointing rifles in our faces. They ordered everyone into their jurtas. They ran, screaming, frantic.

"Jonas?" Mother yelled. "Lina, where is Jonas?"

"He was sent to fish," I said.

"Davai!" barked Ivanov, pushing me into the jurta.

"Jonas!" yelled Mother, stumbling to get away from Ivanov.

"He's coming, Elena," said Mr. Lukas, running toward us. "I saw him behind me."

Jonas arrived, out of breath from running. "Mother, there's a ship. It has an American flag."

"The Americans have arrived. They've arrived!" said the repeater.

"Will the Americans fight the NKVD?" asked Janina.

"Stupid girl. The Americans are helping the NKVD," said the bald man.

"They're hiding us," said Mother. "The guards don't want the Americans to see us, to know what they're doing to us."

"Won't the Americans wonder what these mud huts are?" I asked.

"They'll think they're some sort of military unit," said the man who wound his watch.

"Should we run out, so the Americans can see us?" I asked.

"They'll shoot you," said the bald man.

"Stay put, Lina!" said Mother. "Do you understand me?"

She was right. The NKVD was hiding us from the Americans. We stayed in our jurtas for more than five hours. That's how long it took for the American ship to be unloaded. As soon as the ship sailed, the NKVD came screaming for us to get to work. There were supplies to be moved to the bakery and NKVD barracks. I watched as the American ship drifted out of sight, pulling thoughts of rescue away with it. I wanted to run to the shore, waving my arms, screaming.

The supplies were stacked on large wooden pallets and stood as tall and wide as four homes in Kaunas. Food. It was so close. Jonas told me to keep an eye on the wood from the pallet, that we could use it to build a door for our jurta.

The man who wound his watch spoke English. He translated the markings on the containers. Canned peas, tomatoes, butter, condensed milk, powdered eggs, sugar, flour, vodka, whiskey. More than three hundred Lithuanians and Finns moved mountains of food and supplies they would never again touch. How much food was there in America that a ship could drop such an enormous supply for fewer than twenty guards? And now the Americans had sailed away. Did they know the Soviets' gruesome secret? Were they turning the other cheek?

After the food, we moved supplies—kerosene, fishing nets, fur-lined coats, hats, thick leather gloves. The NKVD would be cozy for the winter. The wind blew through my threadbare coat. I strained to lift crate after crate with Jonas.

"Please, stop," Mother told Mr. Lukas.

"I'm sorry," he said, winding his watch. "It calms me."

"That's not what I mean. Stop translating the words on the crates. I can't bear to know what we're carrying anymore," Mother said as she walked away.

"I want to know," objected the bald man. "I want to know what might be available if the opportunity presents itself for one of you."

"What does he mean?" asked Jonas.

"Probably that he wants us to steal things for him," I said.

"She's doing it again," said Jonas.

"What?" I asked.

Jonas motioned to Mother. She was talking to Kretzsky.

72

JONAS FOUND AN EMPTY barrel floating in the Laptev Sea. He was able to pull it ashore with a log. He rolled it up to our jurta. The men cheered.

"For a stove," Jonas said, smiling.

"Good work, darling!" said Mother.

The men set to work on the barrel, using empty tin cans from the NKVD's trash to create a stovepipe.

It was risky to carry or save your bread ration when Ivanov was around. He loved to take bread rations. Three hundred grams. That's all we got. Once, I saw him snatch a piece of bread from an old woman in line at the bakery. He popped it into his mouth and chewed it up. She watched, her empty mouth chewing along with his. He spit it on her feet. She scrambled to pick up every chewed piece and eat it. Mrs. Rimas said she heard Ivanov had been reassigned from a prison in Krasnoyarsk. The assignment in Trofimovsk had to be a demotion. Had Kretzsky also been demoted? I wondered if Ivanov had been at the same prison as Papa.

My stomach burned. I longed for the gray porridge they gave us on the train. I drew detailed pictures of food—steaming chicken with crispy, glazed skin, bowls of plums, apple cakes with crumbling crusts. I wrote down the details of the American ship and the food it carried.

The NKVD set us to rolling logs out of the Laptev Sea. We were to chop them up to dry for firewood. We weren't allowed any wood for ourselves. We sat in our jurta facing the empty stove. I saw plates with food being taken from our dinner table and the pieces scraped into the trash. I heard Jonas's voice saying, *But Mother, I'm not hungry* when told to finish his dinner. Not hungry. When were we ever not hungry?

"I'm cold," said Janina.

"Well, go find some wood for the stove then!" said the bald man.

"Where can I find it?" she asked.

"You can steal it. Near the NKVD building," he replied. "That's where the others are getting it."

"Don't send her to steal. I'll go find something," I said.

"I'll come with you," said Jonas.

"Mother?" I expected her to protest.

"Hmm?" she said.

"Jonas and I are going to look for wood."

"All right, dear," she said softly.

"Is Mother okay?" I asked Jonas as we walked out of our mud hut.

"She seems weaker and confused," said Jonas.

I stopped. "Jonas, have you seen Mother eat?"

"I think so," he said.

"Think about it. We've seen her nibble, but she's always giving us bread," I said. "Just yesterday she gave us bread. She said it was an additional ration she got for hauling logs."

"Do you think she's giving us her ration?"

"Yes, or at least part of it," I said. Mother was starving herself to feed us.

The wind howled as we walked toward the NKVD building. My throat burned with each breath. The sun did not appear. The polar night had begun. The desolate landscape was painted in blues and grays by the moon. The repeater kept saying we had to make it through the first winter. Mother agreed. If we could make it through the first winter, we'd survive. We had to endure the polar night and see the sun return.

"Are you cold?" asked Jonas.

"Freezing." The wind sliced through my clothing and stabbed at my skin.

"Do you want my coat?" he asked. "I think it will fit."

I looked at my brother. The coat Mother had traded was too big for him. He'd grow into it.

"No, then you'll be cold," I said. "But thanks."

"Vilkas!" Kretzsky. He wore a long wool coat and carried a canvas sack.

"What are you doing?" he demanded.

"Looking for driftwood to burn," said Jonas. "Have you seen any?"

Kretzsky hesitated. He reached into the bag and threw a

piece of wood at our shins, walking away before we could say anything.

That night, September 26, the first snowstorm arrived.

It lasted two days. The wind and snow bellowed and blew through the cracks in our jurta. The freezing temperatures crept into my knees and hips. They ached and throbbed, making it hard to move. We huddled together for warmth. The repeater pushed in close. His breath smelled rotten.

"Did you eat fish?" asked the bald man.

"Fish? Yes, a little fish," said the man.

"Why didn't you bring any for us?" demanded the bald man. Others also yelled at the repeater, calling him selfish.

"I stole it. There was just a little. Only a little."

"Liale doesn't like fish," whispered Janina. I looked at her. She clawed her scalp.

"Does it itch?" I asked.

She nodded. Lice. It was only a matter of time before our entire mud hut was crawling with them.

We took turns digging a path out the front door to make our way to the bakery for rations. I scooped up large amounts of snow to melt for drinking water. Jonas made sure Mother ate her entire ration and drank water. We had been relieving ourselves outside, but with the snowstorm in full rage, we had no choice but to sit on a bucket in the jurta. As a courtesy, the sitter did not face us, but some argued the rear view was worse.

73

WHEN THE STORM broke, the NKVD yelled at us to get back to work. We emerged from our mud hut. Even though it was dark, the white snow brightened the charcoal landscape. But that's all we could see—gray everywhere. The NKVD ordered us to roll and chop logs for firewood. Jonas and I passed a jurta completely covered in snow.

"No," cried a woman outside. The tips of her fingers were bloody, her fingernails shredded.

"Idiots. They built their door so it opened out. When it snowed, they trapped themselves inside. The weaklings couldn't pull or claw the door down!" Ivanov laughed, slapping his thigh. "Four of them are dead in there! Stupid pigs," he said to another guard.

Jonas's mouth hung open. "What are you looking at?" yelled Ivanov. "Get to work."

I pulled Jonas away from the crying woman and the snow-covered mound.

"He was laughing. Those people died and Ivanov was laughing," I said.

"Four people died in the very first snowstorm," said Jonas, looking at his feet. "Maybe more. We need more wood. We have to make it through the winter."

They split us into groups. I had to walk three kilometers to the tree line to find wood for the NKVD. The bald man was in my group. We trudged through the snow, a dry crunching underfoot.

"How am I expected to walk in this with my bad leg?" complained the bald man.

I tried to rush ahead. I didn't want to be stuck with him. He would slow me down.

"Don't you leave me!" he said. "Give me your mittens."

"What?"

"Give me your mittens. I don't have any."

"No. My hands will freeze," I said, the cold already scraping against my face.

"My hands are already freezing! Give me your mittens. It's only for a few minutes. You can put your hands in your pockets."

I thought about my brother offering me his coat, and wondered if I should share my mittens with the bald man.

"Give me your mittens and I'll tell you something," he said.

"What are you going to tell me?" I asked, suspicious.

"Something you want to know."

"What would I want to know from you?" I asked.

"Hurry, give me your mittens." His teeth chattered.

I walked on, silent.

"Just give me your damn mittens and I'll tell you why you were deported!"

I stopped and stared at him.

He snatched the mittens off my hands. "Well, don't just stand there. Keep walking or we'll freeze to death. Put your hands in your pockets."

We walked.

"So?"

"You know a Petras Vilkas?" he asked.

Petras Vilkas. My father's brother. Joana's father. "Yes," I said. "He's my uncle. Joana's my best friend."

"Who's Joana, his daughter?"

I nodded.

"Well, that's why you're deported," he said, rubbing the mittens together. "Your mother knows. She just hasn't told you. So there you have it."

"What do you mean, that's why we're deported? How do you know?" I asked.

"What does it matter how I know? Your uncle escaped from Lithuania before you were deported."

"You're lying."

"Am I? Your aunt's maiden name was German. So your uncle's family escaped, probably repatriated through Germany. Your father helped them. He was part of it. So your family was then put on the list. So your father's in prison, you'll die here in arctic hell, and your best friend is probably living it up in America by now."

What was he saying? Joana escaped and went to America? How could that be possible?

~

"Repatriate, if they can get away with it," said my father, stopping abruptly when he saw me in the doorway.

~

Dear Lina,

Now that the Christmas holiday is passed, life seems on a more serious course. Father has boxed up most of his books, saying they take up too much space.

~

I thought of my last birthday. Papa was late coming to the restaurant.

I told him I had received nothing from Joana. I noticed that he stiffened at the mention of my cousin. "She's probably just busy," he had said.

~

"Sweden is preferable," said Mother.

"It's not possible," said Papa. "Germany is their only choice."

"Who's going to Germany?" I yelled from the dining room.

Silence.

~

"I thought all of Auntie's family was in Germany," I said.

"Apparently she has a relative in America. She gets letters from him. He's in Pennsylvania."

~

It was possible.

Joana's freedom had cost me mine.

"I'd give anything for a cigarette," said the bald man.

"BUT WHY DIDN'T you tell me?"

"We were trying to protect your uncle. They were going to help us," said Mother.

"Help us what?" asked Jonas.

"Escape," whispered Mother.

There was no need to lower our voices. Everyone pretended to occupy themselves with their fingernails or clothing, but they could hear every word. Only Janina watched intently. She sat on her knees next to Jonas, swatting lice off her eyebrows.

"When they got to Germany, they were going to process papers for us to try to repatriate as well."

"What's *repatriate*?" asked Janina.

"To go back to where your family is originally from," I told her.

"Are you German?" she asked Mother.

"No, dear. But my sister-in-law's family was born in

Germany," said Mother. "We thought we could get papers through them."

"And Papa helped them? So he was an accessory?" I asked.

"Accessory? He committed no crime, Lina. He helped them. They're family," she said.

"So is Joana in Germany?" I asked.

"Most likely," said Mother. "It all went horribly wrong. After they left, your father received reports in April that the NKVD had entered and searched their house. Someone must have informed the Soviets."

"Who would do such a thing?" asked Jonas.

"Lithuanians who work with the Soviets. They give information about other people in order to protect themselves."

Someone hacked and coughed in the hut.

"I can't believe Joana didn't tell me," I said.

"Joana didn't know! Surely her parents didn't tell her. They feared she might tell someone. She thought they were going to visit a family friend," said Mother.

"Andrius said they thought his father had international contacts. Now the Soviets think Papa has communication with someone outside Lithuania," said Jonas quietly. "That means he's in danger."

Mother nodded. Janina got up and lay down next to her mother.

Thoughts swam through my brain. I couldn't process one before another stepped over it. We were being punished while Joana's family lived comfortably in Germany. We had given up our lives for theirs. Mother was angry that the bald man had told me. She had trusted him with the secret. He had given it up for five minutes of mittens. Hadn't Mother and Papa thought to trust *us*? Did they consider the consequences before they helped them escape? I scratched at the back of my head. Lice were biting a trail down the nape of my neck.

"How selfish! How could they do this to us?" I said.

"They had to give up things, too," said Jonas.

My mouth fell open. "What do you mean?" I asked. "They gave up nothing! We gave it all for them."

"They gave up their home, Uncle gave up his store, Joana gave up her studies."

Her studies. Joana wanted to be a doctor as much as I wanted to be an artist. Although I could still draw, she could not pursue medicine with a war raging in Germany. Where was she? Did she know what had happened to us? Had the Soviets managed to keep the deportations a secret from the world? If so, how long would that last? I thought of the American supply ship, sailing away. Would anyone think to look for us in the Siberian Arctic? If Stalin had his way, we'd be entombed in the ice and snow.

I got my paper. I sat near the firelight of the stove. Anger sizzled within me. It was so unfair. But I couldn't hate Joana. It wasn't her fault. Whose fault was it? I drew two hands clutching on to each other, yet pulling apart. I drew a swastika on her palm and the hammer and sickle on top of my hand, the Lithuanian flag shredded and falling in between.

I heard a scraping sound. The man who wound his watch carved a small piece of wood with his knife. The logs popped, spitting ashes out of the barrel.

~

"It looks scratched," said Jonas. He sat cross-legged on my bed, looking at one of the Munch prints I had received from Oslo.

"It is. He used his palette knife to scrape texture into the canvas," I said.

"It makes her look . . . confused," said Jonas. "If it weren't scratched, she would look sad. But the scratches make confusion."

"Exactly," I said, using long strokes to comb through my warm, clean hair. "But to Munch, that made the painting feel alive. He was a confused man. He didn't care about proportion, he wanted it to feel real."

Jonas flipped to the next print. "Does this feel real to you?" he said, his eyes wide.

"Definitely," I told him. "That's called Ashes.*"*

"I don't know about real. Maybe real scary," said Jonas as he got up to leave. "You know, Lina, I like your paintings better than these. These are too weird. Good night."

"Good night," I said. I took the papers and flopped down on my bed, sinking into my puffy goose-down duvet. A comment in the margin from an art critic read, "Munch is primarily a lyric poet in color. He feels colors, but does not see them. Instead, he sees sorrow, crying, and withering."

Sorrow, crying, and withering. I saw that in Ashes, *too. I thought it was brilliant.*

~

Ashes. I had an idea. I grabbed a stick from next to the stove. I peeled back the outer skin to reveal the pulp. I separated the fibers, forming bristles. I grabbed a handful of snow from outside the door and carefully mixed in ashes from the barrel. The color was uneven, but made a nice gray watercolor.

NOVEMBER CAME. Mother's eyes lacked their wink and sparkle. We had to work harder for her smile. It came only when her chin rested on the heel of her hand or when Jonas mentioned Papa in our evening prayers. Then she would lift her face, the corners of her mouth turned up with hope. I worried for her.

At night, I closed my eyes and thought of Andrius. I saw his fingers raking through his disheveled brown hair, his nose tracing a line down my cheek the night before we left. I remembered his wide smile when he teased me in the ration line. I saw his tentative eyes, handing me *Dombey and Son*, and his reassurance as the truck pulled away. He said he'd find me. Did he know where they had taken us? That they laughed and wagered upon our deaths? *Find me*, I whispered.

The man who wound his watch looked at the sky. He

said a storm was coming. I believed him, not because of the pale gray of the sky, but because of the bustle of the NKVD. They shouted at us. Their "davais" pushed with an urgency. Even Ivanov was upon us. Normally, he shouted orders from afar. Today, he hastened to and from the barrack, coordinating every effort.

Mrs. Rimas tried to negotiate advance rations for the impending storm.

Ivanov laughed. "If there's a storm, you won't work. Why should you get a ration?"

"But how will we survive without bread?" asked Mrs. Rimas.

"I don't know. How will you?" said Ivanov.

I pilfered wood from the NKVD barracks. There was no other way. We would need a lot for the storm. I went back for more. Snow began to fall.

That's when I saw it.

Mother stood, talking to Ivanov and Kretzsky behind the NKVD barracks. What was she doing? I stepped out of sight and squinted to see. Ivanov spit on the ground. He then leaned close in to Mother's face. My heart began to pound. Suddenly, he lifted his gloved hand to his temple, mocking a gun firing. Mother flinched. Ivanov threw his head back and laughed. He walked into the NKVD barracks.

Mother and Kretzsky stood motionless, snow falling all around them. Kretzsky reached out and put a hand on her shoulder. I saw his lips moving. Mother's knees buckled. He caught her by the waist. Her face contorted and fell against his chest. She pounded his shoulder with her fist.

"MOTHER!" I screamed, running toward her. I tripped over the firewood tumbling from under my coat.

I grabbed her from Kretzsky, pulling her to me. "Mother." We fell to our knees.

"Kostas," she sobbed.

I stroked her hair, hugging her to me. Kretzsky's boots shifted. I looked up at him.

"Shot. In Krasnoyarsk prison," he said.

The air crushed in around me, pushing my body deep into the snow. "No, you're wrong," I said, my eyes searching Kretzsky's. "He's coming to get us. He's on his way. He's wrong, Mother! They think he's dead because he has left. He got my drawings. He's coming for us!"

"No." Kretzsky shook his head.

I stared at him. *No?*

Mother wept, her body chugging into mine.

"Papa?" The word barely escaped my lips.

Kretzky took a step closer, reaching to help Mother. Loathing purged from my mouth. "Get away from her! Stay away. I hate you. Do you hear me? I HATE YOU!"

Kretzsky stared at Mother. "Me, too," he said. He walked away, leaving me on the ground with Mother.

We sank deeper, snow blanketing us, the wind sharp against our faces like needles. "Come, Mother. A storm is coming." Her legs couldn't carry her. Her chest heaved with every step, throwing us off balance. Snow whirled around us, limiting my sight.

"HELP ME!" I screamed. "Somebody, PLEASE!" I heard

nothing but the wail of the winds. "Mother, match my steps. Walk with me. We must get back. There's a storm."

Mother didn't walk. She just repeated my father's name into the falling snow.

"HELP!"

"Elena?"

It was Mrs. Rimas.

"Yes! We're here. Help us!" I cried.

Two figures emerged through the wall of wind and snow.

"Lina?"

"Jonas! Please!"

My brother and Mrs. Rimas came through the snow, their arms extended.

"Oh dear God, Elena!" said Mrs. Rimas.

We dragged Mother into our jurta. She lay facedown on a wood plank, Mrs. Rimas at her side, Janina peering over her.

"Lina, what is it?" said Jonas, terrified.

I stared blankly.

"Lina?"

I turned to my brother. "Papa."

"Papa?" His face fell.

I nodded slowly. I couldn't speak. A sound came out of my mouth, a twisted, pitiful moan. This wasn't happening. This couldn't be happening. Not Papa. I had sent the drawings.

I saw Jonas's face rewind before me. He suddenly looked his age, vulnerable. Not like a young man fighting for his family, smoking books, but like the little schoolboy who ran into my bedroom the night we were taken. He looked at me, then at Mother. He walked over to her, lay down, and carefully put his arms around her. Snow blew through a crack in the mud, falling on their hair.

Janina wrapped her arms around my legs. She hummed softly.

"I'm sorry. So sorry," said the repeater.

76

I COULDN'T SLEEP. I couldn't speak. Every time I closed my eyes, I saw Papa's face, battered, peering down from the bathroom hole on the train. *Courage, Lina,* he said to me. Exhaustion and grief inched heavily into every fiber of my body, yet I was wide awake. My mind flickered as if on short circuit, spitting never-ending images of anguish, anxiety, and sorrow at me.

How did Kretzsky know? There was a mistake. It was another man, not Papa. It was possible, right? I thought of Andrius, searching the train cars for his father. He thought it was possible, too. I wanted to tell Andrius what had happened. I put my hand in my pocket and clutched the stone.

My drawings had failed. I had failed.

I tried to sketch but couldn't. When I started to draw, the pencil moved by itself, propelled by something hideous that lived inside of me. Papa's face contorted. His mouth pulled in agony. His eyes radiated fear. I drew myself, screaming at Kretzsky. My lips twisted. Three black snakes with fangs spurted out of my open mouth. I hid the drawings in *Dombey and Son.*

Papa was strong. He was a patriot. Did he fight? Or was he unaware? Did they leave him in the dirt like Ona? I wondered if Jonas had the same questions. We didn't discuss it. I wrote a letter to Andrius, but it became smudged with tears.

The storm raged. The wind and icy snow created a deafening roar of white noise. We dug a path out the door to collect our rations. Two Finns, lost in the blizzard, couldn't find their jurta. They squeezed into ours. One had dysentery. The stench made me gag. My scalp was crawling with lice.

On the second day, Mother got up and insisted on shoveling the door. She looked drawn, like a part of her soul had escaped.

"Mother, you should rest," said Jonas. "I can dig through the snow."

"It does no good to lie here," said Mother. "There is work to be done. I must do my part."

On the third day of the storm the man who wound his watch directed the two Finns back to their jurta.

"Take that bucket outside. Wash it out in the snow," the bald man told me.

"Why me?" I asked.

"We'll take turns," said Mother. "We'll all have to do it."

I took the bucket out into the darkness. The winds had retreated. Suddenly, I couldn't breathe. The moisture in my nostrils had frozen. This was only November. The polar night would last until the beginning of March. The weather would get worse. How could we withstand it? We had to make it through the first winter. I hurried with my bucket duty and returned to the jurta. I felt like Janina, whispering to Papa at night like she whispered to her dead doll.

November 20. Andrius's birthday. I had counted the days carefully. I wished him a happy birthday when I woke and thought about him while hauling logs during the day. At night, I sat by the light of the stove, reading *Dombey and Son.* Krasivaya. I still hadn't found the word. Maybe I'd find it if I jumped ahead. I flipped through some of the pages. A marking caught my eye. I leafed backward. Something was written in pencil in the margin on page 278.

Hello, Lina. You've gotten to page 278. That's pretty good!

I gasped, then pretended I was engrossed in the book. I looked at Andrius's handwriting. I ran my finger over his elongated letters in my name. Were there more? I knew I should read onward. I couldn't wait. I turned through the pages carefully, scanning the margins.

Page 300:

Are you really on page 300 or are you skipping ahead now?

I had to stifle my laughter.

Page 322:

Dombey and Son *is boring. Admit it.*

Page 364:

I'm thinking of you.

Page 412:

Are you maybe thinking of me?

I closed my eyes.

Yes, I'm thinking of you. Happy birthday, Andrius.

IT WAS MID-DECEMBER. Winter had us in its jaws. The repeater had frostbite. The tips of his fingers were puckered, jet black. Gray, bulbous lumps appeared on the end of his nose. We wrapped ourselves in every piece of clothing and rags we could find. We tied our feet in old fishing nets that had washed ashore. Everyone bickered in the jurta, getting on each other's nerves.

Small children began dying. Mother took her ration to a starving boy. He was already dead, his tiny hand outstretched, waiting for a piece of bread. We had no doctor or nurse in camp, only a veterinarian from Estonia. We relied on him. He did his best, but the conditions were unsanitary. He had no medicine.

Ivanov and the NKVD wouldn't step inside our jurtas. They yelled at us to leave the dead outside the door. "You're all filthy pigs. You live in filth. It's no wonder you're dying."

Dysentery, typhus, and scurvy crawled into camp. Lice feasted on our open sores. One afternoon, one of the Finns left his wood chopping to urinate. Janina found him swinging from a pole. He had hanged himself with a fishing net.

We had to trek farther and farther to find wood. We were nearly five kilometers from camp. At the end of the day Janina clung by my side.

"Liale showed me something," she said.

"What's that?" I said, stuffing twigs into my pockets for our stove and my paintbrushes.

Janina looked around. "Come here. I'll show you."

She took my hand and walked me into the snow. She reached out her mitten, pointing.

"What is it?" I asked. My eyes scanned the snow.

"Shh . . ." She pulled me closer and pointed.

I saw it. A huge owl lay in the snow at the edge of the trees. Its white feathers blended so well that at first I didn't see it. Its body looked to be nearly two feet long. The large raptor had tiny brown speckles on its head and trunk.

"Is he sleeping?" asked Janina.

"I think it's dead," I replied. I took a stick from my pocket and poked at the wing. The owl didn't move. "Yes, it's dead."

"Do you think we should eat him?" asked Janina.

At first I was shocked. Then I imagined the plump body, roasting in our barrel, like a chicken. I poked at it again. I grabbed its wing and pulled. It was heavy, but slid across the snow.

"No! You can't drag him. The NKVD will see. They'll take him away from us," said Janina. "Hide him in your coat."

"Janina, this owl is enormous. I can't hide him in my coat." The thought of a dead owl in my coat made me shiver.

"But I'm so hungry," cried Janina. "Please? I'll walk in front of you. No one will see."

I was hungry, too. So was Mother. So was Jonas. I leaned over the owl and pushed its wings against its belly. It was stiff. Its face looked sharp, menacing. I didn't know if I could put it against my body. I looked at Janina. She nodded, her eyes wide.

I glanced around. "Unbutton my coat." Her little hands set to work.

I lifted the dead raptor and held it against my chest. Shivers of revulsion rolled through my body. "Hurry, button me up."

She couldn't button the coat. The owl was too large. I could barely get my coat around its body.

"Turn him around, so his face doesn't stick out," said Janina. "He'll blend in with the snow. Let's hurry."

Hurry? How was I supposed to walk five kilometers, pregnant with a dead owl, without the NKVD noticing? "Janina, slow down. I can't walk fast. It's too big." The horned beak poked at my chest. Its dead body was creepy. But I was so hungry.

Other deportees looked at me.

"Our mamas are sick. They need food. Will you help us?" explained Janina.

People I didn't know formed a circle around me, sheltering me from view. They escorted me safely back to our jurta, undetected. They didn't ask for anything. They were happy to help someone, to succeed at something, even if they weren't to benefit. We'd been trying to touch the sky from the bottom of the ocean. I realized that if we boosted one another, maybe we'd get a little closer.

Janina's mother plucked the owl. We all crowded around the makeshift stove to smell it cook.

"It smells like a duck, don't you think?" said Jonas. "Let's pretend it's duck."

The taste of warm meat was heavenly. It didn't matter that it was a bit tough; the experience lasted longer because we had to chew. We imagined we were at a royal banquet.

"Can't you just taste the gooseberry marinade?" sighed Mrs. Rimas.

"This is wonderful. Thank you, Lina," said Mother.

"Thank Janina. She found the owl," I said.

"Liale found him," corrected Janina.

"Thanks, Janina!" said Jonas.

Janina beamed, holding a fistful of feathers.

78

CHRISTMAS CAME. We had made it halfway through winter. That was something to be grateful for.

The weather continued, relentless. Just as one storm passed, another queued at its heels. We lived the life of penguins, freezing under layers of ice and snow. Mrs. Rimas stood outside the bakery. The smell of butter and cocoa made her cry. The NKVD made cakes and pastries in their bakery. They ate fish, drank hot coffee, and enjoyed canned meats and vegetables from America. After a meal, they'd play cards, smoke cigarettes, maybe a cigar, and drink a snifter of brandy. Then they'd light the fire in their brick barracks and cover themselves with their fur blankets.

My drawings became smaller. I didn't have much paper. Mother didn't have much energy. She couldn't even sit up for the Kucios Christmas celebration. She had lain too long. Her hair was frozen to a board. She drifted in and out of sleep, waking only to blow a kiss when she felt us near.

The lice brought typhus. The repeater fell ill. He insisted on leaving our jurta.

"You're such nice people. It's too dangerous for you all. Dangerous," he said.

"Yes, get out of here," said the bald man.

He moved to a jurta where people had similar symptoms—fever, rash, some delirium. Mrs. Rimas and I helped him walk.

Four days later, I saw his naked body, eyes wide open, stacked in a heap of corpses. His frostbitten hand was missing. White foxes had eaten into his stomach, exposing his innards and staining the snow with blood.

I turned and covered my eyes.

~

"Lina, please take those books off the table," said Mother. "I can't stand to see such ghastly images, not at breakfast."

"But that's what inspired Edvard Munch's art. He saw these images not as death, but as birth," I said.

"Off the table," said Mother.

Papa chuckled behind his newspaper.

"But Papa, listen to what Munch said."

Papa lowered the newspaper.

I turned to the page. "He said, 'From my rotting body flowers shall grow, and I am in them and that is eternity.' Isn't that beautiful?"

Papa smiled at me. "You're beautiful because you see it that way."

"Lina, take the books off the table, please," said Mother.

Papa winked at me.

~

"We must do something!" I cried to Jonas and Mrs. Rimas. "We can't let people die like this."

"We'll do our best. That's all we have," said Mrs. Rimas. "And we'll pray for a miracle."

"No! Don't talk like that. We will survive," I said. "Right, Jonas?"

Jonas nodded.

"Are you feeling unwell?" I asked him.

"I'm fine," he replied.

That night, I sat with Mother's head in my lap. Lice marched triumphantly across her forehead. I flicked them off.

"Did you apologize?" asked Mother, gazing at me through heavy eyelids.

"To whom?"

"To Nikolai. You told him you hated him."

"I do hate him," I said. "He could help us. He chooses not to."

"He helped me," said Mother softly.

I looked down at her.

"That day when I went to meet the grouchy woman coming back from the village, it was dark. Some NKVD drove by. They began to taunt me. They lifted my dress. Nikolai came. He shooed the others off. He drove me the rest of the way. I begged him to find news of your father. We met the grouchy woman on the road in the dark. Nikolai dropped us three kilometers from camp. We walked the rest of the way. See," she said, lifting her face to mine, "that helped me. And I think the commander found out about it. Nikolai was punished for it. I think that's why he's here."

"He deserves to be here. Maybe he'll get sick and everyone will ignore him. Then he'll see how it feels. He could get a doctor for us!"

"Lina, think of what your father would say. A wrongdoing doesn't give us the right to do wrong. You know that."

I thought about Papa. She was right. He would say something like that.

Jonas walked into the jurta. "How is she?" he asked.

I put my hand on Mother's forehead. "She still has a high fever."

"Darling," said Mother to Jonas. "I'm so very cold. Are you cold?"

Jonas took off his coat and handed it to me. He lay down beside Mother, wrapping himself around her. "Okay, put the coat on top of us. Get the small hide from Ulyushka," said Jonas.

"Ulyushka," said Mother fondly.

"I'll warm you, Mother," said Jonas, kissing her cheek.

"I feel better already," she said.

I PRACTICED THE Russian words. *Doctor. Medicine. Mother. Please.* My stomach jumped. I clutched the stone. I heard Andrius's voice. *Don't give them anything, Lina. Not even your fear.*

It wasn't just Mother. The man who wound his watch was sick. Janina's mother was sick. If I could just get some medicine. I hated the thought of asking them for anything. The NKVD had killed Papa. I hated them for it. I couldn't let them do the same to Mother.

I saw Kretzsky near the NKVD barracks. He stood with Ivanov. I waited. I wanted to speak to Kretzsky alone. Time passed. I had to go to work in order to get my ration. I trudged through the snow toward them.

"Look, it's a little pig," said Ivanov.

"My mother is sick," I said.

"Really?" he said, feigning concern. "I think I know something that might help."

I looked at him.

"Give her plenty of sunshine, fresh fruits, and lots of vegetables." He laughed at his own sick joke.

"We need a doctor. We need medicine," I said, shivering.

"What else do you need? A bathhouse? A school? Well, you better get building. Davai!"

I looked at Kretzsky.

"Please, help me. We need a doctor. We need medicine. My mother is sick."

"There is no doctor," said Kretzsky.

"Medicine," I said. "We need medicine."

"Do you want another twenty years?" yelled Ivanov. "I can give you that. No bread today, you ingrate. Get to work! Davai!"

I didn't get a doctor. I didn't get medicine. I lost my ration and humiliated myself in the process. I began walking away from the barracks. I had forgotten what the sun felt like on my face. When I closed my eyes, I could see sunlight in Lithuania, and on Andrius's hair. But I couldn't imagine the sun on the Laptev Sea. Even if we did make it through the winter, would we have the strength to build things? Could we really build a bath-house and a school? Who would be left to teach?

I couldn't lose Mother. I would fight. I would do whatever it took. She trembled, slipping in and out of sleep. Jonas and I sandwiched her between us, trying to warm and comfort her. Mrs. Rimas heated bricks to warm her feet. Janina picked the lice off her eyelashes.

The bald man leaned over and tucked his ration under Mother's hand. "Come on, woman. You're better than this. You've got children to take care of, for God's sake," he said.

Hours passed. Mother's teeth chattered. Her lips turned blue.

"J-Jonas, keep this." She handed him Papa's wedding band. "It's full of love. Nothing is more important."

Mother's trembling increased. She whimpered between breaths. "Please," she pleaded, staring at us with urgent eyes. "Kostas."

We held her between us, our arms curled around her withered body.

Jonas breathed quickly. His frightened eyes searched mine. "No," he whispered. "Please."

80

JANUARY 5. Jonas held Mother through the lonely morning hours, rocking her gently, as she used to do with us. Mrs. Rimas tried to feed her and massage circulation into her limbs. She couldn't eat or speak. I warmed bricks and shuttled them back and forth from the stove. I sat next to her, rubbing her hands and telling stories from home. I described every room in our house in detail, even the pattern on the spoons in the kitchen drawer. "The cake is in the oven baking and it's hot in the kitchen, so you've decided to open the window over the sink and let the warm breeze in. You can hear children playing outside," I told her.

Later that morning Mother's breathing became increasingly labored.

"Warm more bricks, Lina," my brother told me. "She's too cold."

Suddenly, Mother looked up at Jonas. She opened her mouth. Not a sound came out. The trembling stopped. Her shoulders relaxed and her head fell against him. Her eyes faded to a hollow stare.

"Mother?" I said, moving closer.

Mrs. Rimas touched her hand to Mother's neck.

Jonas began to cry, cradling her in his eleven-year-old arms. Small whimpers became deep, racking sobs, shaking his entire body.

I lay down behind him, hugging him.

Mrs. Rimas knelt beside us. "The Lord is my shepherd; I shall not want," she began.

"Mother," cried Jonas.

Tears spilled down my cheeks.

"She had a beautiful spirit," said the man who wound his watch.

Janina stroked my hair.

"I love you, Mother," I whispered. "I love you, Papa."

Mrs. Rimas continued.

"Yea, though I walk through the valley of the shadow of death, I will fear no evil: For thou art with me; thy rod and thy staff, they comfort me. Thou preparest a table before me in the presence of mine enemies; thou anointest my head with oil; my cup runneth over. Surely goodness and mercy shall follow me all the days of my life: and I will dwell in the house of the Lord forever.

"Amen."

It described Mother perfectly. Her cup overflowed with love for everyone and everything around her, even the enemy.

Mrs. Rimas began to cry. "Sweet Elena. She was so dear, so good to everyone."

"Please, don't let them take her body," said Jonas to Mrs. Rimas. "I want to bury her. We can't let her be eaten by foxes."

"We'll bury her," I assured Jonas through my tears. "We'll make a coffin. We'll use the boards we sleep on."

Jonas nodded.

The bald man stared blankly, and for once, said nothing.

~

"She looks pretty," said Jonas, standing at the side of Grandma's coffin. "Papa, does she know I'm here?"

"She does," said Papa, putting his arms around us. "She's watching from above."

Jonas looked up toward the ceiling and then to Papa.

"Remember last summer, when we flew the kite?" said Papa.

Jonas nodded.

"The wind came and I yelled to you that it was time. I told you to loosen your grip. The string started unwinding, and the wooden spool spun through your hands, remember? The kite went higher and higher. I had forgotten to tie the string to the spool. Do you remember what happened?"

"The kite disappeared up into the sky," said Jonas.

"Exactly. That's what happens when people die. Their spirit flies up into the blue sky," said Papa.

"Maybe Grandma found the kite," said Jonas.

"Maybe," said Papa.

~

The bald man sat, his elbows on his knees, talking to himself. "Why is it so hard to die?" he asked. "I helped turn you in. I said 'No' too late. I saw the lists."

Mrs. Rimas spun around. "What?"

He nodded. "They asked me to confirm people's professions. They asked me to list the teachers, lawyers, and military who lived nearby."

"And you did it?" I said.

Jonas held Mother, still crying.

"I told them I would," said the bald man. "And then I changed my mind."

"You traitor! You pathetic old man!" I said.

"Pathetic, and yet I survive. Surely, my survival is my punishment. That has to be it. This woman closes her eyes and she is gone. I've wished for death since the first day, and yet I survive. Can it really be so hard to die?"

81

I WOKE, UNEASY. The night had been unkind. I slept next to Mother's body, muffling my sobs so as not to scare Jonas. My beautiful mother—I would never see her smile again, feel her arms around me. I already missed her voice. My body felt hollow, like my sluggish heartbeat was bouncing and echoing through my vacant, aching limbs.

The bald man's questions kept me awake in thought. Was it harder to die, or harder to be the one who survived? I was sixteen, an orphan in Siberia, but I knew. It was the one thing I never questioned. I wanted to live. I wanted to see my brother grow up. I wanted to see Lithuania again. I wanted to see Joana. I wanted to smell the lily of the valley on the breeze beneath my window. I wanted to paint in the fields. I wanted to see Andrius with my drawings. There were only two possible outcomes in Siberia. Success meant survival. Failure meant death. I wanted life. I wanted to survive.

Part of me felt guilty. Was it selfish that I wanted to live, even though my parents were gone? Was it selfish to have wants beyond my family being together? I was now the guardian of my eleven-year-old brother. What would he do if I perished?

After work, Jonas helped the man who wound his watch make a coffin. Mrs. Rimas and I prepared Mother.

"Is there anything left in her suitcase?" asked Mrs. Rimas.

"I don't think so." I pulled Mother's suitcase from under the board she lay on. I was wrong. Inside were fresh, clean clothes. A light dress, silk stockings, shoes without scuffs, her tube of lipstick. There was also a man's shirt and tie. Papa's clothes. I began to cry.

Mrs. Rimas brought her hand to her mouth. "She really intended to return home."

I looked at Papa's shirt. I lifted it to my face. My mother was freezing. She could have worn these clothes. She kept them, to return to Lithuania in a clean set of clothes.

Mrs. Rimas pulled out the silk dress. "This is lovely. We'll put this on her."

I took Mother's coat off of her. She had worn the coat since the night we were deported. Stitch marks and stray threads pocked the inside where she had sewn in our valuables. I lifted the fabric of the lining. A few papers remained.

"Those are deeds to your home and property in Kaunas," said Mrs. Rimas, looking at the paperwork. "Keep them safe. You'll need them when you go home."

There was another small piece of paper. I unfolded it.

It was an address in Biberach, Germany.

"Germany. That has to be where my cousin is."

"Probably, but you mustn't write to that address," said Mrs. Rimas. "It could get them in trouble."

That night, Jonas and I stole shovels and ice picks from outside the NKVD barracks. "It has to be someplace we'll remember," I told him. "Because we're taking her body back to Lithuania with us." We walked to a little hill near the Laptev Sea.

"This has a nice view," said Jonas. "We'll remember this."

We dug all night, chipping away at the ice, digging as deep as we could. As morning approached, Mrs. Rimas and the man who wound his watch arrived to help. Even Janina and the bald man came to dig. The ice was so hard, the grave was fairly shallow.

The next morning Mrs. Rimas slipped Mother's wedding band off her finger. "Keep this. Bury it with her when you take her back home."

We carried the coffin out of the jurta and walked slowly through the snow toward the hill. Jonas and I held the front, Mrs. Rimas and the man who wound his watch held the center, and the bald man carried the back. Janina trailed beside me. People joined us. I didn't know them. They prayed for Mother. Soon, a large procession walked behind us. We passed the NKVD barracks. Kretzsky talked with guards on the porch. He saw us and stopped talking. I looked ahead and walked toward the cold hole in the ground.

82

I PAINTED A MAP to the gravesite using the ash mixture and a feather from the owl. Mother's absence left a gaping hole, a mouth missing its front tooth. The eternal grayness in camp became a shade darker. Amidst the polar night, our only sun had slipped under a cloud.

"We could drown ourselves," said the bald man. "That would be easy, right?"

No one responded.

"Don't ignore me, girl!"

"I'm not ignoring you. Don't you understand? We're all tired of you!" I said.

I was so very tired. Mentally, physically, emotionally, I was tired. "You always talk of death and of us killing ourselves. Haven't you figured it out? We're not interested in dying," I said.

"But I'm interested!" he insisted.

"Maybe you don't really want to die," said Jonas. "Maybe you just think you deserve to."

The bald man looked up at Jonas and then at me.

"You think of nothing but yourself. If you want to kill yourself, what's keeping you?" I said. Silence sat between our stares.

"Fear," he said.

Two nights after we buried Mother, there was a whistle on the air. A storm would arrive the next day. I bundled in all that I could find and set out into the blackness to steal wood from the NKVD building. Each day, when chopping and delivering wood, we dumped extra behind the pile. It was understood that if someone was brave enough to steal it, it was there. A man in group twenty-six got caught stealing wood. They sentenced him to an additional five years. Five years for one log. It could have been fifty. Our sentences were dictated by our survival.

I walked toward the NKVD barrack, making a wide circle to arrive at the back, close to the woodpile. My face and ears were wrapped in a cloth, with only my eyes exposed. I wore Mother's hat. A figure scurried past me, carrying a large plank of wood. Brave. The planks were leaned up against the barracks. I turned near the back of the woodpile. I stopped. A figure in a long coat stood behind the giant stacks of wood. It was impossible to see in the darkness. I turned slowly to leave, trying not to make a sound.

"Who's there? Show yourself!"

I turned around.

"Group number?" he demanded.

"Eleven," I said, backing away.

The figure moved closer. "Vilkas?"

I didn't respond. He stepped toward me. I saw his eyes under the large fur hat. Kretzsky.

He stumbled and I heard swishing. He carried a bottle.

"Stealing?" he asked, taking a swig.

I said nothing.

"I can't arrange for you to draw a portrait here. No one wants one," said Kretzsky.

"You think I want to draw for you?"

"Why not?" he said. "It kept you warm. You got food. And you drew a nice, realistic portrait." He laughed.

"Realistic? I don't want to be forced to draw that way." Why was I even talking to him? I turned to leave.

"Your mother," he said.

I stopped.

"She was a good woman. I could see she used to be very pretty."

I spun around. "What do you mean? She was always pretty! It's you that's ugly. You couldn't see her beauty, or anyone else's for that matter!"

"No, I saw it. She was pretty. Krasivaya."

No. Not that word. I was supposed to learn it on my own. Not from Kretzsky.

"It means beautiful, but with strength," he slurred. "Unique."

I couldn't look at him. I looked at the logs. I wanted to grab one. I wanted to smash him across the face, like the can of sardines.

"So, you hate me?" He laughed.

How could Mother have tolerated Kretzsky? She claimed he had helped her.

"I hate me, too," he said.

I looked up.

"You want to draw me like this? Like your beloved Munch?" he asked. His face looked puffy. I could barely understand his slurred Russian. "I know about your drawings." He pointed a shaky finger at me. "I've seen them all."

He knew about my drawings. "How did you know about my father?" I asked.

He ignored my question.

"My mother, she was an artist, too," he said, gesturing with the bottle. "But she is with yours—dead."

"I'm sorry," I said instinctively. Why did I say that? I didn't care.

"You're sorry?" He snorted in disbelief, tucking the bottle under his arm and rubbing his gloves together. "My mother, she was Polish. She died when I was five. My father is Russian. He remarried a Russian when I was six. My mother wasn't even cold a year. Some of my mother's relatives are in Kolyma. I was supposed to go there, to help them. That's why I wanted to leave the barge in Jakutsk. But now I'm here. So, you're not the only one who is in prison."

He took another long swig of the bottle. "You want to steal

wood, Vilkas?" He opened his arms. "Steal wood." He waved his hand toward the pile. "Davai."

My ears burned. My eyelids stung from the cold. I walked to the woodpile.

"The woman my father married, she hates me, too. She hates Poles."

I took a log. He didn't stop me. I began to pile wood. I heard a sound. Kretzsky's back was turned, the bottle hanging from his hand. Was he sick? I took a step away with the logs. I heard it again. Kretzsky wasn't sick. He was crying.

Leave, Lina. Hurry! Take the wood. Just go. I took a step, to leave him. Instead, my legs walked toward him, still holding the wood. What was I doing? The sound coming from Kretzsky was uncomfortable, stifled.

"Nikolai."

He didn't look at me.

I stood there, silent. "Nikolai." I reached out from under the wood. I put a hand on his shoulder. "I'm sorry," I finally said.

We stood in the darkness, saying nothing.

I turned to leave him.

"Vilkas."

I turned.

"I'm sorry for your mother," he said.

I nodded. "Me, too."

83

I HAD PLAYED through scenarios of how I would get back at the NKVD, how I would stomp on the Soviets if I ever had a chance. I had a chance. I could have laughed at him, thrown wood at him, spit in his face. The man threw things at me, humiliated me. I hated him, right? I should have turned and walked away. I should have felt good inside. I didn't. The sound of his crying physically pained me. What was wrong with me?

I told no one of the incident. The next day, Kretzsky was gone.

February arrived. Janina was fighting scurvy. The man who wound his watch had dysentery. Mrs. Rimas and I tended to them as best we could. Janina spoke to her dead dolly for hours, sometimes yelling or laughing. After a few days she stopped speaking.

"What are we to do?" I said to Jonas. "Janina's getting sicker by the minute."

He looked at me.

"What is it?" I said.

"I have the spots again," he said.

"Where? Let me see."

The scurvy spots had reappeared on Jonas's stomach. Clumps of his hair had fallen out.

"There are no tomatoes this time," said Jonas. "Andrius isn't here." He started shaking his head.

I grabbed my brother by the shoulders. "Jonas, listen to me. We are going to live. Do you hear me? We're going home. We're not going to die. We're going home to our house, and we're going to sleep in our beds with the goose-down comforters. We will. All right?"

"How will we live alone, without Mother and Papa?" he asked.

"Auntie and Uncle. And Joana. They'll help. We'll have Auntie's apple cakes and doughnuts with jam inside. The ones you like, okay? And Andrius will help us."

Jonas nodded.

"Say it. Say, 'We're going home.'"

"We're going home," repeated Jonas.

I hugged him, kissing the scabbed bald spot on his head. "Here." I took the stone from Andrius out of my pocket and held it up to Jonas. He seemed dazed and didn't take the stone.

My stomach sank. What would I do? I had no medicine.

Everyone was ill. Would I be the only one left, alone with the bald man?

We took turns going for rations. I begged at other jurtas as Mother had done on the beet farm. I walked into a jurta. Two women sat amongst four people who were covered as if sleeping. They were all dead.

"Please, don't tell," they pleaded. "We want to bury them once the storm ends. If the NKVD discover they're dead, they'll throw them out into the snow."

"I won't tell," I assured them.

The storm raged. The sound of the wind echoed between my stinging ears. The wind blew so cold, like white fire. I fought my way back to our jurta. Bodies, stacked like firewood, were covered in snow outside the huts. The man who wound his watch hadn't returned.

"I'll go look for him," I said to Mrs. Rimas.

"He could barely walk," said the bald man. "He probably went to the closest jurta when the winds came. Don't risk it."

"We have to help one another!" I told him. But how could I expect him, of all people, to understand?

"You need to stay here. Jonas is not well." Mrs. Rimas looked over to Janina.

"Her mother?" I asked.

"I took her to the typhus hut," whispered Mrs. Rimas.

I sat next to my brother. I rearranged the rags and fishing nets he was covered with.

"I'm so tired, Lina," he said. "My gums hurt and my teeth ache."

"I know. As soon as the storm ends, I'll search for some food. You need fish. There's plenty of it, barrels. I just need to steal some."

"I'm s-so cold," said Jonas, shivering. "And I can't straighten my legs."

I heated chunks of brick and put them under his feet. I took a brick to Janina. Scurvy bruisings spotted her face and neck. The tip of her tiny nose was black with frostbite.

I kept the fire going. It did little to help. I could use only a small amount of wood, to save what we had. I didn't know how long this storm would last. I looked at the empty spot where my mother had lain, Janina's mother, the man who wound his watch, the repeater. Large gaps had appeared on the floor of the jurta.

I lay next to Jonas, covering him with my body as we had done for Mother. I wrapped my arms around him, holding his hands in mine. The wind slapped against our disintegrating jurta. Snow blew in around us.

It couldn't end like this. It couldn't. What was life asking of me? How could I respond when I didn't know the question?

"I love you," I whispered to Jonas.

THE STORM DREW back a day later. Jonas could barely speak. My joints were locked, as if frozen.

"We have to work today," said Mrs. Rimas. "We need rations, wood."

"Yes," agreed the bald man.

I knew they were right. But I wasn't sure I had the strength. I looked over at Jonas. He lay completely still on a plank, his cheeks hollow, his mouth agape. Suddenly, his eyes opened with a void stare.

"Jonas?" I said, sitting up quickly.

A loud commotion stirred outside. I heard male voices and shouting. Jonas's legs moved slightly. "It's okay," I told him, trying to warm his feet.

The door to our jurta flew open. A man leaned in. He wore civilian clothing—a fur-lined coat and a thick, full hat.

"Any sick in here?" he said in Russian.

"Yes!" said Mrs. Rimas. "We're sick. We need help."

The man walked in. He carried a lantern.

"Please," I said. "My brother and this little girl have scurvy. And we can't find one of our friends."

The man made his way over to Jonas and Janina. He exhaled, letting out a string of Russian expletives. He yelled something. An NKVD stuck his head in the door.

"Fish!" he commanded. "Raw fish for these little ones, immediately. Who else is sick?" He looked at me.

"I'm okay," I said.

"What's your name?"

"Lina Vilkas."

"How old are you?"

"Sixteen."

He surveyed the situation. "I'm going to help you, but there are hundreds sick and dead. I need assistance. Are there any doctors or nurses in camp?"

"No, only a veterinarian. But—" I stopped. Maybe he was dead.

"A veterinarian? That's all?" He looked down, shaking his head.

"We can help," said Mrs. Rimas. "We can walk."

"What about you, old man? I need teams of people to make soup and cut fish. These children need ascorbic acid."

He had asked the wrong person. The bald man wouldn't help anyone. Not even himself.

He raised his head. "Yes, I will help," said the bald man.

I looked at him. He stood up.

"I will help, as long as we tend to these children first," said the bald man, pointing to Jonas and Janina.

The doctor nodded, kneeling to Jonas.

"Will the NKVD allow you to help us?" I asked the doctor.

"They have to. I am an inspection officer. I could make a report to the tribunal. They want me to leave and report that everything is fine here, that I saw nothing out of the ordinary. That's what they expect."

His hand moved quickly toward me. I put up my palms, shielding myself.

"I am Dr. Samodurov." His hand was extended, for a handshake. I stared at it, stunned by his show of respect.

We worked under his supervision. That day we each had a bowl of pea soup and half a kilo of fish. He helped us store fish for the upcoming storms and plot out a burial yard for more than a hundred bodies, including the man who wound his watch. He had frozen to death. The doctor enlisted the help of Evenks, native hunters and fishermen, who lived less than thirty kilometers away. They came on sleds with dogs and brought coats, boots, and supplies.

After ten days he said he had to move on, that there were other camps with deportees who were suffering. I gave him all the letters I had written to Andrius. He said he would mail them.

"And your father?" he asked.

"He died in prison, in Krasnoyarsk."

"How do you know that?" he asked.

"Ivanov told my mother."

"Ivanov did? Hmm," said the doctor, shaking his head.

"Do you think he was lying?" I asked quickly.

"Oh, I don't know, Lina. I've been to a lot of prisons and camps, none as remote as this, but there are hundreds of thousands of people. I heard a famous accordion player had been shot, only to meet him a couple of months later in a prison."

My heart leapt. "That's what I told my mother. Maybe Ivanov was wrong!"

"Well, I don't know, Lina. But let's just say I've met a lot of dead people."

I nodded and smiled, unable to contain the fountain of hope he had just given me.

"Dr. Samodurov, how did you find us?" I asked him.

"Nikolai Kretzsky," was all he said.

85

JONAS SLOWLY BEGAN to heal. Janina was speaking again. We buried the man who wound his watch. I clung to the story of the accordion player and visualized my drawings making their way into Papa's hands.

I drew more and more, thinking that come spring, perhaps I might be able to send off a message somehow.

"You told me those Evenks on the sleds helped the doctor," said Jonas. "Maybe they would help us, too. It sounds like they have a lot of supplies."

Yes. Maybe they would help us.

I had a recurring dream. I saw a male figure coming toward me in the camp through the swirling ice and snow. I always woke before I could see his face, but once I thought I heard Papa's voice.

~

"Now, what sort of sensible girl stands in the middle of the road when it's snowing?"

"Only one whose father is late," I teased.

Papa's face appeared, frosty and red. He carried a small bundle of hay.

"I'm not late," he said, putting his arm around me. "I'm right on time."

~

I left the jurta to chop wood. I began my walk through the snow, five kilometers to the tree line. That's when I saw it. A tiny sliver of gold appeared between shades of gray on the horizon. I stared at the amber band of sunlight, smiling. The sun had returned.

I closed my eyes. I felt Andrius moving close. "I'll see you," he said.

"Yes, I will see you," I whispered. "I will."

I reached into my pocket and squeezed the stone.

Epilogue

April 25, 1995 Kaunas, Lithuania

"What are you doing? Keep moving or we won't finish today," said the man. Construction vehicles roared behind him.

"I found something," said the digger, staring into the hole. He knelt down for a closer look.

"What is it?"

"I don't know." The man lifted a wooden box from the ground. He pried the hinged top open and looked inside. He removed a large glass jar full of papers. He opened the jar and began to read.

Dear Friend,

The writings and drawings you hold in your hands were buried in the year 1954, after returning from Siberia with my brother, where we were imprisoned for twelve years. There are many thousands of us, nearly all dead. Those alive cannot speak. Though we committed no offense, we are viewed as criminals. Even now, speaking of the terrors we have experienced would result in our death. So we put our trust in you, the person who discovers this capsule of memories sometime in the future. We trust you with truth, for contained herein is exactly that—the truth.

My husband, Andrius, says that evil will rule until good men or women choose to act. I believe him. This testimony was written to create an absolute record, to speak in a world where our voices have been extinguished. These writings may shock or horrify you, but that is not my intention. It is my greatest hope that the pages in this jar stir your deepest well of human compassion. I hope they prompt you to do something, to tell someone. Only then can we ensure that this kind of evil is never allowed to repeat itself.

Sincerely,
Mrs. Lina Arvydas
9th day of July, 1954—Kaunas

Author's Note

"In the depth of winter, I finally learned that within me there lay an invincible summer." —*Albert Camus*

In 1939, the Soviet Union occupied the Baltic states of Lithuania, Latvia, and Estonia. Shortly thereafter, the Kremlin drafted lists of people considered anti-Soviet who would be murdered, sent to prison, or deported into slavery in Siberia. Doctors, lawyers, teachers, military servicemen, writers, business owners, musicians, artists, and even librarians were all considered anti-Soviet and were added to the growing list slated for wholesale extermination. The first deportations took place on June 14, 1941.

My father is the son of a Lithuanian military officer. Like Joana, he escaped with his parents through Germany into refugee camps. Like Lina, members of his family were deported and imprisoned. The horrors the deportees endured were ghastly. Meanwhile, the Soviets ravaged their countries, burning their libraries and destroying their churches. Caught between the Soviet and Nazi empires and forgotten by the world, the Baltic states simply disappeared from maps.

I took two trips to Lithuania to research this book. I met with family members, survivors of the deportations, survivors of the gulags, psychologists, historians, and government officials. Many of the events and situations I describe in the novel are experiences related to me by survivors and their families, experiences they said were shared by many deportees across Siberia. Although the characters in this story are fictional, Dr. Samodurov is not. He arrived in the Arctic just in time to save many lives.

Those who survived spent ten to fifteen years in Siberia. Upon returning in the mid-1950s, the Lithuanians found that Soviets had occupied their homes, were enjoying all of their belongings, and had even assumed their names. Everything was lost. The returning deportees were treated as criminals. They were forced to live in restricted areas, and were under constant surveillance by the KGB, formerly the NKVD. Speaking about their experience meant immediate imprisonment or deportation back to Siberia. As a result, the horrors they endured went dormant, a hideous secret shared by millions of people.

Like Lina and Andrius, some deportees married and found comfort in knowing looks and whispers in bed late at night. Beautiful children, like Jonas and Janina, grew up in forced-labor camps and returned to Lithuania as adults. Countless mothers and wives like Elena perished. Brave souls, who feared the truth might be lost forever, buried journals and drawings on Baltic soil, risking death if their capsules were discovered by the KGB. Like Lina, many channeled emotion and fear into art and music, the only way they could express themselves, keeping their nation alive in their hearts. Paintings and drawings were not shared publicly. Art was passed secretly, encoded with messages and news from the various prison camps.

Sketches of symbols from their homeland were sometimes enough to push a deportee onward, to fight for another day.

It is estimated that Josef Stalin killed more than twenty million people during his reign of terror. The Baltic states of Lithuania, Latvia, and Estonia lost more than a third of their population during the Soviet annihilation. The deportations reached as far as Finland. To this day, many Russians deny they ever deported a single person. But most Baltic people harbor no grudge, resentment, or ill will. They are grateful to the Soviets who showed compassion. Their freedom is precious, and they are learning to live within it. For some, the liberties we have as American citizens came at the expense of people who lie in unmarked graves in Siberia. Like Joana for Lina, our freedom cost them theirs.

Some wars are about bombing. For the people of the Baltics, this war was about believing. In 1991, after fifty years of brutal occupation, the three Baltic countries regained their independence, peacefully and with dignity. They chose hope over hate and showed the world that even through the darkest night, there is light. Please research it. Tell someone. These three tiny nations have taught us that love is the most powerful army. Whether love of friend, love of country, love of God, or even love of enemy—love reveals to us the truly miraculous nature of the human spirit.

Ruta E. Sepetys

Acknowledgments

I am enormously indebted to many wonderful people who have assisted in the journey that is this novel.

Lindsay Davis, who believed in this book from the first page—you are my hero. Steven Malk, whose guidance and music brought me to Writers House. Rebecca Sherman, who assured me I could do it, and the incredible Ken Wright, who appeared on a white horse to make it all possible. I couldn't ask for better mentors, representation, and friends.

My spectacular editor, Tamra Tuller, invested unfathomable time and effort in this novel. We are a team and I am forever grateful. A deep bow to Michael Green, who was brave enough to pull the jar from the earth and finally bring this story to the world. Courtenay Palmer, Camilla Sanderson, Farah Géhy, Liz Moraz, Julia Johnson, and all of the wonderful people at Philomel and Penguin. Thank you for believing.

My writing group—Sharon Cameron, Amy Eytchison, Rachel Griffiths, Linda Ragsdale, Howard Shirley, and Angelika Stegmann. Thank you for your dedication and, most of all, your friendship. I couldn't have done it without you! Thanks to Laura Goering for her assistance with the Russian language.

Society of Children's Book Writers and Illustrators, whose Work-in-Progress grant, conferences, and wild parties helped me realize that I really could write a book. Special thanks to Genetta Adair and Tracy Barrett from SCBWI Midsouth.

Yvonne Seivertson, Niels Bye Nielsen, Fred and Lindsay Wilhelm, Mike Post, Mike Cortese, Jeroen Noordhuis, Louise Ardenfelt Ravnild, Laurence Harry, Heather Napier, Gerry Rosenblatt, JW Scott, Daniel Schmidt, John Wells, Gavin Mikhail, the Reids, the Tuckers, the Peales, and the Smiths have all assisted or supported my efforts on this book from day one.

I owe everything to Mom and Dad, who taught me to dream big and love even bigger. And John and Kristina—my inspiration, my best friends. My dream is to someday write as well as you.

And my husband, Michael, who suggested I begin writing in the first place. Your love gave me the courage and the wings. You are my everything.

Lithuanian Acknowledgments

Without Linas Zabaliunas, this book simply would not have been possible. Linas directed me to countless individuals for my research, provided translation, accompanied me throughout Lithuania, provided spurgos and cepelinai, and even arranged for me to be locked away in a former Soviet prison. Ačiū labai, my friend!

My sincere gratitude to the Lapteviečiai organization and the following survivors from the Lithuanian deportations for spending time and sharing their experiences with me: Mrs. Irena Špakauskienė, Mr. Jonas Markauskas, Dr. Jonas Puodžius, Mrs. Rytė Merkytė, and Mr. Antanas Stasiškis.

Special thanks to Ms. Agnieška Narkevič for translation in Vilnius; Mrs. Dalia Kazlauskiene for sharing her husband's stunning photos of Siberia with me; Nemunas Tour and the Zabaliunas family; Dr. Danute Gailiene, head of the Department of Clinical Psychology at the University of Vilnius in Lithuania for meeting with me to answer all of my questions; Gintare Jakuboniene, director of the Memorial Department of the Center of Genocide and Resistance; Vilma Juozevičiūtė at the Museum of Genocide Victims; the Genocide and Resistance Research Center; Lithuanian Parliament; the Lithuanian Foundation; Rumšiškės Museum, and Karosta Prison in Latvia.

I am indebted to the following books that helped fill in the blanks: A Stolen Youth, a Stolen Homeland *by Dalia Grinkevivičiūtė,* Sentence: Siberia *by Ann Lehtmets and Douglas Hoile,* Leave Your Tears in Moscow *by Barbara Armonas,* Lithuanians in the Arctic *by the Lapteviečiai Organization, and* The Psychology of Extreme Traumatization *by Dr. Danute Gailiene.*

And finally, to the extended family of Jonas Šepetys. Thank you for the continued love and support you have always shown our family. Your patriotism, loyalty, and sacrifice shall never be forgotten.

Ačiū labai!